SNOW ANGEL

Edward Farrell

This book is dedicated to Lee J. Farrell, my father, who first showed me mountains and who loved a good story.

ISBN 978-1-7342621-6-2
Edited by Kate Benson
Cover design by Mel Volker

Printed in the United States of America

Otherwords Press
www.otherwordspress.net

OTHER BOOKS IN THE MICKEY POWELL SERIES

White Angel

JANUARY, 2001

VISITATION

The young woman rests on her back in the snow, arms spread wide as if to embrace the forest above her, heels touching, eyes fixed on the winter sky. Her lips are pressed together in a line that turns down slightly, suggesting concern rather than sorrow, and her blonde hair is loose and windblown, circling her head like a golden halo.

She does not move as the breeze from the west stiffens, carrying a heavy veil of new snow that wraps around the forest like a shroud, cloaking the pines and hemlocks, painting the windward sides of oaks and maples and ash trees, bleaching yellow birch stands a fine bone white, erasing the shapes of the landscape like a teacher erasing a chalkboard.

She lies perfectly still as the fragile crystals waft down and alight on her, -- eyes unblinking, lips unmoving, hands unfeeling. On her, the snowflakes do not melt. Soon she disappears, her bare fingers first, then arms and legs... torso, chest, and face. Finally, her toes are covered, and the woman is gone.

CHAPTER 1

Monday, 9:45 a.m.

More gray than black and white.

When you looked carefully, the winter woodland's palette was softer than the stark contrast it first presented, the whites not quite white after all, the blacks a little less than black— it was a simple matter of perception. Mickey Powell shifted in his folding backrest , stretched his legs out in the snow in front of him, and considered the matter of perceiving which was, after all, just a question of clarity, of clearing your mind of the past's clutter and the future's anxiety so that you could really experience the present moment, really see, really hear, really smell, really feel it. Here in the forest he could see that pine needles and grit dusted the pure white of the snow, that tree trunks were more gray brown than black, the pine boughs a dark gray green; that though the day seemed sunless, the tree trunks and rock shapes cast faint gray shadows, that the layered nimbocumulus themselves were tinted in shades of slate and ash and pewter. The sounds were indistinct as well: the chittering of an animal, perhaps a bird or squirrel, a crunch of something like footsteps from below the knoll where he sat, which might be from one of his students, the sourceless soughing of wind above him, the distant drone of highway sounds, probably on the interstate a mile or so away beyond a hill. Even the smells were shadowy, pine the predominant one but tinged with the metallic scent of the new snow itself as well as whiffs of those he brought with him - sweat from his fleece and traces of bacon and pipe smoke from the sweater beneath that. *How I feel*, Powell thought. *Like I'm not quite here sometimes, like I am just a part of the background.*

At a small table in the back corner of the bustling two hundred square foot room that was the Coffee Mug Café, Detective Lieutenant Kate Romeo sat with a newspaper, sipping a fresh ground, dark roast Tanzanian brew, savoring its heady aroma, and watching and listening to the human swirl of coming, going that presented it-self like improvised theater from a troupe of familiar actors. She learned that it was Elaine's birthday. Jerry and Mike pondered the Patriot's' playoff chances, concluding that they'd go deep but might not have the legs to win it. Jean's mother was sick, probably pneumonia, and her son Ron was back from Florida.

Each item mundane, Romeo thought, but each of them intimate in a way, and each of them a thread in the café's weave of connection. *And am I one, too?* She thought not. She came in as often as she was in town, and some of the regulars recognized her but she wasn't part of the easy banter. Even the waitresses seldom engaged her beyond passing comments about the weather. Perhaps it was the uniform. Or perhaps the fact that she lived elsewhere but it seemed unlikely to her that anyone would even notice if she stopped coming altogether. *And why should they?* Knowing there was no answer, Romeo waved at the waitress for a refill and pretended to turn her attention to her paper.

"Everything bleeds into everything else," Powell scribbled in his journal, his fingers numbing in the January cold. Wonder how many of them will discover that? That was the whole point of the exercise – formally labeled Meditation in Nature on the syllabus and

popularly called "pond sitting" by his students – but this was just the second session of the semester. Powell smiled ruefully and scrawled more words. *Don't understand it myself and I've been teaching it for nine years. Nevertheless, it's true.* He closed the journal and looked around again. No movement to snatch his attention; the landscape flattening itself into two dimensions. Tipping his head and shutting his eyes, he let his breath become his focus, the slow rhythm of in and out, the stinging cold of air in his nostrils, the pale warmth of exhaled vapor rising over his eyelids and dissipating before it reached his brow, mind moving into the rhythm and out of time, slowly opening itself to scent and air and all the space behind them.

But in reality, the space was no space, he knew. The oxygen that he drew in was simply the breath of the trees; the carbon dioxide that he expelled was drawn in by them, its carbon feeding their roots and trunks and branches and needles; oxygen excreted by them back to the atmosphere for his use. Oneness of being, each requiring the other. Closing his eyes, Powell let his breathing carry him into that thought.

A sudden sound brought him back. A noise in the middle distance that didn't belong, something like a gasp with retching close behind. Standing quickly, he surveyed the white woods. Trees and snow, the flat plane of the frozen pond, the roundnesses of covered boulders. Then something moving down the hill and to his left, a flash of blue among the variegated grays. Powell squatted and peered through the tree trunks – a girl in a blue jacket fifty yards away, bent over and leaning on a yellow birch tree. *Nina.*

Despite the deep snow, Powell covered the ground in seconds. The girl had dropped to her knees in the snow, had placed her head against the birch, had wrapped her arms around its trunk.

"Nina! Nina, what's wrong?"

The girl, a junior from Georgia, vaguely waved her hand at a copse of spruce trees. Her words made no sense. "Ahead. Janet.

Ahead. Hand to –"

Powell's eyes followed the direction of the wave but no one was there. "Janet? Ahead of what?"

The St. Johnsbury Caledonian-Record had a smattering of national news from the AP, local news for a dozen or so of the towns and villages of the Northeast Kingdom of Vermont and the North Country of New Hampshire, good coverage of high school sports, a handful of comic strips, a page or two of obituaries, and a conservative editorial slant. Kate Romeo started with the obituaries – lives summed up in three paragraphs. Today she was rewarded with Pandora Kuhn, – an octogenarian from Island Pond. After listing her extensive family connections, the writer noted "as a cook Aunt Pandora was not so good, but she was renowned for her pies." Romeo set the paper down and wondered for a moment what her obit would say. "As a daughter and wife she was not so good, but she was renowned for her inability to tell a joke." She sighed and picked the paper up again. There wouldn't be much more. Generally it was a fifteen minute read – unless some local saga captured your attention. But today's paper had one – a short item under the headline **Body Found**. St. Johnsbury Police were reporting the discovery of a body in a vacant building on Railroad Street. The corpse – a woman's, name and age not released – had turned up at 1:15 a.m. on Sunday after a patrol car noticed a plywood panel pulled from a door frame of the building, which was described as being "under renovation." Romeo couldn't help sniggering at that. If being boarded up signified 'renovation,' half of downtown St. J was being renovated.

But it was the article's last phrase that caught the Lieutenant's eye. "A drug overdose is suspected." I-93 through St. Johnsbury had long been a drug conduit from Montreal to Boston, but overdose deaths were spiking suddenly and unexpectedly in the North Country. Romeo was making a mental note to call her counterpart in Vermont to check on what, if any, pattern they were seeing when the call from the barracks in Twin came. The receptionist Joanne's voice: "Just got a call from the Seven Springs Academy that one of their teachers was found dead in the woods. There was a 911 call, too, so chances are Chief Sanborn's on it."

By now Nina was sobbing uncontrollably and could only shake her head in reply to Mickey's questions. Powell gave her shoulder a gentle squeeze and turned to where the girl's footprints led out of the snowy grove. Ducking under boughs laden white, he entered a space that was almost a room, walled with spruce trunks and mountain laurel, roofed by overhanging branches, no doubt the spot that Nina had found for the meditation exercise, private and protected, almost cozy- if not for the corpse.

Powell spied the hand first - the 'hand too' of Nina's babbling - oddly pale but still with enough color to contrast with the drift from which it emerged, palm up, fingers open, as if signaling welcome. The head, a short yard to the left of the hand, was harder to make out. Really only the face was visible and even that had been obscured by blowing snow, turning eyebrows as white as a crone's and filling the groove of the pale pursed lips. Even so, no doubt about identity. The head in the snow was Janet Debian.

CHAPTER 2

Monday, 10:11 a.m.

"That's right, Janet Debian. D-E-B-I-A-N." Speaking to the cop, a blonde and earnest young man in a heavy leather jacket and matching fur trimmed hat, Mickey Powell was numb, not from the cold, which he barely felt now, but from the stark vision of the face in the snow.

"Do you know about any family?"

"Parents, I think. She spoke about her father often. The office will know how to get in touch with them." And, no doubt, they would be asking him to do it. God, what a horror that would be, Powell thought. Delivering the one message no parent ever wants to hear. All the love lavished on the one you yourself brought into the world and suddenly what point did it have? *As at the crucifixion*, Powell thought. Even from a distance of two millennia and six thousand miles, it was not hard to feel Mary's anguish at the foot of that cross when everything she knew about the world had been turned inside out.

As it was here. One moment sitting in contemplation of nature, the next reaching down toward a friend's throat to check for a pulse that he knew would not be there, guiding a sobbing girl up a path to the school, returning to collect the rest of the class and, when they had been sent on their way, to keep vigil by the corpse until the police came, no longer seeing the trees or the snow, not hearing the birds or the wind, barely feeling the chill outside while the chill inside grew.

He had tried to hold onto the living Janet, had pictured her in her classroom passionately explicating some obscure aspect of the environment, saw her laughing between classes in the hallways, remembered her fluid progress on mountain trails under a backpack almost as big as she was. But the still face in the snow continually reminded him that that life was no more, that now Janet was in the province of death.

"And you found the body?" The policeman's voice brought him back.

"No, a student of mine did. Nina Edwards."

The officer jotted the name. "And what was she doing out here? Shouldn't she have been in school?"

"She was. Our whole class was out here doing a meditation exercise."

A raised blonde eyebrow. "Out here? It's, what, not even twenty out."

"They dress for it."

Both eyebrows up now and a slight shake of the cop's head. "So they saw this, too?"

"No, we sit separately down here that's part of the point. I took Nina back up to the office and came down to collect them while I was waiting for you. The Head of School – that's Sam, Sam Robeson – came down and took them back up."

More jottings in the notebook; steam of breathing rising around the patrolman's face. "You know her pretty well?"

"At a boarding school you know everyone pretty well." Which was only too true, Powell thought. As he could with anyone else on the staff, he could easily picture Janet at most times of the day or night. Coming up the hill towards Old Main and the dining hall as the sun rose red and wonderful on a winter morning, sitting on a rug in the Great Hall at school meeting shoulder to shoulder with one of her advisees, Brigid or Peg or Julianne or one of the others, directing discussion in her classroom, hands and arms windmilling, eyes flashing with excitement. Or hockey-stopping at the bottom of a ski run in a spray of snow, face glowing in the frosty air of a winter afternoon. Though she hadn't been with them long – two, maybe three years – she was a good fit, more than he was himself really, more connected, more comfortable in her own skin there. She was young, maybe that was it but –"

"Was there any reason – " The cop's voice again, interrupting his thoughts just as Powell began to feel sorry for himself. " – why anyone would want to hurt her?"

"You think someone did this to her?" The question came out as though shot, and its recoil shook Powell into the realization that he himself thought that exact thing. Something was bothering him though he could not say what.

"I doubt it." The officer – Steven Cox, according to the blue nametag on his black jacket – glanced up from his notepad while Powell searched the folds of his consciousness, hoping to shake out whatever was bothering him. "Have to ask, though. And wouldn't it be odd for her to be out here by herself at night? Anyone mad at her?"

"Janet was a zealot. And zealotry irritates some people." What was she doing in the woods? Powell considered the problem. Given that she was practically buried, she would have to have come out before the snow began to fall and when he had gone to bed at eleven, moonlight was still slanting in the window.

"What have we got, Cox?"

The voice came from behind Powell, who turned to find a

fat, bare-headed man with hair the color of last night's snow approaching through along the path of beaten down footprints. As he took this in, the cop's voice offered, "G'morning, chief."

"What have we got?" the chief asked again brusquely, ignoring Powell and taking the notepad out of the officer's hand as he spoke.

"She's over here, chief."

The old man – now Powell could place him from press photos - brushed past him as if he were merely another tree in the forest and the two men stepped up to the copse where Janet was. "Uh huh. What's the step in there?"

"That's where Father Powell here reached in to check for pulse. Other than that no one's been near her."

"Father Powell?" The chief's head swiveled back to Mickey Powell.

"Michael Powell – I'm the school chaplain. Most people call me Mickey," By reputation, the chief ran the town as if it were his own dysfunctional family, knowing the dirt on everyone and not afraid to use it. Simply to irritate him, Powell equably offered, "And you would be?"

The white-haired man, not speaking, stared hostilely at Powell as if one of the snow-covered boulders had begun to talk back to him. *Silence as intimidation*, Powell thought. *Which only works if you let it.* He let the stillness tighten between them like a rope twisted at both ends. Ten seconds, twenty, thirty - nearly an eternity, until finally the tension embarrassed Officer Cox into speaking.

"Sorry, Father, this is – "

"Shut up, Cox." The barked order was as malevolent as a gut punch.

"That's okay, Officer." *Might just as well push things over the edge*, Powell thought, *and see where they fall.* "Chief Sanborn's reputation as an anal opening makes him unmistakable."

In an instant the chief's face went from winter's red to angry purple. "What did you say?"

"I believe you heard me just fine, chief." Why had he said something so stupid and provocative? Powell caught the look on Cox's face: a perfect blend of amazement and horror but let his ego-self push on. "Or were there too many syllables for you?"

The old man took two steps toward him and spits words out. "I should level you right there, mister!"

Control, control, control, Powell thought. Not even a blink. "Perhaps you should, chief, but I don't think you will. Beating up a priest isn't the kind of ink you need just now. And, anyway, it might not be so easy. I'm not drunk. And this time there's a witness."

Sanborn turned another shade of purple but did not move. Powell knew he got the reference to a local scandal – an intoxicated prisoner seriously injured 'attempting to escape.' There were no witnesses and no charges were filed but all of it fit with the chief's rap as a law unto himself. "Get him out of here, Cox."

The young officer stepped forward but Powell raised his left hand, palm outward. "I'm not going anywhere until the state police get here. We called them. If this is a crime scene, I believe it would be theirs."

"What crime? The girl falls down, hits her head, passes out on a cold night." The chief channeled venom into his voice.

"Could be. But what was she doing out here? Do you spend a lot of time in the woods at night when it's ten degrees out?"

"Who says it was night, smart guy? We got no time of death. Unless you know more than you've said so far."

"Had to be before it snowed, and I do know this – Janet would have been at dorm closing last night. That's at eleven."

At this information, Sanborn's eyes became glittering poisonous slits , first tightly focused on Powell's face, then moving to something behind him. "Jesus Christ." He spat the words. "Not that bitch."

Powell turned to see a dark-haired woman, stocky but trim, in olive gray pants and a green parka crunching her way along the uneven track in the snow towards them. Blue lights flashed through the bare trees from the roof of a car on the road at the top of the hill. Cox looked down and stepped away from his chief who glared, unspeaking in the direction of the approaching figure. A radio in her left hand crackled words that Powell could not make out; lifting it to her face without slowing down she replied, "Is that right? Interesting," and reaching him, extended her gloved right hand. "Kate Romeo. State Police."

A firm grip, Powell noted. "Mickey Powell. I'm with the school."

Turning toward her professional colleagues then, speaking in a clipped, efficient tone like a quarterback in a huddle, "Officer Cox, isn't it? Weren't you on that vehicular homicide case last year?"

Cox nodded. "Yes, ma'am."

"That was good work." And to Sanborn: "Walter, I just heard you called an ambulance in but never got around to calling me. That right?"

"Hell, it's an open and shut deal – Snow White here's a hypothermia case. An accident. No call for you."

Kate Romeo glanced at the face in the snow. "And you know that how?"

"C'mon, what else?" The condescension dripping from Sanborn's words raised Powell's hackles but the Snow White reference brought back to mind what had been troubling him earlier, and he found himself stepping forward as the old chief went on. "She slips, hits her head, she's drunk, it's a suicide like that idiot up on Lafayette a few years ago – it still comes down to freezing to death. You know it does."

"You don't know squat, Warren. You don't even know if there's a body attached to that head much less how she died." Kate Romeo was as direct as a shoe on a bug.

"Try blood loss," Powell found himself saying. "I think she may have bled to death."

All three of the police officers looked at Mickey Powell as though they had just noticed he was there until Romeo broke the silence. "*What?*"

"She's way too pale, even for a corpse."

The statie eyed him for a long moment. "Huh."

Powell opened his mouth to speak again but Romeo had already turned away from him towards Cox. "Let's take a look at her."

She led the younger man past his chief without a word and the two of them squatted by the face in the snow. "Like this," she said, and began gently brushing snow away from the corpse's face. "You start down there."

Slowly the white powdered body of Janet Debian began to emerge from the drifted landscape, arms outspread like a snow angel, hands open, blonde hair pulled back from her face, feet to-gether, wearing loafers, jeans, a blue and green plaid sweater with the collar of a blue blouse circling her neck, an unzipped jacket To Powell, the moment was one of almost unbearable intimacy, of stepping uninvited into a space that had called only to her but which one day would know his name as well . Cox and Romeo slid hands under Janet's shoulders and hips, rolled her briefly up onto her side, eased her back down onto the frozen ground.

Snow had begun to fall again. Warren Sanborn smirked at Powell. "No blood, smart guy."

CHAPTER 3

Monday, 11:16 a.m.

The body was gone and over the spot where it had been a blue plastic tarp was rigged to preserve the scene as much as possible for the CSI crew. *Who wouldn't find much.* Kate Romeo, squatting where one corner of the bright blue square was tied to a birch tree, mused that reality is not like television with its high-tech gimmickry and seemingly limitless resources. Possibly some hair or fiber evidence on surrounding bushes or trees, but a foot of new snow would make even that difficult to find. Whatever hope they had for clues lay with the corpse that had now been bundled off to the hospital to wait for the medical examiner. What story would it have to tell?

It. The unspoken word turned on Romeo and tugged on her mind like a neglected child clutching at her mother's dress. The image brought back some dim memory of her own childhood, but before she could place it the body yanked insistently again. *Not it. She. Janet.* A person, who only a day ago had been breathing, walking, speaking, tasting. Where was that person now? What would it feel like to be her?

The detective thought of the peaceful body, reclining beneath the snow like a pampered princess beneath a goose down comforter, her pale face as tranquil as a high mountain pond on a still day. Though there was no knowing now whether Janet Debian was actually at peace, Romeo could not help but compare the corpse's seeming serenity with the troubled state of her own psyche the evening before. While Janet was laying down in the falling snow, Romeo had been pacing the rooms of her small house drinking wine and eating gingersnaps, talking to herself, checking her email repeatedly – though the only additions were come-on coupons from Borders and Barnes and Noble – and telling herself that it was about time to get some sleep. Which did not come early or easy.

Now, wired between too little sleep and too much coffee, she found herself wondering what that final lie down would be like. Hypothermia survivors spoke of becoming profoundly weary but calm, accepting the need for rest not as the frightening reality that many of them, in more lucid moments, knew it to be but as an organic necessity that was at once inviting and inevitable . *Why not? Why not just lay down and rest?*

Romeo shook her head against the realization that she was asking the question as much about herself as Janet Debian, taking it as a sign that it was time to get back to work. She stood and weighed the limited data that she now had. An accident as Sanborn had concluded? Possible – but a quick look hadn't shown any kind of contusion on her head so a fall didn't seem to fit. But how likely was it that she had gotten lost a quarter mile from the school on a path she'd used a hundred times before? Perhaps if she had been drunk or high, but they'd have to wait for the tox report to determine that. And suicide was not impossible – every few years someone in the North Country used winter as a way to bring life to a close. Psychologists said it was a peaceful way to die – but so far, of the few people they'd talked to, none seemed to think that Janet Debian was depressed at all, much less despondent enough to kill herself.

But maybe despondency wasn't so hard to come by. Maybe she was just tired, Romeo thought, or lonely or sick of the same old same old. And if that was the case, there'd be a sign of it somewhere. The priest, though, hadn't thought it possible. How had he put it? Closing her eyes, she let memory bring his voice back.

"You can never know for certain what's in the depth's of another person's soul," he'd said. They were standing in the snowy woods, a discreet distance from Janet's lifeless shape, waiting for the ambulance to come for her body. "But you rarely meet people as full of life as she was."

What's in another person's soul. Not a phrase you heard often. In the world of science souls had ceased to exist, replaced by a welter of emotions and impulses, brain chemicals and traumatic memories, all of them almost random and out of anyone's control. Though she had not said as much to Powell, she had allowed that she wasn't really sure she knew what a soul was. His reply surprised her.

"I'm not sure what a soul is either." His hazel eyes were astonishingly soft, almost vulnerable. "But I am sure *that* it is."

Not knowing how to respond, saying only, "Really? How's that?"

Powell had laughed, the straight hard lines of his face transforming themselves into curves and whorls. "Would you prefer the physics of it or the metaphysics?"

Again the unexpected, provoking a bit of disquiet like a pebble disturbing the surface of a pond. But also a draw, a sense of wanting to see what was around this curve. "I'm not sure my grasp of metaphysics would be enough to get me far."

"You're probably underestimating yourself. Most folks get metaphysics intuitively. But we can stick with physics for now, okay?"

"Sure." Romeo, wishing she hadn't fallen into this particular pit, had looked around as if to plot an escape route, a glance that Powell had not noticed or at least that he had pretended not to.

"So think of the soul as energy connected to consciousness. No one really knows what consciousness is, but no one can deny that it is since that very denial would be a conscious act, right?"

Romeo recalled that she had merely nodded but had felt herself drawn further into his thinking.

"And no one would deny that there is energy connected with consciousness since it's as measurable as heat or electricity; or perhaps both – those measurably change when consciousness as we know it ceases. So what happens to it? The first law of thermodynamics says that it must be preserved even if we don't know how or where, right?"

"I guess." Now Romeo was smiling.

"So there it is – the physics of the soul. What it is exactly, I don't know – but it does exist." Powell, lips slightly upturned, had cocked an eyebrow like a question mark to see if she was with him.

Her answer had been, she hoped, even and noncommittal. *But he is interesting. In a weird way.* "You must drive your students crazy."

"I suppose I do. But if I get them to think, it's worth it."

"And how many of them buy your physics lesson?"

"Not many." The chaplain's smile a little sad now . "But that's not the point. I'm only trying to show them that there are many things science cannot account for. So it might be best for them to cultivate some other ways of knowing."

"And do they?"

Powell had been pensive in replying. "Some do."

The conversation had trailed off then into comfortable silence as they both had turned toward the path at the sound of the ambulance crew crunching through the snow, carrying a backboard between them. They had helped lift Janet Debian's stiff corpse onto it then had watched as the straps were tightened across her chest and legs. Before they picked it up, Powell stepped forward and traced a cross on her forehead, whispering words that Romeo could not quite make out.

"I have to get back," Powell said as the body began its progress toward the road.

"But I hope you find out what happened. And let me know when you're ready for the metaphysics talk."

And then the priest was gone, trailing the stretcher through the woods and up the slope, the only mourner in a sorry cortege. Romeo watched until the ambulance pulled away and Powell disappeared up the hill towards the school. She tried to imagine Janet Debian full of life, as he had described her, and wondered what it was that had emptied her of it. *Accident, suicide, or homicide?* Nothing obvious pointed to any of them – but somewhere there would be something that gave them a hint. In the M.E.'s report or in Debian's home or in a comment she had made to a student or friend. There was always something somewhere. *Perhaps in the depths of a soul?*

Romeo shook her head at the thought, but owned the fact that she had found the conversation interesting. She had been brought up a sort of sometime Episcopalian but her parents had not taken her often after she punched a fellow angel who had pulled her ponytail during the Christmas pageant, and except for weddings and funerals she had stopped going altogether after high school. While she wanted to believe there was something beyond what she saw every day, sometimes longed to believe, two decades of poking into the underside of human affairs – the robberies and assaults, the rapes and murders, the drug abuse, child abuse, spousal abuse – had nearly convinced her that if ever there had been a God, he had long since retired. *But I keep coming back.* Like a stray mutt in an alley, she could not stop sniffing the edges of every rank mound she found, trying to smell out what happened, hoping to hold someone accountable for the mess.

Looking in at the cleared space where Janet Debian had lain like a sleeping snow angel, she wondered if her work made any difference at all. Perhaps the atoms and molecules of the universe just had to spin this way, like a windup toy that kept on going until its spring went slack or it came to the unseen edge of whatever table top it had been set on and fell off. Did catching the bad guys change that?

Too tired. Too tired to think about it. But it seemed to Romeo that she had been tired for years. She closed her eyes and wished that Janet Debian had just overslept on this cold Monday, wished that she was snowshoeing along the bank of a frozen brook this January morning, wished she had not met Mickey Powell with his glib talk of souls, wished for another cup of coffee to shake this zombie sluggishness.

Coffee, she thought, smiling tersely, and opening her eyes to the white world again. At least that was possible. She thought of the Coffee Mug – a seat in the window, another carafe of something exotic, the morning crossword to keep her mind occupied, maybe one of their fabulous scones. Romeo looked again at the

bare space under the tarp, idly

CHAPTER 4

Monday, 2:36 p.m.

The mid-afternoon sunlight slanting into the classroom cast shadows across the desks that made the gloom of Mickey Powell's mood all the more palpable. Outside, the morning clouds had fled the skies but had settled on his soul— students, faculty, and staff, first in silent shock as the announcement of Janet Debian's death was made at a hastily called assembly, then in a near hysteria of tears and cursing, then in a weepy attempt to resume the normal schedule, destined to fail of course but attempted nonetheless because no one could conceive of a better plan. A boarding school was, he knew, a community for better or for worse, and any community as small as Seven Springs would be traumatized when the worst suddenly happened to one of its members.

In the end, they had limped through the school day as well as could be expected. Classes had become rap sessions on loss and grief, and crisis counselors had been called in to work with the most troubled— for the most part students whose personal baggage included loss or abandonment. Most of the faculty had held themselves together admirably, though Powell knew that a couple of Janet's closer friends were as near the edge as they could be—

candidates for a visit from the chaplain before the day was over.

Surveying his own emotional landscape, Powell saw that his reaching out to others was partly a way of avoiding his own rough and jagged places, the dark hollows, the empty tracts of that interior topography in which, as the scripture put it, "we live and move and have our being." No one's map of the world was without its crossroads of loss. *Even yours, Mick*, Powell thought. In the classroom, Janet's classroom, he sought some sign of her, some palpable presence that would bring back the vibrant young woman he had come to know, that would obliterate the final image of a pale corpse strapped on a stretcher.

He thought again of Janet's departure, of the woman with the odd name – Romeo, wasn't it? – exchanging hot words with Sanborn, the chief brushing past them glaring smugly while Kate Romeo returned to the scene.

He had stood on the road watching until the police cars and ambulance disappeared around a bend in the narrow road, then had spent a long moment looking back into the winter woods before trudging up the drive to confirm the grim news. Now all the students were gone to sports – skiing, dance, or fitness in the winter – and Powell, in Janet's classroom, closed his eyes and looked back to the scene in the woods. Something was not right there. Now Powell saw the face and hand in the snow again, saw Cox and Romeo carefully uncovering the body, saw its arms loosely hanging off the stretcher before the attendants strapped them in, ashen fingers trailing in the snow. Powell frowned and focused his mind's eye on the scene, straining to see what he had missed before. When it came to him, he smiled grimly. He was looking for something that wasn't there. No gloves. Janet Debian, on a January night in New Hampshire, wasn't wearing gloves. And was wearing loafers, not boots. The echo of his earlier question sounded in Powell's thoughts. *What were you doing out there, Janet?*

The empty classroom gave no answer but there were shades of her there. The earth flag that hung from the rear wall was a personal emblem and the floppy stuffed moose doll in the corner – four feet tall if it was an inch – held a touch of her whimsy. One corkboard displayed a motto: *Life Won't Work Unless You Do*; another framed a collage of diversity – people and places, cities, forests, mountains, deserts, palaces and slums, all of which spoke volumes about the woman who had taught there.

Powell sat behind her desk and considered what he actually knew about Janet Debian. It hadn't been much until the previous school year. She was one of a particular type of boarding school teacher: from a fairly privileged background, liberally educated, idealistic and committed. In Janet's case that meant Winnetka, Illinois, a Dartmouth dual major in history and environmental science, several summers in the Appalachian Mountain Club's backcountry huts, and a post-grad year working at an orphanage in Honduras. Her energy and enthusiasm were contagious – in her first year she was an instant hit both with her students and her colleagues – particularly the handful of single young male teachers who called Seven Springs home. Not until the summer following had Powell had much to do with her – at the year-end meetings she had asked him if she could co-teach his class, *Spirituality and the Environment* with him. "The kids," he recalled her saying eagerly, "tell me it's great." When he'd asked what she knew about the subject she'd replied with complete innocence, "Nothing. That's why I want to teach it." The charming and Zen-like ingenuousness of that answer had won him then and made him smile now.

He'd arranged to have the class offered in one of her free blocks and had signed her on as a co-teacher although in practice she had turned out to be more of a super-student than an instructor. But her thoughtful questioning was a prod that pushed him and the class to a higher level, and her earnest curiosity was as good a lesson for the students as any he had offered.

And she was right, Powell reflected. Teaching *was* learning. And Janet herself was like a text book that the course had offered him that term. Her table of contents presented a well-organized persona – the background, the education, the interests – but a careful reading revealed a subtly shaded character, more fragile she first appeared and perhaps for that more lovely.   Her class journal was a stream of doubt – words said that should have been left unsaid or words unsaid that should have been said, things done that she wished not done or things not done that might better have been done – a watershed of uncertainty that collected misgiving in drips and rills and rivulets that ran down toward an unseen sea within her. Now Powell wondered what if anything in that landscape had led to her death. *Something always does*, he thought. *Something leads each of us to our own private Calvary. One thing always leads to another.* Nothing on her desk suggested disorder – a stapler, a calendar blotter, a mug of pencils and pens, a Beanie Baby owl. *But it isn't always disorder that leads us astray.* The calendar bore colored jottings – class times in green, dorm duty in blue, sports assignments in pink, and purple for personal entries – dentist, car in shop, blood drive at the Elks, movie w/ Christie, dinner for Jen and Bill. Nothing for the night before except a blue note, 'dorm 7-11,' followed by a purple exclamation point, perhaps to denote that the night was hers at last.

Without knowing why, Powell tried the desk drawer and found it locked. He idly wondered what he would expect to find there, then considered the desk in his own classroom and its miscellaneous contents – index cards, rubber bands, cough drops, broken pencils, stray paper clips, notepads, gradebooks, handouts, printer paper, thumb tacks, odd pen tops, and more – the detritus of a classroom life. It struck him that the desks were just alike, probably purchased from the same place at the same time, and the thought moved his hand to action before his conscious mind took note, fingers fishing keys from a pocket and sorting them before he was aware of thinking that the locks might be the same.

And were. The small silver key – rarely used on his own desk – turned clockwise moved the stiff bolts that froze the drawers. Janet's, he discovered, were neater than his. Office supplies in an organizing tray, index cards rubber banded in bunches, Bic pens arranged by color, half bags of Hershey kisses – plain and almond – neatly clipped close, a separate drawer for record books and lesson planners, another for Kleenex and paper towels. The bottom drawer held two dictionaries, a Merriam-Webster and a pocket English-Spanish as well as a short stack of spiral bound notebooks with fancifully doodled covers.

One of which Powell recognized. Its cover would have been green on a Staples shelf but now elaborate pen and pencil drawings of leafy flowering vines enveloped it so completely that it appeared to have grown them. Her pond journal, from their semester of teaching together. Reaching for it, recalling the elegant, questioning entries he had read and commented on weekly, he was startled by a voice from the hall.

"Looking for something?" Kate Romeo stood framed in the doorway, parka unzipped, notebook in her left hand, pencil in her right, neat uniform and polished black gunbelt contrasting disheveled brown hair.

"Not something. Someone." Powell spoke evenly enough, he hoped, to conceal a sudden sensation of being caught at something. "I'm not going to find her, though."

"It must be very hard here today." Her voice was warm, Powell thought; not overly friendly but sympathetic. "I'm sorry."

"It is. People liked her – not that it matters. Place this small, even losing someone you don't like is hard."

"You have many losses?" Her blue eyes were soft with what seemed to be genuine concern but the question, Powell thought, was not without purpose.

"Not like this. Only a couple of deaths in the fifteen years I've been here, and neither was on campus. But faculty come and go, and we expel a fair number of students – for fighting, cheating, drugs. The usual for boarding schools. The separation seems almost as final."

"Hmmm." Kate Romeo nodded and took this in, then went on. "I heard some students talking in the office – they said you were great this morning."

The same warm voice, on the low and husky side. But now Powell wondered where her comments were going. *Somewhere. She's looking for something herself.* "If it helped them, that's good. But to be honest, I couldn't tell you what I said."

Kate Romeo seemed to consider this for a moment, pursing her lips slightly and letting her blue eyes break connection with his for an instant. *Or is she considering me?* When she spoke, the words were hesitant.

"Out there this morning when . . . did . . . did you have any reason to think someone had done something to her?"

"No, not then. It was just seeing her like that and wondering what she was doing there."

"That must have been a shock." Again, the calm voice – almost soothing, Powell thought. "How well did you know her?"

There it is – the turn signal, the direction indicator. Careful now. "I knew her pretty well. It's a small faculty here."

"Hmmmmm." Clearly Romeo wanted more. "It's just that when I asked, the office said that you knew her better than anyone."

"Don't know why they'd think so." Powell saw the path now but wondered what Romeo knew that put her on it. "We did teach a class together last spring. Haven't seen so much of her this year, though."

Another "hmmmmm," softer this time, then: "Would there have been any reason for her to have wanted to hurt herself?"

"Suicide?" Though Sanborn had mentioned it that morning, Powell had not given it much thought. "I doubt it. I never saw any signs of depression. The usual concerns about relationships but those were well within the normal range."

"She was concerned about someone she was seeing?" Romeo's eyebrows arched over the limpid blue pools of her eyes.

"Not what I meant. She was concerned – last spring anyway – that she *wasn't* seeing anybody. That could have changed, I guess, but I haven't seen her with anyone."

Romeo looked down to jot notes, and in that momentary quiet Powell found himself trying to guess her age. Forties? Maybe in the middle of that decile. Younger than his own fifty-three certainly but a woman with some miles on the odometer. *And why is it that I'm wondering?* No answer to that as Romeo looked up with another question.

"Isn't that unusual? Looked like a very attractive young woman."

"She was." Even in the school's casual atmosphere Janet could turn heads, Powell recalled. "Might have been part of the problem for her. I think she was wary that guys were just drawn to the surface looks."

Kate Romeo nodded, kept her blue eyes on him. "Um, Mister Powell - or do I say 'Father?'"

Now we're getting to the point, Powell thought. "'Father' would be correct, officer, but here everyone just calls me Mickey."

Perfunctory smile. "Actually, in my case it would be 'lieutenant' not 'officer.'

Which clearly made a difference, Powell noted. "Sorry. You were about to ask me something, lieutenant?"

"Yes." In the moment, the distance between them seemed to shrink, Powell thought, as if Romeo were adjusting focus to bring a lens closer to him. "What made you think we'd find blood this morning?"

Powell felt a blush rise to his face at a quick recollection of Sanborn's derisive comment. He wondered how much he should say, heard the inner whisper again. *Careful. Could get messy.* "Lieutenant, have you ever seen a person who has bled out?"

"No, I haven't." Now her eyes intent on him, her voice taut. "Have you?"

"A couple of times." *Don't say too much.* "It's not something you forget."

"And where was that?"

"I was in the service." The truth but not the whole truth. "In Vietnam."

Romeo's face grew visibly weary as if she had just remembered a rock she was rolling. "I'm sorry. I lost a cousin there."

Powell nodded, said nothing, waited, wondered if she had had enough now, got an answer in her next question. "Father, Officer Cox told me that you said Janet Debian might have irritated some people."

"I said she was a zealot and that people sometimes find that irritating." *This. The rest of what she had came for.*

"And just what was she zealous about?" Eyes a little harder

now, more of a cop now, Powell observed.

"The environment. The planet. Creation, if you will."

"Creation? She was religious?"

Powell smiled. "If you mean churchy, no. If you mean faithful, yes. She definitely believed that the earth is holy."

Eyebrows arching over the limpid cobalt of her irises like tree boughs moving over pools in stream. Quietly: "Sounds like someone I would have liked."

"Many people did."

Romeo's voice firmed up again. "But some people didn't?"

"Not everyone shares those views." Powell paused to consider how much to say and decided that most of what he knew would likely be revealed in any case. "A developer in town, for instance, was trying to skirt the wetlands rules – and might have managed it, too, if Janet hadn't gotten in the way. I think he finally came around, though. And one of our trustees, this guy Eric Ames, had a plan to bottle Seven Springs water which Janet was pretty vocal about."

"Huh. Funny your principal didn't mention either of those."

"Sam? In boarding schools they're called Head of School." Powell smiled and shook his head. "He may not even have known about the developer – that wasn't an institutional thing, and anyway it worked itself out. As to the trustee, Sam's pretty old school. The board killed the project and I'd guess he'd want to keep school squabbles in the family."

The lieutenant jotted notes and Powell took the opportunity to take another look at her. Solidly built, not thin. But trim, he thought, even muscular. Silver ear posts in the shape of snowflakes lent a feminine touch. No rings. But why am I looking? He looked away and back again, and as if to dispel the moment briskly asked, "Anything else, lieutenant?"

"No." She shook her head without looking up. "I mean yes." Lips bending in a slight smile. "I mean I don't want to sound like Columbo but there is one more thing. Earlier when I asked you if you thought someone had done something to Ms. Debian, you said, 'no, not then.' I wonder what you think now?"

The answer, he knew, was that he didn't know what to think. But the response he gave was a question. "Did you find Janet's gloves out there, lieutenant?"

VISITATION

"**S**nowing again," the man says to the empty room. "No more of that Mexican tar for me."

In his left hand an eyedropper; in his right an ordinary soup spoon. Both are shaking as he squeezes the dropper's black bulb and droplets of citric acid find their way into the spoon's bowl, rolling down from its rim in a miniature rivulet, first colliding with and then dissolving a small mound of white powder heaped in the spoon's center.¬ The man's breathing is quick and shallow, his red-veined eyes focused on the spoon as he eases the eyedropper blindly but surely down to a shot glass of water on the scuffed Formica tabletop, squeezing, releasing, raising, squeezing again to add just enough water to bring the tide line of viscous liquid up to the spoon's edge. Now he sets the eyedropper down and picks up a plastic lighter again without looking, snapping it twice to bring it to flame, a blue and orange fire that he brings carefully to the bottom of the spoon, watching closely as the spoon's liquor begins to bubble and swirl. After a long moment, he lays the lighter next to the eyedropper and picks up a blue syringe, immersing the needle at the center of the spoon's small pool and raising its plunger slowly with a practiced thumb until the spoon is empty.

"Andjeo," he says, again addressing no one. "Here's to you."

The spoon is on the tabletop now between the eyedropper and the lighter.

The man balls his empty right hand into a fist and lays his arm on the table, bringing the needle's tip to the fold of his elbow, four inches below the rubber tourniquet that is tied around his bicep. The needle finds its mark on the first attempt and the man looks briefly across the dingy room, speaking now in the direction of the door as if he saw through it to the white world beyond. "I'd share if you were here, Julie. You know that."

He takes a deep breath and holds it while his left thumb slowly eases the syringe plunger into its load, sighing only after he has removed the needle, then sighing again as he rises from his chair and makes his way across the room to a battered sofa.

"I'd share," he says again while his head begins a rhythmic nod. As his lips begin to shape another word, the nod stops and his face come up for a moment, eyes wide and mouth open. His hands, resting on his thighs, clench briefly at something unseen before his chin drops to his chest and rests there.

CHAPTER 5

Monday, 4:15 p.m.

Alpenglow on the Presidentials caught Kate Romeo's eyes as she drove west from Bethlehem along the Amonoosuc River towards the Troop F barracks in Twin Mountain. The snow-covered mountains around the valley were suffused with rose light as though the sun were shining on them through the glass of a gothic cathedral under the deepening blue of the sky's dome. She hiked these mountains as often as she could, and the sight of them at winter's dusk was enough to bring up memories of trails trekked in boots or on snow-shoes or Nordic skis. But neither the beauty nor the memories held her long. A young woman lying dead in the woods reached for her consciousness and caught its hem, tugging at it as insistently as a child might until she turned her thoughts back to the present and to the prescience of Father Mickey Powell's question.

If it was prescient. They had, in fact, not found any gloves within twenty feet of Janet Debian's body though with the new deep snow it could be that they were somewhere nearby, dropped or discarded as a last act of one sliding into hypothermic confusion. A real possibility – people did crazy things when the cold took them. She had been on the recovery team that went after the naked body of a winter camper whose scattered clothes marked his last hike on Mount Guyotte on a day when the mercury peaked at minus nine. But Powell's question was what interested her now. Had he simply noticed the missing gloves or was he playing with her, knowing full well that they wouldn't find them there. Had he actually found the body - or left it where it could be found? It was often the case that the finder was the perpetrator, and wasn't the older man/younger woman theme a classic? It wouldn't be the first time a priest had crossed that line - anymore you almost expected them to be across one line or another.

Kate Romeo sighed. All of it was possible but none of it felt right. Fred Boynton, her boss in Concord, wouldn't want to hear that. He would bark gruffly: "Forget how it feels, Kate. What are the facts?" But feelings did mean something. Powell had not felt evasive or hostile or defensive to her; he had just seemed sad, sad and burdened as if the weight of Janet's death added something to a load he was already carrying. Not the affect you would expect from a killer. Still, to give Boynton his due, it wouldn't hurt to see what she could learn about Powell.

Which could wait until after she heard from the M.E. She still couldn't rule out an accident although the fact that there were no gloves troubled her more than she had let Powell know, the more so since this Debian was apparently quite an outdoor person. Her apartment, which the school head or principal or whatever he was had opened for her, had an impressive collection of well-used, well-maintained gear. Alpine and Nordic skis and boots, snowshoes, trekking poles, backpacks, a sleeping bag and pad, climbing shoes and harnesses, carabiners, rope, and an ice ax but the only gloves were thin dress pair of black leather and a pair of blue Goretex mittens jammed well down into a ski boot. Surely there should have been another backcountry kind of pair. Where were they?

On the highway Romeo let the light on the river push the question aside, and felt the peaks and sky gather her in an embrace. In the spring there were trout to be caught on this stretch of river and not far upstream a trail led into the heart of the Pemi wilderness, four hundred square miles of forest and mountains in which two hours of hiking could take you to places where the only sign of humanity was the trail itself and the only sounds were the soughing of the wind in the trees and the rushing of water in the brooks, where the mayhem and busyness of life was reduced to a simple meal and a campfire. From the gear at her place, Janet Debian must have known this same deep joy.

And so Janet was back. Another sigh from Kate Romeo. Boynton always told her not to let the bodies get to her, to detach from them, treat them like objects, not people. But she could not do it. The lives of the dead were unfinished journeys, full stops on trails that might have led somewhere beautiful. The weight of disappointment that went with that bound her, so it seemed, to uncover what it was that brought the journey to its end. Now, as she approached the barracks drive, she spoke aloud to the deceased, "Janet, what the hell were you doing?"

No answer. Yet, Romeo thought. No answer yet. She wheeled her unmarked cruiser into the barracks parking lot and took a last look up at the mountains before she headed for the door. The peak of North Twin was still glowing, but its shoulders had fallen into shadow and Romeo thought of a sweet hidden campsite below it, along the middle reaches of the Little River. Stream crossings would make it difficult to access in snow but not impossible. *Soon,* she promised herself; *sometime soon.*

The office was quiet as Kate entered. Ted Landry was at his desk in the squad room and Joanne Fillion, the receptionist, was on the phone with someone. The room itself was so standard issue that it could have been any of a hundred state offices – grey metal desks and grey metal filing cabinets, grey cubicle dividers and fluorescent lights. What would distinguish it was invisible: shatter proof glass in the windows and ballistic panels in the walls and ceiling, an armory behind one mundane door and a holding cell behind another. All of it combined to close in around her like a spring fog, and she found herself longing, as she always did, to be somewhere else, somewhere with a sky, and trees, and unprocessed air.

"Hey, Lieutenant." Ted Landry speaking, a newbie pick up from the Whitefield P.D. just out of State Police training. "We got another overdose stiff, in Colebrook this time."

"And good afternoon to you, too, Ted," Romeo said with a wry smile. "I'm fine. How are you?"

"Oh, yeah . . . um, fine. Good afternoon." Landry reddened slightly and fumbled with his tie. "I thought – "

"Is Bill around?" Bill Kennedy, the barracks commander, her principal contact at Troop F.

"No, he's meeting with the chief in Lincoln. Something about some radar work on the Kanc." 'The Kanc' meant the Kancamagus Highway, route 112 between Conway and Lincoln, a beautiful winding road through the national forest that in some winters would be closed by now. Romeo recalled that local yahoos liked to road race there, first in cars and then on snow machines. A couple of them were killed every year. It was just that kind of work, picking through bloody wrecks to pull young corpses out, that had motivated her move up to narcotics and investigative services though the double duty was wearing on her. For the moment, though, the only way out was to take a job at HQ in Concord. *Which is not going to happen*, she thought. To Landry: "Now what's this about an OD?

"Local guy – Todd Brooks. Looks like heroin again." A wistful pause. "I played hoops against him back in the day. A big man with a helluva fade-away."

Romeo smiled to herself. For Landry 'back in the day' meant, what, about five years ago? But five years was enough for a jumper to fade away to nothing, leaving a big man with a small life. "You patrolling up there soon?"

"Tomorrow morning." Like her, Landry loved the North Country – never hard to get him on the road there.

"See if you can find out where he got it. Maybe there's a girlfriend or a homeboy who'll talk." Not likely, though. This was the fourth OD in the region in five weeks – looked like some purer H was now in the mix and so far no one was saying anything about where it was coming from.

"Can do, Lieutenant."

Romeo, half expecting the young officer to snap off a salute, stifled another smile. Most of the new ones, she knew, came from the military but it helped when they softened up a bit. *Not that Boynton would agree. But so what?*

"Hey, Loo?" Joanne was off the phone now. She was an almost lanky thirty-something with big hair and a hard-bitten look. "I got that info you were lookin' for. On the trustee? His name is Eric Ames – lives in Yarmouth, Maine, over near Portland."

"Great! How did you find that out?" Robeson had been as evasive as Powell had predicted he would be, saying he didn't recall any incident between Ms. Debian and a trustee but his eye movement – down and away from her – said that he was lying.

"Claudia, Claudia Thibodeaux, works in the office there? She's Cal's second cousin." Cal was Joanne's husband, a logger and scion of one of the North Country's sprawling French-Canadian clans, which as far as Romeo could tell were intertwined on both sides of the border in ways that an anthropologist couldn't decode. Fillions and Thibodeauxs and Champagnes were as thick on the ground there as ticks in August grass. "She said there was quite a dust up in the Head's office, that this guy Ames was screamin' so you could hear it through the door. Somethin' about money. I got a number, but we can't say it came from Claudia."

"Well, well. Seems Mr. Robeson needs a memory jog." Romeo knew how it was, though. Office politics. If money might be coming to the table, you'd try not to embarrass the guy who'd be bringing it. "How about the developer? Find anything on that?"

"Yeah, maybe. I knew it wouldn't be here in Bethlehem - their plannin' meetin's are all on Channel 2 and I watch them all the time." Small town politics, Romeo mused. The best and worst of American democracy. "So, I got hold of Shirley at the Littleton town offices? The one that takes the minutes for the Planning Board?"

"Let me guess - she's related to you?"

"Not really - she's my aunt's step-daughter."

Kate Romeo worked to suppress a smile. "What did she have to say?"

"Well, she wasn't sure, but she thinks it could have been Jim LaFlamme over at Northern Mountains Realty. She remembered some kind of protest about a development he wanted to put in down along 302 which would be just down the hill and across the town line from the school's property. She thought that might have been about wetlands - said it'd be in the minutes if we wanted to check."

"Could she fax them over?"

"In process, Loo. She'll send them sometime today."

"Thanks, Joanne." No surprise at her efficiency - Romeo had long thought that Joanne would have made a first-rate officer.

When she had suggested Joanne take the qualifying exam, though, she had politely declined, explaining that she didn't think the hat would work with her hair. And that was that – a paradigm of North Country reasoning that embraced simplicity but lacked ambition.

Not that small fortunes weren't made and lost here – but to the degree that they were, the gamblers were mostly outsiders, so-called flatlanders from south of the notches. So set in their geography were the locals, Romeo had learned, that 'south of the notches' had a cosmic meaning among them, at least among the older ones. Working a cold case early on in her tenure, she was trying to locate a witness only to be told by a local codger that he had gone south of the notches. When she had asked if he had any idea where, the old man had replied that he guessed it was some-place pretty warm but couldn't say for sure. Thought the minister might know. When asked, the minister laughed. "Oh, he's south of the notches all right. That man died two years ago. He might well be someplace pretty warm now."

Romeo smiled briefly at the memory as she grabbed a mug at the coffee station, filled it, and headed for the empty desk at the back of the room that served as her office when she was here. Before she was in her chair her mind was already working over the terrain of Janet Debian's demise like a surveyor running lines, considering what she knew, what she didn't know, and how to increase the former and decrease the latter. What she knew: not much. Of the who, how, when, and why she knew only the *who* with certainty. *How* was most likely hypothermia from the quick field exam of the body but the M.E. could find a contributing factor or something else entirely. *When* had to be between eleven when the dorm closed and nine fifty when the girl had found the body, but the low temperature would limit greater precision unlikely since it would slow the onset of rigor. Debian had at least been out there when it started snowing – no snow under her - but might not have been dead at that point. *Why* was a puzzler. A simple accident was still a logical explanation but didn't answer the why of her being out there in the first place. There were at least a couple of people who might have wanted her out of the way but were the stakes high enough for killing? Leads to follow there, anyway. And there was still this priest, this chaplain, who seemed to know something about death and loss. What was his story?

Might as well start there. Romeo sipped her coffee and called to Joanne, "Hey, cher, can you do one more thing for me?"

From the front of the office she heard, "Can you hang on a minute?" and then, "Sure, Loo, what do you need?"

Another sip before answering. "Could you call Claudia again? Ask her for some background on this Father Powell? Like maybe where he worked before?"

"Sure can. And now I've got one for you." Romeo smiled. *I work for her as much as she works for me*, she thought. "That's Mc-Dade on the line. He says there's no blood."

"Talk about stating the obvious!" Romeo snorted and picked up the receiver. Hank McDade was the Grafton County medical examiner - a surgeon and forensics man who was usually right on point. "Hank? Romeo. Don't tell me there was no blood. I already know that. I was at the scene, remember?"

"Easy, lieutenant." Hank McDade's voice was low and firm. "I didn't say there was no blood. I said there *is* no blood. Janet Debian had bled out completely."

Powell, Kate Romeo thought. *What he said.*

CHAPTER 6

Monday, 9:23 p.m.

If he was Obi-Wan, who was the Vladimir? Mickey Powell, ensconced in his favorite Queen Anne wing back, pondered this as he fumbled to fill his briar with tobacco, dropping strands of riff cut burley and black perique into his lap. On the end table next to the chair was Janet Debian's green spiral bound notebook, which he had appropriated from her classroom at the close of his interview with Lieutenant Romeo. Strange, he thought, that the police had not cleared out her desk themselves but conceded that they did not know what the journal contained nor had he imagined it when he'd picked it up. Just what were you looking for then? Powell knew the answer to that question without having to speak it to himself. Vanity. Fifty-six and alone, he wanted to see again what a young, attractive woman had written about him. Simple vanity.

Since he had reviewed her journal bi-weekly along with those of the rest of last spring's class he knew some of what would be there. 'Obi-Wan tells us to perceive,' the first entry began. 'Don't think. Perceive. Here goes.' What followed was what she had perceived sitting in the woods for their first meditation in nature a year before. And she was perceptive. Sights, sounds, smells; sky, clouds, trees, twigs, ice, smoke, cars, birds, snow - exhaustive lists of what her senses brought her with only occasional random thoughts thrown in. 'What is Obi-Wan up to?' The question was fair enough and the Star Wars reference was charming, though it had only made him feel old at first. Why not Skywalker? Still, better Obi-Wan than Jabba the Hut – or some of the other attributions that the journal now contained.

And that was the surprise – after the class had ended, Janet had kept the journal going. Some of it followed the perception practice that he had taught while other pages functioned more as a diary. Some of the characters were quite recognizable – Sam Robeson was Mr. Bean, Sagan had to be Dan Caplan, the physics teacher, while from the context 'Nads' no doubt referred to Mark Vitelli, the Outdoor Program Director. Others, though, were less clear. Who was LC? Or Jacob? Who was Underdog? And who was Vladimir?

From the diary, it might be someone she was seeing, though the first mention of the name, in July, sounded like a pretty random encounter. 'Jemimah called my number but when I stepped up, she went on break. No pancakes for me! Instead, ice blue eyes under dark hair, trimmed beard, trim bod. Vladimir.'
The next line was Mr. Bean's – she'd been late for a meeting with him although the entry didn't note that it had caused a problem. No mention of Vladimir again until late in August. 'Vlad called! He peeked to get my name. Is that flattering or creepy? Wanted to know if I'd see him when he was in the area. Told him he should look for me at the draw.' Mysterious, Powell thought, but not particularly threatening. An entry about 'Jacob' a few days earlier had more heat: 'Ran into smarmy Jacob in the woods today walking in his suit and tassel shoes with some surveyor type. He wanted to find where 5 and 6 were, had heard that I might know. Didn't tell him squat. Not a happy camper. Too damned bad for

him. He thinks he knows all the answers, but he just proves Obi-Wan's point.'

Powell smiled, guessing that the point she referred to was a saying he wrote on the board on the first day of each of his classes - *If you think you know, you don't know; if you know you don't know, then you know* - his way of reminding his students and himself that only God can know completely, and a good rejoinder to the insecure arrogance of some adolescents. And to Jacob as well, whoever he was. And to himself, too, at least the last part. He knew that he didn't know who Jacob was or Vladimir or 5 and 6 - or what had happened to Janet Debian.

Powell tamped the tobacco down lightly with his index finger, tucked the pipe into the right side of his jaw, and lit it with a black butane lighter that spat flame sideways like a miniature blow torch. As the heady, sweet smoke curled around him, he considered what he didn't know and what to do about it. *Nothing. Nothing is the first option*, he thought. *It's a police matter. Let it be.* That answer did not sit well, though. Janet's death was a rock in the pond, and even if he waited for the ripples to calm themselves, things would not be the same however much they appeared that way on the surface. The rock would still be there unless and until someone dove in to find it, to bring it to light, to understand it. Sanborn wasn't likely to do it. Would Romeo?

Letting pipe smoke swirl around him, Powell let the lieutenant drift across his consciousness as darkness rose in the east beyond his wall of windows. He liked her; he knew that. There seemed to be something solid there like the granite foundation that laid under this whole region of the state. But something more than that too, something live and curious and connected. *Connected.* The whole premise of his class - and the whole problem of Janet's death. Everything was connected. So how did the details of her end connect with what he knew about her and about the world? The connections were there if only vision was sharp enough to perceive them. Powell drew on the pipe, savored its heady flavor for a moment, puffed smoke out in a cloud, and reached for Debian's journal again.

Which revealed little. A little more than an hour of reading – two pipe fills - brought him from where he had left off in August to her last entry less than a week ago. Jacob appeared again in late September and then again just after New Years; encounters with Vladimir occurred in September and December with enough commentary between meetings to suggest a nascent relationship. A new character, 'LC,' surfaced on October 2nd and reappeared in November. The only revelation was the identity of Underdog – an entry describing a Morning Reading performance that had to be Lee Zelman's. "Underdog blew us away at MR," Janet wrote, "with a passionate reminder that science was the way we came to know our world and that we ignore its lessons at our own risk." Powell remembered the occasion. Some student moron had scrawled, "Science is the whore of capitalism" on the chem lab blackboard and Lee had issued a full force rejoinder. The nickname was perfect. Zelman was a small, quick man whose compassion always put him on the side of the less fortunate – the underdogs.

LC was apparently more of a mixed bag. The October entry read, "First encounter with old LC himself. (The locals say he's been around for a while.) He scared the kids but I feel sorry for him. Never saw so much hair." The second entry, in November, only noted that she'd seen him again loping through the woods on a day too cold for it. What, Powell, wondered, had frightened the kids? And which kids were they?

And then what did the nickname Vladimir suggest? A

Russian? A Marxist like Lenin? Obviously Janet was fond of him
– she talked about his eyes and his touch and his smile – but little
there as to where they'd met or who he might be. Though probably not someone at the school – their actual meetings were far too
infrequent for that. Jacob, too, seemed to be an outsider but in
his case it seemed that their encounters took place at the school so
maybe someone would know something about him.

   Powell stood and stared at the reflection thrown back at
him by the windows – a tall man, not heavy, in a light blue turtle-
neck and dark blue pants, short hair thin and graying, the line of
his nose broken slightly off center, age lines chiseled in his face,
deep set hazel eyes made dark by the rings below them. *Not much
to look at,* he mused. And knew that the thought had its genesis in
the journal, not with what he'd just read, but with what he hadn't.
After his class had ended, Janet wrote only a little about him. No
reason that she should have, he knew, but wouldn't it have been
nice? *The wistful longing of the aging male.* Did priesthood make
that better or worse? Both, he supposed, smiling wryly. Not that
it mattered – too much a part of who he was to change it.

   Movement on the hill across the road drew his attention
away from his reflection, thin beams of light playing here and
there on the snow and trees by the now vacant tennis court. Lower down, on the school road below the gym, red taillights as a
car started, then low beams coming on, sweeping across the field
in front of his house before disappearing down the hill towards
town. The thin beams, two of them, probably flashlights, made
their way down the slope and stopped at the road, probing the
dark in a circle from where they stood before crossing the town
road and starting up the walk to his house.

   Powell opened the door just as the two men reached it.
One was Officer Cox in full uniform, the other Don Teller, the

Dean of Students, in flannel pajamas and a down jacket.

"Who are you looking for? Did one of the kids bolt?"

"Hey, Mick." Teller was shivering slightly. "Did you notice anyone on the hill?

"Come in out of the cold." Powell held the door as the men stepped past.

"I didn't see anyone but a car pulled out of there while you were on the back side of the gym. Headed for Littleton, I'd guess."

"Did you get a look at it?" Cox's voice was urgent.

"Not really – too dark. A little wagon of some kind by its shape. An Outback or an Escort maybe."

"Dammit!" Cox's frustration was right on the surface, Powell thought, like frost on grass. "He could be on the highway or halfway through town by now."

Powell turned to Teller who was flushed from his run through the snow.

"Mind telling me what's going on?"

"I wish I knew. Got a call from Cathy at Carter twenty, thirty minutes ago that she thought she heard someone in Janet's apartment. I called the P.D. and Steve and I went up together. Whoever it was must have heard us, though, because when we unlocked it the place was empty, a window was open, and you could see the spot where someone hit the snowbank."

"Anything taken?"

Teller spoke. "Didn't look like it – just some mail on the floor. I was never in there much, though. Think you'd know if anything was missing?"

Powell thought for a moment. He could picture Janet's cozy living room – she'd invited him up for tea and conversation fairly frequently when she'd helped with his class but since then he hadn't spent much time with her. "Probably not," he said. "I might notice something obvious but nothing else."

"Maybe worth a try." An urgency in the dean's voice that surprised Powell but the reason for it came before he could ask. "And anyway, you could help us settle the girls down."

That made sense. With a teacher dead and a cop arriving and then running out into the winter night, the place would be buzzing. "Okay. I'll take a look."

"Try not to touch anything. We may want to dust for prints," Cox said. "I'll stay down here until the chief comes. Maybe we can pick up a tire track."

Powell found his coat and made his way up the hill toward the dorms with Teller, neither of them speaking for a time, letting the night settle around them like a mantle. Finally the dean, younger than Powell by a quarter century or more, let some of his anxiety loose. "Jesus, Mick," he said, "This is getting weird. What's going on?"

"I wish I knew," Powell said. "But I do know this - in the end, it will be clear."

"You think so?" Teller drew his jacket closer around him as they stepped into the circle of a streetlight's glow at the foot of the school's main driveway.

"I'm certain of it." Powell watched the young man nod and decided not to tell him that there was no knowing when this end might come; maybe tomorrow, maybe not until the Last Day. Those not used to thinking about eternity did not find much comfort in it.

When they entered, Carter Dormitory was as electric with emotion as Powell had imagined. He could hear sobbing from one direction while from another a loud argument cascaded down the stairs. "Why don't you have Cathy call a dorm meeting?" he said to Teller. "Give us a chance to pour some oil on the waters."

"Right. But will you talk to them? You're better at it than I am." Teller fumbled in his jacket pockets for a moment. "Here – here's a master key that'll get you into Janet's. Meet you up there in a couple of minutes."

As Powell started up stairs, the dean disappeared around a corner and down the corridor that separated the first-floor rooms. At the top of the steps, a similar corridor ran off to the right while Janet Debian's apartment occupied the end of the building to the left. Black and yellow police tape across the doorframe blocked entrance but only symbolically. Powell inserted the key, worked the lock, eased the door open, and ducked under the tape to cross the threshold.

The small room he stepped into was just the way he remembered it – a coat rack immediately to his left, a sitting area and desk to his right, a small open kitchen straight ahead, and a dining table cattycorner across the rectangle from him near a window that still stood open. A hallway beyond the coat rack led to the bedroom and bath. There was a scattering of mail on the floor by the desk but otherwise everything seemed to be in its place – pictures neatly hung, counters empty, drawers closed. Janet herself was tidy, Powell recalled, and whatever team Romeo had brought in must have been as well. He crossed the room to the open window, studied the footprints lit by the driveway streetlight in the snow twelve feet below, and crossed back to the bedroom hallway. The bedroom was as neat as the rest of the apartment – bed made up, nothing left out, even its windows sparkling. The view was across the culdesac that separated the girls' dorm from the boys' – the Belt, the kids derisively called it, short for Chastity Belt. Nothing to see really – snowbanks from the maintenance guys plowing and one parked car nearly buried in them, Cox's cruiser next to it, and beyond that the walkway up to the facing dorm, its façade looming in the darkness. There was something disquieting in the scene, but Powell could not pinpoint what it was; perhaps, he thought, just the idea of an intruder slipping through the shadows of that peaceful scene. Shaking his head at the image, he walked back down the short hall to the living room.

Where he saw something new. From this angle, Janet's desk caught his eye differently, as did the white cord hanging down from her phone. Leading nowhere. A close up look revealed that the cord was too short to reach the jack on the baseboard near the floor lamp – a gap that fired synapses in Powell's memory. *Answering machine.* When he'd had to call her about class, her voice would come on, as pleasant recorded as it was in life. Either Romeo's people had taken it or the burglar had. What could have been interesting about it?

The unspoken question was interrupted by Don Teller's knock. The door eased open to his voice. "We're ready for you downstairs, Mick."

The Carter girls were crammed into the downstairs lounge, on its couches, coffee tables and floor. There was an undercurrent of whispering and a palpable vibration of emotion hanging in the air. *Fear*, Powell thought. Always best just to acknowledge it. Raising his hand, he asked, "Who besides me is a little scared right now?"

A half dozen hands went up, and then a half dozen more, and then gradually the rest. "That's normal. We don't know what's going on and it's scary. We don't know what happened to Janet and we don't know who was in her apartment. But we do know some things and one of them is this - someone will be here tonight, awake, to help Cathy make sure this place is safe." He glanced briefly at Teller and was pleased see the dean nodding at this promise. "And another is this – what is unknown, eventually becomes known."

Out the picture window behind the semi-circle of girls, Powell watched as a dark sedan pulled up to the Belt, past the buried car. Kate Romeo got out and headed purposefully for the entrance as a second sedan pulled in behind her. "The police are here now," he said, using their arrival as his closing. "If you noticed anything unusual at all, tell them."

The girls turned to the window and Powell eased himself toward the door, meeting Romeo as she came through. He stepped back to let her in, heard Romeo brusquely say that she needed to talk with him, saw the cars on the Belt in a narrowing frame as the door swung shut. And knew what was wrong with the picture.

CHAPTER 7

Monday, 10:05 p.m.

Powell knew too much, that was the problem. Kate Romeo weighed this carefully as she watched the tow truck back up the narrow driveway. Faces lined the windows of the dormitories on either side, and Romeo wondered what would happen here when word got out about McDade's homicide ruling. Her speculation faded, though, as Father Michael Powell himself came out of the school's main building and stepped onto the plowed path that led across an open field towards her. First the blood, then the gloves, and now the phone and this. Was it just coincidence that these revelations had come through him? Or had he known about them all along? Was he simply trying to help or was he playing with them?

The blood facts were most bizarre. It was twilight by the time she'd caught up with McDade, the medical examiner, at the lab in Littleton Hospital and had followed him to the building's small morgue where he pulled back a sheet to reveal the pale nude body of Janet Debian, once a person, now an object. Even after a thousand corpses, Romeo thought, you wouldn't get used to that.

"So we go to draw some blood for toxicology tests and there isn't any," McDade said. "That's a little different, huh? And no obvious reason – wrists and neck intact, no head wound, no blood on her clothes and none at the scene, no sign of trauma at all, right? But look at this." McDade gently spread the corpse's legs and indicated a thin red line on the inside of its right thigh a half inch below the joining of her leg and torso."

"What's that, Hank?" Romeo asked.

"That, Lieutenant, is no accident. Someone opened up her femoral artery. She would have bled out in minutes."

"Jesus!" Romeo could not remove her eyes from the incision.

"Exactly. The thing is it's an odd way to kill someone."

"Why's that?"

"She would have had to be unconscious when the cut was made. Why not just smother her or stab her in the heart?"

Now the lieutenant pulled away from the slim body on the examining table and studied the doctor's craggy face, thinking *how do you do this*, saying, "Back up a minute. Why unconscious?"

"In a bleed out, unless the victim is completely relaxed there would be involuntary spasming before all the blood drained. We'd see some light bruising on the heels or head or arms."

"So she couldn't have done this to herself?"

"Not likely." McDade grinned tersely. "But even if she could have, how'd she get dressed again?"

Romeo nodded.

"So unconscious but no sign of bruising so no concussion, right? What put her out?"
"Some kind of drug, I'd guess. I'm having her sent down to Dartmouth-Hitchcock so we can test some tissue samples."

"Thanks, Hank. Any thoughts on the perp?"

"Someone who knows something about anatomy for sure. And definitely not a crime of passion – too methodical. But I'd look for a lover."

"Really?" McDade, she thought, always likes to save a surprise. "Why?"

The doctor was now gently draping the sheets over Janet Debian. "From the muscle distension and fluids our friend here had definitely been intimate with someone. Not forced either."

"If she was unconscious . . ." Romeo let her question trail off but the doctor saw where she was going.

"Maybe - if whoever it was happened to be patient enough. Mostly they aren't - there'd be bruising."

"Semen?"

"No. No hair either. Maybe wearing a condom. Maybe a woman. Maybe no connection to her demise but she would probably have been undressed when she was cut so maybe they go together."

Maybe a woman? As far as anyone knew, Janet Debian did not have a boyfriend but what about a girlfriend? Romeo held the thought for a moment, turned it over, rolled it around her mind. Would being lesbian be something that a young teacher would feel she needed to hide? How tolerant would a small school be? If it wasn't, would there be anyone she might have confided in? No suggestion of it in the interviews she'd had so far but at this point everyone was thinking accident. Would they say more if they heard murder? Perhaps nothing there but still a strand that she'd need to trace to see if it was woven into some bigger design.

That was all from McDade - at least for now. He had promised to expedite the tissue work so there might be something coming there. Romeo had left the lab agitated by the uncertainty and had not been calmed by the voice that had caught at her in the lobby like a cat's paw pulling at upholstery.

"Lieutenant!" The voice's pitch was just this side of shrill and its timbre as sharp as glass shards. No mistaking who it was.

"Amy Ashton from the Daily Record!"

The woman Romeo turned to face was brunette trying for blonde, middle aged trying for young, thick trying for thin. No need to acknowledge her; a question would come in any case.

"Lieutenant, I understand you found a body this morning."

"Who told you that?" Romeo asked, in as even a tone as she could manage.

"Are you denying the report?"

"I haven't actually denied anything. But if the report is that I found a body, that I would deny."

"Did anyone else?"

"Did anyone else what?"

"Allow me to clarify." New voice, just as familiar, coming from behind her.

This speaker was thick trying for thicker, grey-haired trying for bald, fifty trying for fifty-one. "Were police called to a scene in Bethlehem where a dead body was recovered?"

"Hi, Al." Al Johnson had covered the police and sports beats for the Weekly Courant for going on two decades. "And, yes, I can confirm that a body was recovered. Beyond that I cannot comment."

"Who was it?" Ashton's Brillo tone again.

"I can't comment."

"How did he die?"

Would the woman never learn that her manner only turned sources off? "The medical examiner has not issued a formal report yet. Until he does, I can't comment."

"Just one more question, Lieutenant." Johnson this time.

"Al, I really cannot – "

"Would the lieutenant – " Johnson was grinning now. " – comment on the possibility of a steak and a beer tonight?"

Romeo laughed. "I would have to deny the beer. I can confirm the steak."

In the end, having left a glaring Ashton, her beer denial had remained firm, but she had confirmed a mellow cabernet to go along with the rib-eye that Al had grilled on the snow covered deck of the house he'd built in the woods above the frozen course of the Amonoosuc. Though their five-year on-again, off-again affair was in off mode now, Al's house remained the most comfortable space she knew in the North Country. While he tended coals and scrubbed potatoes for the oven, she tossed a salad together and immersed herself in jazz from his collection – Clifford Brown and Max Roach from way back when – and wondered what was wrong with her that she backed away from moving in. Almost enough. *Almost enough here.* Almost, she knew, but not quite. For all their ease in being together, there was at the center of Al Johnson something that he would not reveal, some fear or hurt or resentment that he would not let her see. The few times she came close his usually open disposition closed up like a box turtle in the woods, not looking, not moving, not responding. And so they stayed with drinks and dinner, a movie now and then, or a hike, and occasional bouts of intimacy that were satisfying if not breathtaking.

"New spice rub, Kate. You up for it?"

"I take it you mean on the steak?" she said, grinning.

"I did. Do you have something else in mind?" Wide, goofy smile from him.

"What's in it?"

"Sorry, that's a first amendment issue. I got it from a confidential source."

"We have ways of making you talk."

The goofy smile again. "I know. I'm hoping."

Romeo shook her head and laughed. "Rub up the steak, news guy."

The rub was fine – piquant and somehow sweet like the dinner itself. Easy, thoughtful conversation, random laughter, romantic innuendo, time passing without notice. Not a bad end to a troubling day. Softened by two glasses of the wine, Romeo had been considering Johnson's offer of a refill in the hot tub on his deck when her parka on the coat tree across the open room began to buzz insistently. Shrugging resignedly, she dropped her dishtowel and moved quickly to fish her phone from its pocket.

Landry. Phoning to tell her that the scanner had just had a call from Seven Springs reporting an intruder in a girl's' dorm. *Where Janet lived.* Romeo had pulled her coat on before she remembered where she was.

"Sorry," she'd offered to Johnson. "Gotta go."

"Kate, you - "

"Dinner was terrific. But this is the way it is."

The way it is. Wheeling her cruiser around the tight curves of Bethlehem's snow-covered back roads, Romeo had brooded over the way it was. Was it a life? Too many days like this one on the byways of the small towns of rural New Hampshire, poking into the failures and miseries of the lives of little people whose frustration with the meanness of their stake in the world simmered beneath the scenic quaintness and sometimes boiled over in desperation and violence. Not home enough to keep a cat. Romeo had sighed but then had found herself chuckling.

"You don't even like cats," she said aloud, taking the corner from Gilmanton Brook Road onto Springs Lane, a mile below the school. The lane was sanded and straight here, and Romeo gunned it to cover some ground before the tight steep S that rose to the campus. At the top of that rise were taillights against the snowbank and silhouettes in the road. Cox was one – pulling a double shift, Romeo guessed – and from the fedora and trench coat she knew that the other was Sanborn, almost a cartoon in that get up. But a dangerous one. Pulling up beside them, she'd rolled down the window and asked, "Whatcha got?"

"Nothing of interest to you, Lieutenant." Sanborn his usual unhelpful self.

Lieutenant Romeo gave him a long look. "Walter, the word may not have gotten to you, but I have an open homicide investigation at this school and as long as it is open anything suspicious here is of interest to me. Clear?"

Sanborn had merely glowered in reply, but Cox came through. "Break in at the dorm. Debian's apartment. The dean – you know, Teller – and I chased him down here. That guy Powell, he lives right here. He saw a car pull out. He and Teller went up to see what's missing. We've got a tire track out of the parking lot there – I'm waiting for the photographer."

"You let Powell go up?"

If Cox understood the implication of her question, he hadn't shown it but Romeo had not waited to ask. Gunning her engine again, she'd headed for the dorm.

What was missing was Debian's answering machine. Since Sanborn had followed her up to the dorm, Romeo had let him handle the meeting, smiling now at the thought of him in the midst of all that earnest adolescent female angst. Not likely that he'd get anything but if he did, Cox would pass it along later. She buttonholed Powell on the dorm's front steps.

"So what did you find in the apartment, Father?"

The priest's lips had tightened into a terse, brief smile. "It's more what we didn't find. Unless your people took it out?"

"We didn't remove anything. What was it?"

"C'mon, I'll show you."

Powell led her back upstairs, ducked back under the crime scene tape with her, pointed out the dangling wires and the empty space on the desk. "I know she had a phone machine. I've left messages on it myself."

"Recently?" One of her guys should have checked it if it was there when they came through – standard operating procedure.

"No, not recently. Sometime before Christmas maybe. We were trying to set up a meeting then."

"About what?"

"Interdisciplinary studies – we're on a committee for that."

"Uh huh." Eyes sweeping the room, noting the mail on the floor. "You do that?"

"Nope. There when I came in. Maybe in grabbing the machine?"

"Could be." Most logical explanation, Romeo had thought, but you had to believe that someone cool enough to be in here while people were still awake would be more careful than that. "Anything else?"

"I don't know. Something to look at, anyway."

Powell had led her into the bedroom, between the neatly made bed and the tidy dresser, to the window overlooking the drive where her car and Sanborn's were sandwiched around a snow-covered compact. "See that?"
he said, pointing to the sandwich filling. "That's Janet's car. Not where she would have parked it, though. Faculty in this dorm have spots in the lot below it."

Romeo kicked herself that she hadn't thought about a car before. Her working assumption had been that Debian had walked into the woods but the M.E.'s report nixed that. Not thinking about how the body could have been moved was a rookie mistake. She reached for her phone to call a tow truck and turned to Powell to say, "Go find Robeson, will you?" No point in waiting any longer to tell the Head.

And now, twenty-five minutes later, he was back, his breath clouding in the cold as he stepped up to where she stood on the dorm porch.

"Get him?"

Powell nodded. Did he look agitated? Romeo wasn't sure.

"Took long enough," she said.

Another nod. "He wasn't home. I had to go check his calendar to find out where to reach him."

"No cell phone?"

"He was at a trustee's over in Franconia. Service is pretty spotty over there. Should be here in ten minutes or so. But, um, Lieutenant?"

Romeo was surprised to see that the priest seemed tongue-tied. "Yes?"

"I have something else I think you'll want to see."

CHAPTER 8

Tuesday, 8:51 a.m.

LC was Lon Chaney.

Lon Chaney was the Naked Man.

Underdog knew.

Those revelations had come as Powell stood in a clump of faculty outside the academy's main entrance on Tuesday morning watching students file onto chartered coaches for the ride to the airport in Manchester. The school was closed – for at least a week, maybe longer. For once Robeson had acted decisively, making the call within minutes of his brief meeting with Romeo the night before. *Not much choice really,* Powell thought. You couldn't ask parents to leave their kids on a campus where someone had just been murdered by an "assailant or assailants unknown" as the phrase went, especially when it looked as if the perpetrator might have come back. And so, the faculty had worked the phones, calling parents of their advisees, networking rides and pick-ups, offering what reassurances they could. Before eight the buses were pulling into the parking lot and Lee Zelman, the science department head, was standing next to him saying, "What the hell is this all about, Mick?"

"God knows." Which was the truth, Powell thought. *What seems unknown is always known.* "But I wish he'd tell someone."

"You were talking to the cops. Did they tell you what happened to her?"

"Not really." Which was not the truth. Or at least not the whole truth. He thought back to his conversation with Lieutenant Romeo the night before, to raised eyebrows and taut lips at his new disclosure, to their wordless walk down to his house, to his sheepish nod in handing over Janet's journal. She had thumbed it quickly at first, slowing when she reached the more recent entries. Romeo had only nodded when he explained what the nicknames were but there was no humor in her voice when she finished. "So what else are you hiding, Father?"

What Powell heard in her tone was authority taking advantage of its power, a faint echo of the chief priests and Pilate. Impulse had produced his response: "Don't make your ineptitude my problem, Lieutenant."

"What the hell does that mean?" Anger flashing in her eyes then.

"It means I'm not hiding anything. That journal was there for you to find but you didn't take the time. When I realized what it said, I gave it to you. Just like Janet's car, Lieutenant. Maybe 'thank you' would be in order."

"*Thank you?*" Romeo had visibly bristled, like a mongoose in a fight. "A woman is dead here, Powell. And at every turn you're standing there – the body, the blood, the gloves, the car, the notebook. I should thank you with some handcuffs."

The body, the blood. An echo of the ancient liturgy – and a tacit acknowledgement, probably unintended, that Janet had bled to death. To Romeo he'd calmly said, "The woman who's dead here is my friend. If you know who killed her, I hope you will handcuff him. But in the meantime you might want to keep me around since I seem to be turning up more than you are."

Glaring, Kate Romeo had slapped the notebook shut and left him, slamming the door hard on her way out. And now standing with Zelman, watching the buses, he found himself wondering if that door would open again.

Wondering, yes, and hoping, too. Hoping that it would. Hoping so for Janet, of course, but for himself as well. Recognizing now an old feeling, long dormant, exhilarating and a little frightening – there was something about Lieutenant Romeo that attracted him.

Old fool, Powell thought, shaking his head. *Can't afford that now.* To Zelman he said, "Say, Lee, let me ask you something – you know how Janet had nicknames for people? You know, like Sagan and Mr. Bean and 'Nads?"

Zelman smiled. "Why yes, Obi-Wan, I do. She called me Underdog. Used to sing the song at department meetings – 'speed of lightning, roar of thunder.'"

Powell grinned back. "I wish I'd heard that. And may the Force be with you."

"Why'd you want to know?"

"It's in her journal. Ever hear her call anyone LC or Jacob? Or maybe Vladimir?"

Zelman shook his head thoughtfully. "Never the last two. LC could be Lon Chaney, though.

"Lon Chaney? Like the old-time actor?"

"Yeah, that's it. That's what she called the Naked Man."

Powell knew who the Naked Man was – a patient from the treatment center that was down the hill from the school. Harmless enough apparently but when he got loose he loved to run through the woods nude. It had caused a bit of a stir when the girls soccer team had encountered him on the shortcut to the upper field. There had been other sightings but no confrontations.

"Apparently," Zelman was saying, "a very hairy guy. The

girls started calling him the Wolfman. Janet morphed that into Lon Chaney – she said she talked with him once.”

“Really? Where?”

“Don’t know. I don’t think she said. She said he was a nice guy who just never got over the sixties.”

Like a lot of us, Powell thought. The buses were full now and the first belched black smoke as it eased into gear and down the school’s driveway toward the road. To Underdog he said, “Interesting that someone as young as Janet even knew who Lon Chaney was.”

Zelman chuckled. “Every human mind has folds and creases that we can’t begin to understand – who knows what gets caught in them? But Janet’s was something, wasn’t it?”

“Indeed.” Both parts of what Lee Zelman said were true – the byways of the mind *were* unsearchable – even those paths that led to homicide, a dark journey as old as Cain’s and as new as yesterday. But a mind could be a lovely thing as well, as light and filled with color as a summer sunrise. And certainly Janet Debian’s was that, a variegated collage of interests; science and literature, music and woodscraft. And loneliness. That was clear from her journal. For all her classiness, there was an undercurrent of anxious insecurity that centered on her inability to find intimacy with anyone. Until Vladimir, whoever he was.

Powell pondered the Vladimir mystery for a moment while the last coach rounded the corner and disappeared among the maples that in a month or two would be tapped and hung with sap buckets for sugaring season. The image of that steady drip caught his attention and diverted his consciousness into a new stream, a roiled, red, ugly flow that spread into an image of Janet in a pool of blood. Somewhere such an image had been real. And since it had apparently not been an accident or a suicide, someone had seen it, had done it, had painted that particular picture on the world's canvas, knew what strokes and daubs had brought it into being.

Before he could begin to consider whose work it was, Zelman's voice asking something, something about police, brought him back to the now. " . . . will let us know something?"

"Hmm?" Powell caught himself, shook his head, answered as if he had actually heard the question. "Not likely. Better bet is they'll be up here asking each of us where we were Sunday night."

"Are you kidding? They think one of us did it?"

"Most likely someone the victim knew – isn't that what they always say on the cop shows?"

"I don't know." Zelman tugged at his lower lip pensively. "I mean, what do you think?"

"I don't know either. But if whoever it was came back last night, he'd have to be a pretty cool customer to go into that dorm – unless he was from here."

"That's true." Another lip tug. "What do you suppose he was after?"

"Good question. Her phone machine was the only thing that seemed to have gone missing."

"That makes no sense. Why not just erase the messages?" Zelman was ready to go on but a portly woman standing next to a Mercedes in the parking lot was waving and calling his name. "Dammit! Tom Osborne's mother – if I'm supposed to be one of the chosen people why am I dealing with her?"

His comment left Powell smiling but his first question was a good one. Not hard to understand erasing an incriminating message but why actually take the machine? And why would anyone leave a link if he was planning to kill her. Crime of passion maybe? But if she had been bled, that wasn't likely. That'd require some careful planning. Though if not that, what was the motive? Why would anyone want to kill Janet Debian?

No answer. Powell sighed. The parking lot was now cleared except for Zelman and Mrs. Osborne who was talking excitedly but thankfully outside the range of Powell's hearing. Turning away, he pushed through the school's ornately carved entrance doors and headed across the lobby towards the office, smiling at the sight of Claudia Thibodeaux who sat entrenched there behind her desk. And entrenched was the right word, he thought. For Claudia every day was a kind of administrative battle, an attempt to impose order on the inherently chaotic world of the Seven Springs Academy, the classic confrontation of the irresistible force and the immovable object. Claudia was the school's long serving registrar and it's self-righteous Pharisee, its chief priestess of rules and regulations that were too often ignored, in her view. Because he was a prime offender, Powell knew he was often regarded as the enemy, but he respected her integrity even as he violated her commandments.

Today she surprised him. "Mickey, can I talk to you?"

Her tone was tinged with worry, a sound Powell had never heard there before. "Sure, Claudia. What's up?"

"Not here." Claudia was almost whispering, another surprise from one given more to pronouncement than discretion.

"Okay. Meet me in the chapel." She nodded but let him leave without moving.

The chapel at Seven Springs was an afterthought, a dark room with a single small stained-glass window that housed an undersized contemporary altar and lectern in front, an ornate but tarnished silver cross that had been found in the ashes of the school's earliest home after a fire that had nearly forced its closure. Powell loved it – the one quiet space in a usually boisterous environment where he taught meditation and led contemplative prayer services for the very few students who were interested, teaching them to listen for that 'still, small voice' that Elijah had heard after the whirlwind and the earthquake and the fire – exact counterparts for the experience of adolescence. Now he had only a minute or two in the silence before Claudia ducked in anxiously from the hall.

"Are you okay, Claudia?" Powell said, realizing for the first time just how short the woman was – had to be five two or less but she played bigger when she was behind her desk.

"Yes, I'm . . . no . . . the police . . . you talked to them, didn't you?" Claudia looked around nervously as if she expected detectives to burst in at any minute.

"I did, Claudia. I think they're doing all they can, don't you?"

"It's not that . . . I mean, yes, but . . . well . . . will I get in trouble for talking to them?"

Now her worry made sense – it was about loss of position or influence, not about Janet. Venal, but human. "Well, what did you tell them?"

"Nothing, really.   I mean, I just mentioned that fight that Janet had with Eric Ames about water."

"I think everyone here was aware of that." Just the kind of internal dispute that most schools had. "Was there more to it?"

"Well." Claudia looked around the room warily, like gumshoe casing a joint for hidden microphones. "Eric was shouting that the school could lose hundreds of thousands of dollars, and Janet was shouting that all she wanted was to be able to make a presentation at the full trustees meeting in June. But then he kind of hissed at her that if she wasn't careful, she wouldn't be around for it."

"And you told Lieutenant Romeo that?"

Claudia Thibodeaux nodded and Powell could see a soft trace of fear in her usually hard grey eyes.

"Did anyone else hear him?"

Claudia pursed her lips thoughtfully. "Well, Sam of course; it was in his office. Maybe Mary, too."

Mary was Mary Jenkins, the somewhat mousy office assistant who, Mickey knew, seldom missed a thing. "I don't think I'd be too concerned," he said. "You were telling the truth, and it can be verified."

With that Claudia drew in a breath that puffed her up like an exotic bullfrog, turned, and left him standing there in the chapel's cool light, pondering the meaning of the trustee's implied threat. If Janet was alive, a reasonable person would conclude that he was suggesting that she'd be fired. But she was dead. And hundreds of thousands of dollars were involved. The combination of those facts framed his statement differently. And then one had to ask, if the school could lose hundreds of thousands, what was at stake for Mr. Ames? Powell sighed. *Money. 'The love of money is the root of all evil.'* St. Paul was not quite right about that – evil had other roots as well – but he was not so far off either. No matter what he'd intended, Mr. Ames had certainly earned himself a place on the suspect list.

That thought brought Lieutenant Kate Romeo to mind, and Powell found himself wishing that he had been less of a smart ass in his last conversation with her, and then immediately wondering why he wished that. Because – he was grinning now – *you like her, you pathetic geezer.* At any rate, she'd left little doubt that she'd be back. *Another chance for charm.* Laughing aloud at the unlikeliness of that, he exited the chapel wondering when his next chance would be. No knowing. And for now, no reason to do

The bright sun and crisp air raised Powell's spirits like an updraft under the wings of a bird. Starting down the plowed path that would take him past the snow shrouded tennis courts and into the pine stand beyond, he found it hard to imagine that anything sinister had happened in so beautiful a place. But evil, he knew, was no stranger to beauty. *Let it rest*, he thought. *Just take the moment.* But below him, down the slope and across the road were the woods where Janet Debian's body had been dumped, and closer, across the lawn below the building, were footprints in the snow where someone, perhaps a killer, had fled in the darkness, crossed and recrossed by the snowtrails of Cox and Teller who had pursued him. Evil would not rest. The tracks joined the pathway just before the pines, and twenty yards into the trees Powell saw the place where one set broke off again, heading through the drifts toward the corner of the gym. One set. Apparently, the patrolman and the dean had missed the fugitive's turn and continued down the path. In the dark, not close behind him, that would be easy enough. Powell stopped to survey the trail and surmised that the runner had left his car, the one he had seen pulling out, in the small lot by the gym's entrance on the building's far side where a light would have given the running man a marker to aim for. Powell stepped off the path to follow the trail, careful to stay far enough away to leave it undisturbed. Halfway to the corner of the gym was a flattened spot, then tracks again leading around the corner. The man had fallen, and where he had, something was wrong, somehow out of place, a line that didn't fit. Stepping closer, Powell smiled grimly and thought he'd be seeing Kate Romeo sooner rather than later. In the snow, just catching a ray of sunlight, a translucent blue plastic syringe.

CHAPTER 9

Tuesday, 2:06 p.m.

Why couldn't she stay mad at him? Kate Romeo sat at her desk with a stiff neck and with both hands wrapped around a mug of coffee, looking across the parking lot toward a line of trees by the river and the shadowed mountain beyond, wondering what it was about Father Michael Powell that disarmed her. When she had heard his voice on the phone, calling about the Lon Chaney ID and the syringe, she'd still been mad enough about his 'keep me around' comment to reach through the phone line and snap his head off his spinal column without even hearing what he had to say. But after she told him that she'd send someone by for the syringe she agreed to stop by his place later for "tea or whatever" as he'd put it. What was that about?

The answer came to her with her second sip of joe. Powell had apologized even though he'd been right. Part of what stung about his comment, she knew, part of what raised her hackles, was just that – he was right. Right about the gloves and the blood of course, but her team had ultimately noticed them, too. The car, though – they should have seen that and hadn't. So far it hadn't yielded much – totally wiped clean of fingerprints and no blood anywhere. There was a wool blanket in the trunk that might yield a fiber match with some strands found on the body but beyond that, nothing. Still, they should have been looking for it.

And the phone machine, too. Romeo had exploded on her crimes scene guys when she learned that it was gone. Not only had they failed to impound it so that techies could try to reconstruct old messages, they had even failed to write down what the two messages on it had been. "You know," one of them had said, "just junk stuff. Something from an insurance agency, I think, and some kind of doctor's call back maybe.

"No," she had hissed. "I don't know. Because I don't have the machine. But I do know that it was important enough for someone to take it." All they could do now was check the records for numbers and see if they could figure out who had called her.

But Powell had been the one who had apologized. Very simply, but directly. "I'm sorry," he'd said when he called about the syringe. "I was out of line last night when I saw you. Sometimes my mouth gets ahead of my mind."

That, in Romeo's experience, was extraordinary. Mostly the men she knew had trouble apologizing even when they were wrong. She couldn't think of one who'd ever been conciliatory when he was right. Not one. Something kind of attractive about it, she thought, then laughed out loud as she caught herself thinking about what Father Mickey Powell looked like – tall, trim, hazel green eyes, salt and pepper hair. *Just like high school, girl.* She remembered sitting in the second row in Algebra class, daydreaming about Billy Wilson, who sat behind her. At the twenty-five-year reunion she'd discovered that he was paunchy, bald Bill Wilson now, an actuary whose patter was as boring as his job. But there had been that 'what if' feeling once – and here it was again. Romeo sipped her coffee and laughed again. *What if what? What if he left the priesthood because he thought women in uniform were a turn-on?* But maybe we never really get out of high school – or get those high school feelings out of us. This thought brought a deep sigh with it. God forbid any return to adolescence with its hopeless awkwardness and endless stupid jokes about her name. 'Romeo, Romeo.'

Only the police academy had been worse – but at least that had ended when she'd broken the mouth-in-chief's arm during self-defense training and greeted him as Juliette when he'd arrived the next day in a cast.

The satisfying recollection of his chagrin faded as the memory segued into a present problem. Julie was the name of her Colebrook OD's girlfriend, and she was coming in this morning. Which might be a waste of time. According to Cox, it was hard to tell which she was missing most, the dead boyfriend or her heroin fix. If he was her hook-up, there might not be much difference. And even if he wasn't, it was becoming more likely that what killed him would kill her, too. The lab reports on the last three OD stiffs indicated that a purer line of junk was moving into the area, one that was taking its users to a permanent nod off. But according to the Drug Task Force its appearance was strangely sporadic, which was making the pipeline hard to find. Maybe Julie knew something. Cox didn't think so, but it was at least worth taking another run at her.

So that was the first part of the morning. Next was a scenic drive to Bethel, Maine – not for relaxation, of course, but to a work site to pay a call on Mr. Eric Ames with her counterpart from the Pine Tree staties. With luck, and not too much traffic in North Conway, that might get her back in time for 'tea or whatever' with the good Father Powell. Or might not. Hard to tell what might come up with Ames - there wasn't much on him. He was once in a bar scuffle but no charges had been filed since it was pretty clear that the other guy had started it, thinking that Ames was paying too much attention to his wife. One of his ski condo projects had nearly tanked, but he'd found some white knight at the eleventh hour and had ultimately come out more than whole according to the locals. Other than that, nothing but speeding tickets - and one loud argument with a vague threat that tied him to Janet Debian. Enough heat there to push him to murder? It didn't seem like his profile, Romeo thought, raising the coffee mug again. But still he was a suspect who had to be ruled out. And then there was the syringe: four inches of blue plastic now sitting in a baggie on her desk. Did it have a story to tell?

"Kate?" Joanne Fillion peered through the office door just as Romeo was setting the now empty mug down. "Julie Tuite is here. You know, from Colebrook."

"Thanks, Joanne." The tender nerve in her neck tweaked as she turned toward her secretary – just what she didn't need. "Why don't you take her coat and bring her in. And see if you can find me some ibuprofen, will you?"

Julie Tuite was a short, skinny, brunette in jeans and a Cape Cod sweatshirt whose lined face looked more forty-six than the twenty-six on her sheet. Her brown eyes - down when she entered – came up to meet the lieutenant's but instantly dropped down again, as if down was all she really knew.

"Ms. Tuite?" Eyes up, eyes down. "Thanks for coming in."

"Not much choice. Got no one with Todd gone. That other cop said maybe you could help." Not much conviction in her words, Romeo thought.

"I'm sorry about Todd, Julie. Can you tell me what happened?"

"Told that cop I don't know nothing about that. I went out for smokes and when I came back he was sittin' there cold."

"The medical examiner says he overdosed on heroin."

"I don't know nothing about that. If he was on something, musta been after I left."

She wants help, Romeo thought, but she won't help herself. "Show me your arms, Julie."

Now the woman's head came up, eyes narrow and glittering with fear. "I don't have to show you nothing."

"We found works in the room, Julie. And a baggie with trace amounts of H."

"Not mine."

"That trailer belongs to you, hun. Technically you were in possession of anything that was in it."

Surprise now, and panic sweeping across her face. "No way. That's not true. Todd got that place."

"Pretty sure you're wrong." Romeo reached to her belt, removed the handcuffs from their holster, set them on the desk. "But if you want to, you can wait right here while I send someone up to check the deed. Probably take most of the day – don't think I'll have a car up there for a while."

"No . . . no, I can't stay here. No. He said you could help me."

Sad, Romeo thought. *Can't last a day without a fix.* Hard to do it this way but if that's what it was going to take. "I'd like to help you, Julie. Maybe I could get you to a clinic. But you have to help me."

"Yeah . . . well, I want to . . . but I don't know nothing and . . . what do I have to do?" Tears welling in her eyes now, nose starting to run. Kate Romeo shook her head, opened a drawer, removed a box of Kleenex, and set it on the edge of the desk.

"Julie, just start with showing me your arms."

Julie Tuite shook her head without looking up but she didn't resist when Romeo reached across the desk and clasped her left hand and gently slid the sweatshirt sleeve up the skeletal forearm. Three small red welts, a pool of bruise surrounding each, no scars – a surprise on someone as weathered as Julie.

The same gentle check of the right arm revealed only two more tracks. "Looks like you weren't on the needle long. Is that right?"

Still sobbing, Julie nodded. "Me n'Todd stayed away from 'em. Did some A-bomb, sniffed a little snowball sometimes, y'know? Weak Mexican skag was all it was. Then he gets this new stuff, says the guy told him it was too good for that, that you needed to shoot it, had the spikes, too, blue ones, just like that one on your desk. We only did it a few times and now Todd's dead."

Romeo put a hand on her shoulder and let her cry. Most of the heroin in the region, she knew, was cut stuff coming up I-91 from Springfield, Massachusetts to St. Johnsbury— not from Mexicans but from the Puerto Rican gangs there – there weren't enough Latinos in the North Country for people to know the difference.

Some people injected it but more smoked it with pot or snorted it with cocaine like Julie and Todd, convincing themselves that it wasn't addictive that way. But now something finer was making its way in.

"Julie? Honey, that might be where you can help us. Do you know the guy's name, the guy Todd was getting it from?"

Julie Tuite shook her head. "I asked him but he wouldn't really say. Maybe his name was Onjoe or something."

"Onjoe?"

"Something like that." Julie squirmed in her chair. "I just know he said the snow angel was as sure as the blood in your veins."

As sure as blood. Maybe a street gang reference? Romeo

didn't think the locals were calling themselves Bloods but it was worth checking – someone in Manchester would have a handle on it. Now, though, she considered the syringe. *Just like that one on your desk.* Could Janet Debian's killing be tied to a drug deal gone wrong? From what people said about her she was an almost nerdy straight arrow – but how often did people end up saying 'I had no idea' about the exposed lives of crimes victims? If she was using, though, the tox screen on her organ tissue would pick it up. Or would it? Romeo made a mental note to ask McDade that question and turned her attention back to the twitchy young woman in front of her.

"Did Todd know a woman named Janet Debian?"

"Never heard of her. But that doesn't mean Todd didn't know her. He'd turn his head for any piece of snatch that walked by."

Thinking, '*So maybe you have motive, huh?* Saying, "And did that bother you?"

Julie shrugged indifferently. "Why should it? He always came home to me."

Home. A couple of strung out junkies crashing in a dilapidated trailer – but still it was home. What did it take? Not much. "Julie, we may need to talk with you again but for now how 'bout I try to get you into the methadone program in St. J.? I know some people over there who owe me a favor."

Quick furtive look up, then eyes away again. "Yeah, that'd be cool. I mean, I don't really need it except to take the edge off, y'know?"

"I do know." What they always said at first – I don't need it. *But all of us need something, don't we?* "Why don't you wait out front while Joanne makes a couple of calls, okay? Maybe you could ask her to come in?"

Not likely that someone as shaky as Julie, whether she had motive or not, could plan something as elaborate as Janet's death - bleeding her, getting her dressed, moving the body, stealing the phone machine. Still, the syringe might be a connection. Best not lose sight of that. And there was still the matter of where the junk that killed Todd Brooks was coming from. Romeo rolled her head around her aching neck as she watched Julie Tuite collect herself and leave. In a moment Joanne Fillion bustled through the doorway with a white plastic bottle and a red file folder.

"Ibuprofen - eight hundred milligrams is prescription strength. What is it, your back?"

"Nope - neck. A literal pain in the neck. Serves me right for being such a pain to everyone I meet."

Joanne laughed. "If that was how it worked, the pain would be lower down. Still got coffee to take these with?"

"Fresh out." Kate was laughing, too. "I'll get it in a minute."

"Nope, give me your mug; I'll pour you some. Here's the file on Dr. Ames."

Romeo's laugh stopped mid-chuckle. "*Doctor?* I thought the guy was some kind of entrepreneur."

"He is - in fact his office says he's over here this morning on a project. But he's a doctor, too."

"And just what kind of doctor is he?"

Joanne opened the file, turned a page. "Vascular surgeon, it says here."

Vascular surgeon. The kind of doctor who would know precisely where the femoral artery is and where you had to put a blade to cut it. "Call them back. Find out exactly where he is. Maybe I won't need to go to Maine."

CHAPTER 10

Tuesday, 2:06 p.m

He started with emptiness and ended with Ames and Romeo.

It was emptiness that drew him out, Powell knew. Not the emptiness of the forest, but the emptiness within, the emptiness of loss. Janet Debian's death was the catalyst – he knew that, too – but not the cause. There is only one loss, he thought, starting down the snowy road that led across a white field into the woods. *Only one thing to lose.* But not a thing at all, really. A state of being. *Connection.* Connection was *the* state of being. And the sense of one disconnection led to another and another and another until, like an electrical power grid collapsing breaker after breaker after breaker, there was no energy anywhere and all the lights went out.

Losing Janet was palpable – a friend not here, a colleague missing, a daily presence absent, a smile now not seen, laughter now not heard. But that loss also touched the keys of the past, sounding notes long quiet that came together in a deep resonant chord of grief, bringing echoes of voices – his parents', a long dead lover's, a murdered friend's - each of them recognizable but each fading and then gone, disconnected, leaving at last only the frightening silence of nothingness.

The woods were an antidote. The dim January sun slanting

through the snow-laden trees, the sting of the winter breeze, the sparkling snow, glinting in the air as it fell from branches – all these brought him to the present moment just as surely as his footsteps had carried him to the present place, his place, a rise above the path where he sat each week for meditation in nature – had been sitting for years in fact - as his class spread out to their own spots in the forest around the pond below him.

Tipping his portable backrest towards the stone slab behind him, he considered the exercise's three sequential questions. What do you perceive out there? What do you perceive in here? How is what's out there the same as what's in here? *Out there.* In some ways that was the hardest question for his students to engage. When the class started each January, the journal responses were mostly focused on how cold it was and how much the writers wanted to go back in. It took some class discussion to raise awareness on this point – the cold itself might be said to be objectively "out there," an interaction of energies that produced a physical response. But the desire to go back in – like all desire – was very much "in here," within the subject, not out there.   And that desire - like all desire, a wish for something other than what was at hand - kept them from seeing what was right in front of them.

Over time, though, some of them did begin to see, and their journals became catalogues of the bounty of the present moment: detailed accounts of snowflakes, clouds, branches, shadows, rocks, lichens, animal tracks, birdsong, traffic noise; meticulous comparisons of the sky's blue or the sun's brightness, or the strength of the breeze. Only when they began to see this richness of Now, did he ask them to turn inward, to examine their thoughts and feelings, to see how consciousness compared with creation. Their discovery, often, was this: the created order is always Now but consciousness was frequently Once or Someday. Once something hurt me. Once someone left me. Someday it will happen again. The past and the future, he hoped to show them, reside only in consciousness, and with them dwell anxiety and fear. The present moment could include pain, of course, but mostly it did not. If the mind could let go of the past and the future, could relax its grip on dread, it often found the present moment alive with color, flavor, and delight.

Alive. That was the promise of the present moment: that in it one could be alive. Once we were not alive, and Someday each of us dies but Now, in this present moment, we *live.* That, Powell thought, is the essence of the Gospel. 'I came that you might have life and have it more abundantly.' And that abundant life persisted. Janet Debian was dead but in the energy pulses and movements of consciousness, his own and other people's, she persisted - just as the atoms that had been Janet still moved in the world. On these points science and religion were in complete agreement. And this, too, was true: if Janet still moved in the world, so did the person who killed her. And who, Powell asked himself, is that?

The woods offered no opinion on the question. The breeze had abated a bit, making the sun on his face seem warmer than it had when he'd sat down. Not much was moving - a pair of birds darted among the white trunks of a grove of birch trees and a branch of the big pine by the pond jiggled as something unseen climbed there. A squirrel most likely. Nothing up the hill either - just the stolid silence of the bare maples that would sport taps eight weeks hence as sugaring season came again. Turning back, Powell examined the crime scene some fifty yards off, where yellow police tape still marked a trodden square. He wondered if the unknown perpetrator had expected Janet to be found so quickly. No knowing, but in some years deep snow cover lasted well into

April. Only the chance combination of his class's visit with the night's high wind, which had carved away enough snow to expose Janet's hand, had revealed what otherwise might have remained hidden for weeks if not months.

Chance - or something else? Wasn't there an order to the cosmos that was purposeful, that put pieces of puzzles together in ways that were meant to be decoded? This was the juncture where science and religion parted company - not over the question of What or How but over the question of Why. *Meaning. Part of our wiring.* Homo sapiens were programmed to seek meaning. Powell could say that he and his student just happened to be there to discover a body or that they were put there to do so. The difference between the two was all the difference in the world.

Put there. Why? Sound in the forest drew Powell's attention away from the stillness around that question - steady crunching footsteps in the snow, very faint but getting louder, coming from the hill below the pond's berm. Powell peered through the tree trunks and bare underbrush to the spot where the school's ski and snowshoe trail fell away steeply below the embankment and watched as a man grew out of that line - hooded head appearing first, round, red face, solid torso in n blue parka, mittened hands, black ski pants above laced hiking boots. The man stood by the white expanse of pond for a moment, beating his hands together and letting his breath rise around him in panted clouds, proceeding along the pond's edge past the old changing shack to where the hill resumed its climb toward the road where the school was. Not one of ours, Powell thought. The faculty and staff of the Seven Springs Academy were so familiar that Powell could recognize them even without seeing their faces, by gait and mannerism - and this was not one. So who?

Powell watched the newcomer without moving and realized

that he was about to become an example of a phenomenon that he had often described to his students. *You can't see what you don't think is there.* The man would pass within twenty yards of him without seeing him just as his students did not see the ceremonial cement urn in the woods beyond the pond until it was pointed out to them. A remnant from the estate days, it was outside the paradigm they had for the woods and was thus invisible. *You can't see what you don't think is there. Unless it moves.* Human eyes were programmed to notice contrast, and movement against an unmoving background provided it. If the urn flitted like a bird, it would catch all eyes just as Powell himself would now if he stood and waved at the man who was continuing up the hill. But still and seated, he didn't draw even a glance as the man passed. Going where? Powell's eyes followed him up the path that led to the road and the school, lost him behind a copse of spruce trees, and picked him up on the far side where he edged off the path, floundering a bit in the deep snow, heading toward a low roof nearly concealed by underbrush, a springhouse over one of the seeps that had given the old estate – and now the school – its name. Holding back some branches, the man ducked under the roof and disappeared.

Within a minute, he was back. Powell watched as he shed his right mitten, fumbled in his parka pocket, produced a small notebook and a pencil or pen, made a notation, and reversed the process. Then back to the path and down the hill towards Powell and the pond.

Why go that way? Without thinking, Powell stood when the man was past him and moving away. To go to the springhouse, why not come down from the road, which was much closer than any sally point below? And what would he want there anyway? As the man headed down the embankment at the pond's lower edge, perhaps eighty yards past him, Powell stood and moved quickly up the hill towards the springhouse. Two sets of the same waffle-soled tracks went in and out of the low structure. *So he has been here before. For what?* The building was essentially a pitched roof on posts, maybe six feet tall at the peak and three and a half at the eaves. Thick underbrush around the open sides made it hard to see in the dim light but what Powell could make out was a rectangular stone reservoir perhaps two yards across and four yards long. Ice covered it but he could hear water trickling into it through a stalagmite that grew up from the surface to a pipe that projected from the top stone at the far end near what appeared to be a sleeping bag or some rumpled blankets dusted with blown in snow – probably a love nest for some of the adolescent libidos of the school but certainly not what the man had been seeking, given the snow on them and the brevity of his visit. Whatever he was looking for could not take long to find.

And didn't. It was literally at Powell's feet. A faint rising and falling of red light led his eyes to the ground at the back side of the four by four that came down from the roof's peak where the display panel of a small black metal box flashed numbers that rose and fell. He fumbled in his jacket pocket to find a box of wooden matches from the Boston tobacconist from whom he bought pipe fill, struck one, leaned down. Lettering on the box labeled it an Anson 20-12 Flowmeter. A wire dropped from the box through the ice on the surface of the reservoir; Powell surmised that the other end must be fixed to the stone tank's outlet. *Has to have been there a while.* He shook the match out and tried to recall when the first hard freeze had come, knew that it was weeks rather than days, wondered if it was possible that Janet Debian had found the device here. Whether she had or not, someone was interested in knowing what the spring's flow rate was. And that suggested that the bottling project was not quite as dead as the faculty had been given to believe. *Why else?*

To that, no answer that made sense. Powell ducked out of the springhouse, picked up the visitor's distinctive tracks, and followed, wondering where he could have started from. Off to the left through the woods, perhaps a mile away, Gilmanton Hill road climbed steeply up from Littleton and dropped more gradually towards Franconia. The school's trails came within a quarter mile of it but they weren't on any area map so you wouldn't know that unless you'd been told. To the right, a half mile away or less, was the red farmhouse of Edge Farm, where the estate's manager had lived pack in the Gilded Age. It was now a weekend house for one of the heirs. And straight down the hill were the highways: first 302, a primary east/west route from Portland to Lake Champlain, and below that I-93 coming up from Boston through Franconia Notch. Unless the man was a local, that's where he'd be coming from.

And local, he was not, Powell was certain of that. Too out of breath, too off balance in the snow, too much reaction to the cold on what was not a cold day by North Country standards. Probably he'd have left a car below on one of the highways though exactly where was hard to know. If he was slogging slowly, it might be possible to catch up and see.

There was no sight of him below the pond though his tracks were clear on the mountain bike path that dropped down the slope. Powell hustled to follow, staying to the side of the path where tree trunks provided easy support in the deep snow. A quarter mile down, where the trail broke left to climb a stony knob, the tracks turned right and entered the woods, continuing down the gradient. Powell's sightline into the woods gave him no glimpse of the stranger but the breeze brought the faint sound of crunching footsteps to where he stood. As long as the man was moving, Powell knew, that sound would cover the noise of his pursuit. Ducking from tree to tree, he stayed with the footprints until the man in the blue parka came into view ahead, a hundred yards or so in front of him, post-holing through the snow with a lumbering roll, stopping, starting, stopping again ten yards further on. Powell paused when the man stopped but picked up his pace while the man moved, closing to perhaps fifty yards as they both worked their way down the slope. The volume of the traffic noise below increased as they came closer to the highways, the interstate, a bit more distant, marked by the higher pitched whine of speed, while lower register sounds from the more proximate 302 faded in and out to match the winding of the road. Close now. Though he had traveled through it scores of times, Powell's memory skipped like an old scratched record as it tried to bring up the landscape he was moving into. His mind's eye could see the far side of the road fairly well: mostly forest – but that described most of the state – with breaks for a deer farm and two houses— a nondescript white ranch and a cedar shingled cape—then the stone wall that fronted New Beginnings, the residential psych center from which the Naked Man had made his occasional flights. But the nearer side escaped him. Off to the left, where the highways crossed, the Elks Club hunkered like a warehouse. But what came after that? More woods, of course. Driveways? Houses? Signs? Was there something about trucks entering? The answer, he knew, was just below him. And below him the light through the trees was now brighter, and the man in the blue parka had become a black silhouette as he stopped in clear sunshine between two tall pines.

The man stood there for only a moment before quickly ducking back behind the tree on his right, and then beginning a slow semi-circle movement down and to his right carefully avoiding the light. *Someone there.* Who was it that pushed his quarry back into the shadows, now out of Powell's sight somewhere downslope? Powell worked his way over windfall and through snowdrifts to the spot between the pines where the man had been standing. Powell worked his way over windfall and through snowdrifts to the spot between the pines where the man had been standing. Below him now was a drop of thirty feet or more cut from the contour of the gradient he had been descending. At its base a level area, more than an acre, possibly two. Probably a gravel pit first, Powell thought, then perhaps a log landing. But in it now, a surveying crew was setting up. In it now, where a dirt road exited, a man in a blue parka stepped out of the woods and slid into a green pick up. In it now, a state police car's blue lights flashed from the edge of the road beyond the truck. In it now, dead center, Eric Ames stood in close conversation with Kate Romeo.

CHAPTER 11

Tuesday, 4:12 p.m.

You'll *want to see this.*

Joanne's note on a yellow post-it on a manila folder labeled *Powell* in the middle of Romeo's desk in the now empty
office – the staffers were off at four and the two swing shift troop-
ers were on patrol. Without sitting, Romeo opened the manila
folder to find a pair of blurry faxes and a folded sheet from a
yellow legal pad with green ink entries in Joanne's careful hand-
writing. *Started SSA 1990 . . . from New York . . . Society of Jesus . . .
chaplain, humanities, Spanish sometimes.* All of that public record
stuff; SSA meaning Seven Springs Academy. Below that on the
page, though, a trip wire that sounded alarm bells *–Former Special
Forces Officer . . . possible C.I.A. role . . . Cambodia . . . El Salvador.
NYPD, talk to Detective Hernandez.* Then two notes highlighted in
pink: *assaulted police officer . . . homicide involvement.* Kate Romeo
dropped the file and reached for her coat.

Best to start quietly, she thought, as she pulled into the
plowed parking lot across from Powell's house. Landry would be
there soon enough – she'd reached him in Lancaster just up the
road – and until she had back up there was no point in a confrontation. The January dusk was already thickening to night, but a
streetlight covered the lot and she noted that Powell had left a

porch light on. *Expecting me.* But she had said she'd stop by so why wouldn't he be?

And if he thought anything was up, he gave no sign of it. When the door opened, the man it revealed was smiling and easy of manner as he surveyed her. "Greetings, Lieutenant. You didn't need to wear the full-dress uniform for me."

She willed herself to smile back. "I wasn't quite sure what one wears for – how did you put it? 'Tea or whatever?'"

He laughed. "I suppose it depends whether it's the tea or the whatever. Which would you like?"

A man comfortable with himself, she thought. Like Al, but somehow more confident. "What are you having?"

"If it's up to me, I'm having scotch and soda. But if you're on call and that's off limits, I'll have a cup of tea with you."

Keep him loose. "I'm always on call. Scotch will be fine."

"Then make yourself at home while I pour them. The study is through there and the closet is the last door before you get to it." Powell pointed to a short hallway off to her left while he slid back towards what appeared to be a kitchen. The room she found after hanging her coat was three walls of books and one wall of windows. A large wooden worktable was positioned in front of the windows, which looked out across a field to the woods, while a sofa and three easy chairs at the opposite end formed a loose semi-circle facing a fireplace arranged around a richly-hued oriental rug with a polished coffee table in the middle. The books dominated the room – all sizes and shapes, bound soft and hard, and arranged by topic as far as she could tell. She was browsing a poetry section when Powell returned carrying two plus-sized tumblers of amber liquid, in which clear bubbles rose around ice.

"Don't read much, do you?" Romeo said as he set the tray down on the table.

"Not as much as I'd like to." Watching him lift ice with tongs, deftly and gently, she could not see a stone-cold killer in the jungle, wondered if there had ever been one and if so, where he had gone. *Perhaps still there. Some hide things better than others.* "What about you, Lieutenant?" he was asking as he poured. "What's there not enough time for?"

She shrugged as she took the drink and raised it. "Reading for sure. But maybe the woods more than that - hiking, back-country skiing, anything like that. Cheers."

"Well, then here's to the woods. And cheers to you."

Ice rattled as their glasses pinged together; the whisky tasted smoky and smooth. Could be a good moment, Romeo thought, if I wasn't working. *But you are.* "So, Father," she said. "You're not a North Country guy, are you? How did you come to be here? Did the church send you?"

Powell smiled but it looked like the question bothered him - something rueful in the way he slowly shook his head. "No. This isn't a Catholic school - it's Episcopal. I think maybe the church has forgotten me - or would like to."

"Wait - you're a Catholic priest and the church doesn't have anything for you to do? I thought they were way short of you guys."

Now a slight movement of the shoulders that suggested a shrug. "I expect they are. But the Jesuits have their own ways. If they call, I'll go; if not, this . . . " - arms spread to indicate the room - " . . . will be enough."

"You like it then? The teaching?"

"I do." A slow sip of whisky. "Somewhat to my surprise."

"How's that?" The goal, Romeo thought, was just to keep him talking.

"I'd never worked with adolescents before I came here.

Didn't even really think I liked them – all the self-absorption and hormonal angst. I was wrong."

"Really? I think I would have agreed with your first impression. What changed it?" Romeo shifted her weight from foot to foot, swirled her drink before tasting it again.

"Why don't we sit?" Powell eased himself into wing-backed Queen Anne chair at one end of the couch, leaving Romeo to select her own spot. Deliberate, she thought; leaving me to choose spacing. *A man in tune with what women liked.* She settled on the middle of the couch, close enough to be interested but beyond the distance of intimacy.

"What I didn't know," Powell was saying, "was how easy it would be to engage young people in the big questions. Adults like you and me can politely avoid them forever but you barely have to scratch a kid's surface to hook them."

"What do you mean?"

"I mean the big questions – Who am I? What is a meaningful life? You and I either think we have figured that out or we're too busy or too scared to try. But a sixteen, seventeen-year-old is *living* those questions. Sometimes they come up with stupid answers but at least they're asking. So if you show them some streams of thought that might help them, they dive right in. After they tell you it's bullshit, of course." Powell laughed, shook his head, sipped his whiskey.

Some passion there, Romeo thought. You could hear it. "So what are these streams?"

Another laugh from him, another head shake; irritation rising in her like wind in front of a storm. "Did I say something funny?"

"No." Still a grin, though. "Well, sort of. How well do you know the Bible?"

Thinking *not interested*, saying, "Look, I – "

Powell waved a hand to cut her off. "It doesn't matter. It's just that you sounded just like a Samaritan woman talking to Jesus at Jacob's well. He was telling her about everlasting waters and she wanted to know what they were. He was talking about himself, of course."

"Is that what you give these kids? Jesus?" She hoped to sound neutral but knew there was an edge in her tone.

And knew that Mickey Powell knew it, too. "Sounds like you might not approve of that, Lieutenant."

"I went to Catholic schools until I was fourteen, Father. Guess I got tired of being force fed morality." Uniforms and nuns, she thought; they almost drive you to break the rules. But not quite. *Still wearing a uniform. And still enforcing the rules.*

" . . . agree with you about force feeding," Powell was saying. "Here it would be more like offering them a taste. Of Jesus, yes. But Plato, too, and Moses and Muhammad and Buddha. Somewhere in there they may get a bite of something that really nourishes them."

Romeo liked the answer, felt some tension within her easing, cautioned herself to be careful, but could not refrain from asking, "And does Jesus nourish you?"

Powell looked at her carefully before answering. "Yes, I suppose he does. All of them do really. What about you? What sustains you?"

"I don't know." The question was too direct to dodge. "Nature, I guess."

"Mmmmm." Still the careful look, the teacher looking for signs of understanding. "I like the forests up here myself but they're pretty unforgiving. Make a mistake and you can be in trouble quickly. Is that how your moral compass works?"

"Yes." Her promptness surprised her. *Do I believe it?* "On the job anyway."

"And off? Any tolerance for sinners there?" Powell was grinning now, not mocking her, she thought, as much as inviting her to acknowledge something he already saw.

"Well . . . some tolerance I guess. Especially if one of them is me."

The grin widened, then a look of *faux* solemnity. "Delicacy demands that I not inquire about what sins you may have committed. But the confessional is always open should you need it. It *is* good for the soul."

"I'll keep that in mind." Romeo felt her own smile forming involuntarily, recognized how skillfully he had drawn her in, wondered if he did the same to others. Like Janet Debian. "You're good at this aren't you? Surprising that Holy Mother Church hasn't found a use for you."

The ice in Powell's glass clinked musically as he swirled it gently. "As I said, the Jesuits have their ways. Once there's a question mark by your name it never goes away, even if the question's answered. Like the military in that respect. And now that I think of it, the order was founded by a soldier."

An opening, she thought. Not much but room for a gentle probe. "Spoken like someone who knows the military. You served, didn't you?"

Powell sipped his scotch deliberately but kept his eyes on her over the rim of his glass. Lowering it, he spoke quietly. "I think you already know the answer to that, Lieutenant, but yes, I did. Now you'll want to know the details"

Something tipped him. What? "What makes you say that?"

"Did you know that my kitchen window also looks out across the road there?" A tip of the priest's head was a directional indicator. "The strangest thing - a state police patrol car pulled in there while I was filling an ice cube tray. Or do you always travel with an official chaperone?"

Best just to come to the point now. "So where did you serve, Father?"

"You may know this, too," ," - still an amiable tone and a relaxed demeanor - "but for the record, I believe that's still classified."

"And were you involved in a homicide in New York? Or is that classified, too?"

The smile gone now, replaced by a tightly focused seriousness. "A *justifiable* homicide. I still regret it but what happened, happened."

"And what was that exactly?"

"A coked-up pimp was whipping one of his girls with a fan belt. I intervened and he came at me with a broken vodka bottle."

"And another time you assaulted a police officer?"

This brought a terse smile. "If ever there was a cop who needed his nose broken, that was the one."

"And you find that amusing?"

A long even look from Powell. "In fact, Lieutenant, I do. I wonder if you spoke to Detective Hernandez about it?"

Hernandez - the name in Joanne's note. "And who would he be?"

"*She* would be the city cop who actually handled these cases. Maria Hernandez. If you had talked to her, you might have saved yourself some time."

Romeo felt a warm blush rising to her face, resisted an impulse to break eye contact. "Tell me about these cases then."

Powell almost imperceptibly shook his head. "I don't think so, Lieutenant. I don't mean to be patronizing but you need to do your homework. Then if you have any questions, I'll answer. But for now, I'm having another scotch. Want one?"

Flushed and embarrassed, she wanted out. But the voice inside, the cop voice, said stay. *And something else speaking, too. Saying stay, saying nothing to lose.* "You know what, Father? You're right –." Romeo lifted her glass and drained it, shaking her head with the swallow. "I was scrambling and I didn't make that call. I will. But that's not to say that I don't think you know more than you're telling me. And, yes, you can pour me another."

Powell gave her a quizzical look, collected her glass, tossed a line over his shoulder as he headed for refills. "Actually, I do know something you might be interested in."

Hooked, Romeo followed him around the wall through a small dining room and into a room that looked surprisingly functional for a single man's kitchen – pots hanging from a rack over a center island, a half dozen blocked knives, a black iron cook stove as big as a Volkswagen, a well-stocked wine rack topped by shelves of neatly arrayed of glassware.

"You cook?"

"I do." Powell was lifting ice from a bucket with tongs, dropping it a cube at a time in their classes. "Self defense. Boarding school food will get you over time."

Now the scotch, an inch and a half in each glass; now a spritz of seltzer from a siphon. He lifted a glass and handed it to her.

"Thanks." Romeo took an easy sip. "And what is it that you know that I might be interested in?"

"First let me ask you something, okay?" Powell's head was cocked ever so slightly to the right and his mouth had shaped itself into a quizzical grin like a schoolyard bad boy trying to pull a fast one on a girl he'd just met.

But why not? Bad boys are often fun. She told herself that it was the scotch thinking for her, but what she said was, "Sure. Ask away."

"What did Eric Ames tell you he was building down there off the road?"

So that was his I-know-something-you-don't-think-I-know secret. "What makes you think he told me anything?"

"I saw you talking to him at the site this afternoon. Hard to believe you wouldn't've asked."

Play it straight. "In fact, I did. He said there were no specific plans now that the water bottling plant was off the table but that it made sense to go ahead with the site work. Just where were you when he was telling me that?"

"In the woods right above you. I had just tailed one of his guys down the hill from the springhouse above the pond. Where he went to check a flowmeter that's installed there. Interesting that Ames is telling you and Robeson is telling the faculty that the water deal is off just as the one vocal opponent to it is killed.
But Ames still wants to know what the water flow is. Cheers." Powell raised his glass to her and took a long swig.

"Cheers." Romeo let a swallow of the smoky liquor slide down her throat while she considered Powell's information. It was interesting - nothing conclusive about it but a possible piece in a larger picture. "Mmmm, that is nice.
Could you show me where this meter is?"

"I can show you where it *was*. "If Ames is as smart as he seems to be, he didn't leave it there long after you were asking - whoa now!"

"What?"

Powell was looking past her toward the sink.

"Turn around fast and you'll see a naked man out there in the snow."

VISITATION

Space expanding as the coat comes off like an exoskeleton too small being shed. Dropping coat on gloves and hat; hurriedly tugging off a sweater and adding it to the pile; fingers methodically working buttons, cold air caressing chest and torso as the shirt is lost; pulling shoes away from feet, toe-to-heel, toe-to-heel; dropping pants and boxers to let the tide of winter rise around legs and buttocks forcing the chilled, satisfying shrink of penis and testicles; peeling thick socks off to stand naked in the snow, relishing the sharp prickle of crystals beneath his soles; breath coming quickly, arms and legs churning now, moving from a jog into a joyful capering run in the thigh-high snow. Alive.

Up the long hill in bounds, falling twice, laughing as the cold, soft cushion of drifts embrace him; skirting the hill's crest to find a path down beneath laden pine boughs, reaching the field where the small house stood, smoke from its chimney rising straight as a pillar towards the starry sky, standing at the edge of the arc of light from a window, peering in for a moment, grinning as faces turned toward him. Seen.

Now up the steep trail behind the house, gasps bringing sweet, cold air deep into powerful bellows, stumbling once, rolling almost playfully in the snow like an ermine at one with its realm, nearly flying across the open ground at the hill's summit down toward the oak the marked the trail's return to forest, sliding on the slope, catching balance with the slender trunk of a young poplar, loping along to the beaten path where he'd seen the giant leave the princess; now reaching his stride, legs and heart and lungs working in perfect concert, an easy canter down to the wide road that led to the pond; warm in spite of the winter air, turning toward the springhouse; one second, two, then ducking under the low eave, something tangled in his hair, grasping; the post coming to him quickly, too quickly. Light.

CHAPTER 12

Tuesday, 8:48 p.m.

Steam rising from the red snow. That was the image that shadowed Powell as he fixed drinks in his kitchen. *Life is short.* The Naked Man could not have been dead more than a minute or two when they had reached the springhouse a half mile from his home, Powell a half step ahead of Romeo while Landry, who had been waiting outside Powell's house in his cruiser, trailed several yards behind. The bright beam of Romeo's flashlight had found the pale, hairy body under the low roof, sitting against the post that supported the roof beam, legs sprawled across the sleeping bag that Powell had seen there on his earlier visit, head canted sharply to one side above a patch of steaming scarlet snow. The man's clothes were piled in a heap in the corner.

"Jesus." Landry's winded comment when he caught up to them.

"Yes," Powell had said, thinking, *Like Jesus, another child of God dead before his time.* He knelt beside the body, prayed quietly, and traced a cross on the man's still warm forehead. To Romeo, he said, "Unless I'm mistaken this is the guy Janet called L.C. in her journal. He's a mental patient who just likes to be naked in nature."

Romeo, tight lipped and glaring, offered nothing. She let

her light play around the body until it found fresh boot prints leading out of the far end of the shelter up towards the road. "See where those go," she'd directed Landry. "And call this mess in."

The local cops arrived, floodlights were set, photographs made, further sweeps of the area conducted, dust spread for fingerprints, clothing bagged, the body removed. Powell had stood at the edge of the scene watching Kate Romeo in charge, giving only quiet terse orders, her eyes always looking, looking. He'd still been there two plus hours later when everyone else was finally gone while Romeo was waiting for a night shift cop to secure the scene, listening as she'd spoken into a pocket recorder in the same quiet voice, appreciating her air of calm command. "Victim is a Caucasian male, about five-six, one fifty; probable cause of death, exsanguination; puncture wound of jugular vein. Contusion on forehead. No weapon recovered. Non-photo identification, library card: Jason Francis. Tracks leaving the scene end at road." She'd paused, slipped the recorder into a pocket, kept looking, searching for whatever might have eluded her.

"Lieutenant, may I make an observation?" Powell had kept his voice low and spoke tentatively. *Always good to go slow when you were on someone else's turf.*

"What?" Her voice clipped but not unfriendly.

"I think your murder weapon may be up there." He'd pointed into the shadows up under the pitch of the roof.

"Where?" Her flashlight followed his gesture and found a nail, wet and coated red, protruding from the joist above the wall.

"How did you see that?" She spoke without looking his way.

"I didn't. But there's a drop of blood dead center on the back of your parka. I noticed it after you were bent over the body and figured it had to come from somewhere. Tells you a few things, doesn't it?"

"It does." Still looking at the bloody nail, she retrieved the recorder from her pocket. "Perp most likely is a tall man, at least six feet, probably more, very strong." Turning to Powell, "Anything you'd like to add?"

He couldn't discern sarcasm in her tone; hoped there was none there. "He'd need an excellent understanding of anatomy."

She nodded, didn't speak, waited.

"The victim, uh, Mr. Francis, must have been unconscious. If he was resisting at all, there'd be no chance at that kind of precision. And we should have heard any kind of fight."

"Anything else?" Still nothing in the timbre of her voice to give him an emotional clue.

"Two things. Well questions, really. That flowmeter is still here so he didn't come for that." Powell turned and pointed to the spot by the far post where red numbers blinked in the darkness. "So what was he doing here?"

"And what else?"

"Just this: I didn't see that nail, and you didn't either. And we had lights. How did he see it?"

"What makes you think he didn't have a light?"

"Francis is running away from us. Does he run towards a light?"

Romeo pursed her lips and frowned. "He could have been with the guy in whatever he was doing out here. And maybe the guy just panics and forgets the meter"

"You think? It only would have taken a second to pick it up." He knew she was just playing with ideas, looking for a puzzle piece that fit. "Let's play that out. The two of them are here, and Francis decides to go on his nude snow romp. Our tall guy just waits here until he comes running back, bangs his head on a post, and punctures his jugular. Why? If he's going to kill him, why not do it before he can attract any attention?"

"Okay." The wheels in gear again, moving an inner magnifier across other possible pieces. "It's a chance encounter. The tall guy comes to get the meter, turns his light off when he hears our naked friend running in the woods, panics when he stumbles in, kills him."

"That's what I was thinking. Except for the nail. If he turns his light off, his eyes don't adjust fast enough for him to pick it up even if he knew it was there. If he turns it back on after he whams the guy on the post, same problem – pupils are dilated and can't handle the light."

"So what's the answer?" Romeo brushed a strand of hair off her forehead. Powell could see that she was still brooding over the riddle, not necessarily expecting a solution.

"How about night vision goggles?"

Kate Romeo nodded. "Could be. Guy comes to get the meter, doesn't want anyone to know he's out there. So no light."

"Or maybe he's not after the meter at all. Maybe Francis is what he's looking for."

"Oh, God." She looked away and then back at him. "There was a bare footprint under a tree about twenty yards from Janet's body."

Powell knew that nothing he could say would help and watched her shoulders shift in a sudden shudder wondering if it was the creepiness of the thought of the man waiting in the dark or the night temperature or both. "Cold?" he asked.

Romeo looked at him directly for a long moment in the dim light, as if looking for something in his face, some sign that would tell her what to do. "The whole thing is damned cold, isn't it? But yeah, I'm freezing."

"Me, too." On the road a squad car had pulled up, its blue lights pulsing. "If that's Sanborn's guy, let's get out of here."

"Good idea." They ducked under the yellow crime scene tape and trudged through the well-worn snow up the hill to the lane where the cruiser sat. Romeo exchanged a few words with the patrolman, promising – or warning perhaps – that she'd be back, then turned to Powell. "Need to get my car."

"I'll walk with you – have to go that way anyhow."

Neither of them spoke as they plodded along the plowed and sanded track that stretched a few hundred yards through the darkness towards the parking lot where her car waited on one side and the short path to his door on the other. Once they rounded the curve that took them out of the patrol car's highbeams there was no light at all except the glow of the Milky Way, stretching a hundred thousand light years across the winter sky. Powell felt the solid presence of the police lieutenant's body lurch a little closer to him in the inky night, noted that it did not then move away. *How long?* He could not recall the last time he had walked so near a woman but knew that he liked it. *Don't go there,* he'd warned himself but knew another tape was playing beneath that admonition, asking what difference it really made, wondering how binding were vows made to a church that seemed to have for-gotten him, arousing doubts like ones his self-righteous relatives had dropped by now and again over the years. *Do you really think you're so holy?* That the internal argument was back only told him what he'd already realized and nothing else: that there was some-thing attractive about Lieutenant Kate Romeo. Stupid, he knew, to suppose that this tug was in any way reciprocated – but that did not stop a sudden pang when she turned towards the parking lot driveway and her car.

"Lieutenant?" The voice was his but he didn't recall deciding to speak.

Romeo had turned towards him. "Yes?"

"Your hat and gloves? Do you want to get them now?"

She'd been leaning away from him and he supposed her answer would be no. But then she tipped her head and grinned. "S'pose I'd better. Winter won't be going anywhere for a while."

What did the grin mean? They were walking side by side toward his door, and Powell felt as giddy and nervous as he had in sixth grade gym class when they'd actually had to dance with girls. *Fool.* He told himself that he was too old for nonsense but smiled to himself with the realization that beyond a certain point age actually liberated you from the too-sensical world. Crazy old folks were stereotypes precisely because they were free to be so.

Inside, she rubbed her hands together to bring back feeling after three plus hours of a New Hampshire winter night while he fetched her hat and gloves from the closet shelf. She took them readily enough but hesitated before beginning to put them on – just long enough for Powell to half blurt, "We never finished that last scotch. I believe I could use it now."

He knew she would decline but was surprised to see a question in her eyes that he could not quite make out. Whatever it was did not inhibit her simple reply. "Me, too."

"Make yourself comfortable then." He nearly stammered as a rush of confused feeling made his face glow. "I'll pour."

In the kitchen now, pouring whiskey over ice and topping it with a touch of seltzer, Powell found he had to stifle an urge to whistle. *The power of irrational desire.* A second gruesome murder in a period of forty-eight hours – the image of steam rising from red snow – and instead of outrage or sorrow he was feeling elation at the prospect of a moment with a woman who had given no sign that she even liked him, who only hours before had thought he himself might be the killer. *But life is short.* He shook his head. *And such are the inscrutable paths of being.*

When he came into the living room with the drinks Lieutenant Romeo was standing in front of the bookshelves, her head tipped sideways so that she could read the titles. She took the drink with a nod of acknowledgement, sipped it, glanced back to his books.

"Pretty eclectic interests." She spoke without turning around. The light on her dark brown hair showed reddish highlights.

"I read everything."

"Me, too." Now she pivoted to face him, regarding him evenly, eyes on eyes. "And speaking of reading, can I ask you something?"

Powell held onto her gaze, felt himself nod, said nothing.

"When I met you in Janet Debian's classroom you were reading her journal. Why? I mean, you read it when she sat in on your class, right?" Romeo's eyes were softer than the hard sapphire ovals that Powell had seen at the floodlit crime scene but her tone was an empty plane, flat and unrevealing.

"Is that a cop question or were you just wondering?" he asked.

The lieutenant's smile was immediate and wide. "When you're a cop, I guess every question is a cop question. But I didn't mean it that way. I don't even know why I thought of it."

Powell sipped his scotch and absorbed the smile. Possibly a set-up. But why worry? In the end if the cat didn't get the mouse, something else did.

"Vanity." He laughed sheepishly. "I was in it and I liked that. You probably figured out that her code name for me was Obi-wan. Once you're past fifty, that's as good as you're going to do - you're not going to be Han Solo anymore."

Though it was true, he surprised himself by sharing this. *Not the kind of thing you tell a woman. Or a cop.* And neither was his follow up: "Maybe there's a point at which any attention is good."

Romeo's arching eyebrows told him that she was as surprised as he was.

Did he want her to think there had been something between him and Janet? Not really, he decided. What he wanted was to have her attention to whatever degree he could in the little space of time that would elapse before she left. Which worked. She eyed him carefully as if trying to re-sort her file of impressions with some new filter that was just coming into focus.

"Sit for a minute if you'd like." He sat himself in one of the room's two armchairs, as if doing so would create some kind of gravitational pull on her, would pull her - momentarily at least - into his orbit.

This, too, worked. Romeo sat on the couch opposite his chair, picked up and studied a plastic cube of photos while she sipped scotch.

"Did you take these?"

"I did. Except the one I'm in."

She looked again at one side of the cube. "That *is* you, isn't it?"

"A much younger version." Powell knew the picture without looking - the garden, the date palms, the boys crowded around him, the bright sunlight and the deep shadows, no grey in his hair, fewer lines etched on his face.

"Looks like a beautiful place - that sunset shot over the water is spectacular. Where is it?"

"Egypt. That's the Nile. The place is called El-Minia - a

few hours upstream from Cairo." And, Powell thought, a million miles from this New Hampshire winter. El-Minia – just its name awoke a memory of heat and a sticky wet feeling that never left your skin and a rich, sick-sweet smell of exhaust and garbage.

"What were you doing there?"

"Living with angels." He knew the answer wouldn't make sense to her. *But it is true.*

"You believe in angels?" A wary look from Romeo, as if he might be mocking her.

"Best not ask if you believe in angels, but when was the last time you saw one." Hoping it would help, anxious that it wouldn't. "Anyone or anything who shows you something true is an angel. Perhaps you've seen them once or twice?"

"Not that I recall." Clearly not her comfort zone, Powell thought as she turned the conversation back on itself. "So why did you go there? To Egypt?"

"To get lost." Taking a long sip of his drink, Powell let the smoky sweet taste of the scotch linger a moment before he went on. "And maybe to get found, too."

Romeo put the cube down and smiled. "You're being a bit opaque there, Father. On purpose, no doubt."

"Well, we're venturing into an area where discretion is the safest course," Powell said, surprised by her grin and surprised, too, by his own instant willingness to give her question an answer. "But suffice it to say that some agents of our government were greatly interested in my whereabouts, and the Jesuits of El-Minia were providing sanctuary."

"But you're here now. Did they stop looking?"

Powell shook his head. "I have no doubt that they know I'm here. They certainly knew that I was in New York. It could be that they became convinced that actually finding me might cost them more than it was worth. I went to Egypt before they knew that."

The detective's brow furrowed slightly as she considered this. "Didn't you just say that you were found there?"

"I did." Mickey Powell wondered how what he was about to say would sound to an intelligent, apparently secular woman – but knew that he needed to say it anyway. "I was found. But not by them. By God ."

CHAPTER 13

Wednesday, 9:56 a.m.

Waiting, Kate Romeo could not quiet her mind. Too much going on. Last night's bloody killing was at the top of the list. If Jason Francis explained the naked footprint near Debian's body, who might have been hunting him in the winter dark? Eric Ames was oily, but his alibi checked out. Sam Robeson was anxious but hardly homicidal. Todd Brooks, who'd had a similar syringe, was dead but still in the picture. Vladimir remained unknown. And then there was her date--, a middle-aged priest – who was late.

According to the clock on the wall of the Coffee Mug Café he was eleven minutes overdue. Sipping Jamaican coffee, she now wondered why she had called him. Partly out of contrition, but that could have waited. Detective Maria Hernandez, NYPD, had returned her call that morning. Not only had she absolved Powell, she had sworn by him. "He saved my life, man. Don't ever doubt that he'll do the right thing." Romeo had taken the masculine attribution as a compliment and had taken the information as highly reliable, coming as it was from a woman in the profession. Not that a cop couldn't be wrong, but it at least removed Powell from her automatic suspicious-until-proven-innocent list. But what was an apology about anyway? *It's the job to suspect people – just part of the territory.* What was different about this?

She knew the answer though she was hesitant to give it voice even in her thoughts. Powell himself was different. At first, she had thought him self-possessed and cocky, but she was coming to see something else. What kind of guy describes his own vanity to you? Or tells you he's been found by God?
And maybe that was it – not so much self-possession as a rooted-ness in something bigger that gave him a solidity that was . . . well . . . appealing. That as much as anything else was the reason for the call. Romeo smiled to herself at the silliness of the thought, turning again towards the café's door just in time to see a grinning Mickey Powell coming in.

"You were talking to yourself, Lieutenant. Is it that hard to find a decent conversation?"

Kate Romeo felt a blush rising across her cheeks. *More adolescent foolishness.* "If I have to wait to talk to you, Father, I could be waiting for a while. I hope you're more punctual about getting to the confessional."

Powell laughed, an unforced mid-range chortle that was inviting and warm.
"Feeling the need to unburden yourself, Kate?"

Kate. He hadn't used her first name before and she liked the way it sounded - but felt herself put on the brakes without meaning to. "As a matter of fact . . . ." She turned away, stammering.

"I . . . I talked . . . to Maria Hernandez."

"A wonderful woman." Still smiling, Powell sat down across the small table from her. "She coldcocked me with a flashlight once. Did she tell you that?"

"No. But I . . ." Romeo took a deep breath, peeked up, felt her eyes drop again. "I'm sorry I didn't speak with her sooner."

No answer but silence. *Well screw you then.* Annoyed, she glanced up to find his blue eyes glitteringly good-humoredly – which only irritated her more. "You finding this funny, Father?"

"Well actually, yes." His full smile was hard to resist and she found herself beginning to grin a little. "First, there's nothing to be sorry for. And, second, if you really were all that sorry, you wouldn't be snapping at me now. It's what we call imperfect contrition in the church business."

Now her turn for a jab. "I thought you told me last night that you were done with church business."

"Not quite," he replied with perfect equanimity. "I said they seemed to be done with me. We had a saying about Jesuits who left – 'you can take the priest out of the church, but you can't take the church out of the priest.'"

"Funny – we say the same thing about cops."

"What? That you can't take the church out of them?"

"You're hilarious, you know that?" No denying that she was laughing, however. "You know what I meant."

"True." A mock serious look, then: "You buying the coffee this morning or am I on my own here?"

"Allie," she called to the multiply pierced young woman at the counter, "get this whiner whatever he wants." To Powell, she said, "I'm having the Blue Mountain. Superb, if you haven't tried it."

"A good choice – but not mine. Allie, the usual for me."

"The usual? You come here a lot?"

"Daily when school is not in session— as often as I can when it is. I mean a small town café with fifteen varieties of shade grown, organic, fair-traded beans – that's a liberal's nirvana! I'd better come out and help keep it alive."

Kate Romeo took this in with less interest in the information than in the man. To see how far he'd go, she said, "I mean I sort of get the organic – but what's with shade grown? Does that make it taste better?"

"Some people say so." No mock seriousness now. "But I think it depends on what you think about birds."

"Birds?"

"Songbirds winter in the tropics – but clearing forest for coffee clears their habitat as well. Shaded fields don't do that. So if you like Mr. Bluebird on your shoulder, yeah, shade grown does taste better."

Powell's tone had a kind of goofy gravity to it, as though he knew the importance of what he was saying but expected that she wouldn't care. Which stung, she thought, for being true. But was still more than a little irritating. "Makes some sense," she said with a soft pointedness, "but do you know how smug you sound when you say it?"

Mickey Powell's smile widened even as a faint reddish hue rose across his cheeks. "I bet you won't be surprised to learn that I've heard that before. Often.
I don't mean it but somehow it comes out that way. You were gentler than many of them."

"Really?"

"One woman threw a whiskey sour on me. Another one called me a goddam self-righteous bastard. And then there was the one who tried to hit me with a bottle of Merlot – half full, too."

"All women?" Romeo was laughing now. "Jesus, Father, you really have a way with the chicks, don't you? No wonder you became a priest."

"I have a theory about it. I think the Y chromosome se-cretes a substance that makes men impervious to condescension. We just can't believe anyone would mean us – so we have a hard time hearing it when we do it to someone else. At least until we're blinking a whiskey sour out of our eyes."

"So your defense is that it's just a guy thing?" *Why let him off the hook?*

Still smiling, Powell shook his head. "There is no defense. I can only throw myself on the mercy of the court."

"*That* might get you some hard time. Especially if the judge is me – or Detective Hernandez for that matter. She said to tell you you're a jerk for never coming to see her."

"Well it's true that I am a jerk – though unless she's changed a lot, I'm guessing she used a different term, perhaps anatomical. On the other hand, she hasn't exactly burnt up the highway coming to see me either."

Allie arrived with a steaming mug and a small pitcher on a tray. "Tanzanian peaberry with half and half."

When she had off-loaded her delivery, Powell caught the young woman's hand and examined a rose tattooed across its back. "That's new, isn't it, Allie?
Quite lovely."

Allie beamed. "Yeah. Guy down in Concord did it for me."

"Still think you can improve on the beauty God created?"

The girl bent and kissed his cheek. "I believe it was you who taught me that we are co-creators with God, no? The difference between Thou-World and It-World?"

Romeo watched Mickey Powell grin up at her. "I did at that. For better or for worse. Good to hear that someone was paying attention."

Allie took her tray and disappeared through into the café's kitchen. Powell's eyes following her as she went. Romeo observed this, saying, "You like her, don't you?"

"I like most people." As Powell spoke, the detective noted

the warmth in his eyes and noted too how much she liked it. "But Allie is special. Most kids are sent to boarding school but she escaped to it. Before she came, her stepfather and his friends had been abusing her for two years. That would crush most adolescents – but she took it on, and so far she's winning."

"I'm guessing she had some help."

Powell pursed his lips and let his eyes drop for a moment, giving Romeo a glimpse of what seemed to be genuine humility. "When you teach theology, you're talking about what's in the depths of the human soul. If someone lets you in there, you'd better go in gently and take God with you. The second you think you can do anything in there yourself is the second you should get out."

Romeo sipped her coffee and let Powell's words float into silence between them. *Different.* Over the rim of her mug she watched him watching her. *This one is different.* "So she stayed here after school?"

"Where was she going to go? Her stepfather had been arrested and her mother was in complete denial. Here she can take a college class or two, and have a job, and work on getting better."

"And you're helping her do that, aren't you?"

Powell smiled. "I don't have much to spend money on."

Romeo briefly considered where her own money went. Her living expenses were low, her rare vacations weren't expensive, and she had no costly vices – mostly her salary just ended up in investment accounts that she rarely even looked at. *Could maybe do better than that.*

"So how's the investigation going, Lieutenant?" Powell's expression was curious, open, amiable – the same look, Romeo mused, that she'd get from a dog that wondered what she was holding in a closed hand. *So why not show him?* If Maria Hernandez was even half right, he'd be more of a help than a hindrance.

"So so." Kate Romeo took a deep breath, let it out, and sipped her coffee. She knew that what she was about to do was against police protocol at every level. Never discuss an investigation. *But here goes.* "Ames acknowledged that the flow meter was his. Said the project was dead but had been far enough along that it just made sense to finish the data collection. But he was in Portland last night so he's not our guy. And anyway, he's too short. Your boss Robeson also said the project was off but then hedged a bit – said the school of course reserved the right to review its options. Says he was at home with his wife last night – she says so, too. He doesn't look like he could lift a man off the ground, though, even if the adrenaline was pumping."

"I don't think he could." Powell's voice was measured and low. Just the right combination, Romeo thought, of interest and encouragement. "He's fit but not that strong – I'd say more of a track guy than a football guy. What about this Vladimir? Anything on him?"

Romeo shook her head. "Some of the faculty think Janet might have been seeing someone but no one knows who he is or where the nickname came from."

"You sure it's a nickname?"

"Not *sure.* But every other name in that journal is. Right, Obiwan?"

Powell chuckled. "Got me there. Wasn't Vladimir Lenin's first name?"

"You think she found a Commie philosopher up here?"

"Who knows? There are plenty of strange people in the North Country. And maybe she didn't find him up here. She *did* go to Yale."

"Yeah. Nothing in her email looks like she was in touch

with people there but we're still running it down. Should have her phone records today." *Somewhere there will be a connection.* The murder didn't have the feel of something random – no signs of struggle on her body at all, no defensive wounds, no skin under the fingernails, no blunt force trauma. The killer knew her somehow, and somewhere that connection would emerge. The thought of linkage pulled Romeo out of her soliloquy and prompted another query to Powell: "Here's something for you. The syringe you spotted in the snow matches one we have in an overdose case. Could Janet have been using?"

The chaplain's face darkened and his forehead furrowed itself. "Janet? I don't think so. What did the autopsy show?"

"Nothing yet." Romeo liked Powell's concern – even dead he still cared for her. Did he care too much? Not her sense of things but still something to be considered. She went on. "The only quick check is a blood test and there wasn't enough left in her for the M.E. to get a read. He took some organ tissue samples but they take a while."

The priest looked at the ceiling briefly before speaking. "I met with her parents this morning."

"I have to see them later." Just the thought of that meeting tightened Romeo's stomach.

"What will you say?"

"The usual stuff – how sorry I am, how we'll do whatever it takes to find the killer. Words that won't bring their daughter back. What did you say?"

Powell's eye's seemed to go a darker shade of blue - as though some new depth had opened behind them. "Nothing consoles parents on the loss of a child in any circumstance but murder brings the cruelest sorrow – the It-World at its worst. All you can say is that in time they may see that life overcomes death, that the joy of their life with Janet is not gone completely even if it seems so in the moment."

Romeo liked the thought, but it was part of the phrasing that caught her. "It-World – Allie just said that, too. What does it mean?"

Powell's look was quizzical, as if he wasn't sure he'd heard her right. "Difficult to explain it in just a few words," he said, "but I'll give it a shot if you're really interested."

Thinking, *why did you think I asked?* Saying, "I am."

The chaplain lifted his mug and took a long swallow of his Tanzanian coffee, and Romeo found herself noticing his slender wrists and long fingers, began to wonder what about them caught her eye before his voice called her attention back to his face, his words.

"The concepts come from *I And Thou* – it's an essay that a Hasidic rabbi named Martin Buber published in 1923. Pretty dense stuff - Buber himself wrote later that he wasn't sure he knew what it meant – but its basic premise is that we relate to the world in two basic ways, I-It and I-Thou. I-It is the world of experience and utility: we find something, we use it, we get rid of what's left, and we think no more about it. A murdered person is often just an object that has to be disposed of. But I-Thou is the world of mutuality and connection. We encounter something or someone, it reveals itself, we reciprocate. As the process continues, bonds are formed, and even if the Other, the Thou, disappears, the bonds do not, because we ourselves are changed. So every murder victim may be an "It" to the murderer but to those who really knew her a "Thou". And between I and Thou something beautiful is created, something that did not exist in the world before. That's what Allie was saying - co-creators with God."

"I get it, I think," Romeo said, but she wondered if she

really did. *Something beautiful that did not exist before.* It sounded wonderful – but her work was mostly in the It-World, as Powell had called it. Did anything else really exist? Before she could ask him more, the phone in her pocket began to vibrate – the It-World breaking in again in the form, the caller ID told her, of the Grafton County Sheriff's Department.

"I have to take this," she said to Powell. To the phone she offered only a clipped, "Romeo."

Romeo's gut tightened as she listened to the voice and did not relax as she repeated the message to Powell. "Walter Sanborn just got a judge to issue a warrant for your arrest."

CHAPTER 14

Wednesday, 1:59 p.m.

The jail cell was clean and stark – six by nine, green-painted cinder block on three sides, a barred door on the fourth, a six-inch window slit in the wall opposite the bars looking out on a paved yard surrounded by high walls topped with razor ribbon. Inside: a bunk, a stainless-steel sink and toilet, a metal desk fixed to the wall – a utilitarian space as austere as any abbot could imagine.

But not safe. The very fact that he was here bespoke danger. He had done nothing, was not a suspect, and both the prosecutor and the arraigning judge knew it – and yet he had been remanded to the sheriff's department until the case could be presented to the grand jury. The judge's comment was, "What harm could it do to let them decide."

The scene had been out of Dickens: fat Walter Sanborn in the courtroom's back row, glowing red and reeking of gin even at a distance, the county prosecutor utterly unable to meet Powell's eye, the rail thin judge peering placidly through the thick glasses that perched on his beak of a nose, and both Romeo and his own attorney, David Shepherd, standing in open-mouthed amazement at the court's ruling.

This had followed a calm surrender. After the call at the café, Lieutenant Romeo's response had been anger. "What the hell does that clown think he's doing?"

"Don't worry about it," he'd said. "Let me use your phone to call my lawyer and have him meet us at the courthouse. If you're there to describe where the investigation actually is, I shouldn't be there long."

But the scene did not follow that script. Although Romeo had played her part, going on the record that he was not a suspect, the district attorney had brusquely dismissed her. "It's not up to the state police to decide who to charge or when to charge them."

His own attorney – really more of a family and probate law practitioner than a criminal lawyer – had been similarly rebuffed, being bluntly told that the facts – means, motive, and opportunity – supporting the charge would be turned over only after the grand jury had seen it. Bail was denied on the basis of Powell's supposed 'history of violence' in spite of Shepherd's pointing out that all charges against his client in New York had been dropped without prejudice.

All of which Powell now turned over in his cell with a rising sense of foreboding like a gardener spading up a human bone in his back yard. *What harm could it do?* What if that was the point? Surely whoever was behind this knew that the evidence wasn't there to make him the scapegoat for this mess. But the scapegoat dies. The scapegoat of myth, Powell knew, was not a goat at all really but a fallen angel, Azazel, who was loaded with the sins of others and driven into the wilderness to perish. His own guilt or innocence was not the point – it was about removing a disquieting mess from a community that did not want to deal with it. *Which didn't work if the angel came back.* So where, Powell wondered, would the threat come from?

The answer had come at lunch. Before that he had been in the hands of the correction department's bureaucrats – being fingerprinted, documented, stripped of clothes and identity, issued the orange jump suit that made him just another felon among felons, just another monk among these strange monastics whom he did not encounter until the guards came to take him to the mess hall.

They were the same odd lot that would populate any county lockup, Powell thought, with the particular exception that, this being rural New Hampshire, they were nearly all white. Drunks who couldn't help fighting when they were liquored up, addicts who couldn't help stealing when they were strung out, dealers whose jail time was a normal part of a career, grifters too smart or too dumb to settle for the straight life, high functioning crazies off their meds, and a smattering of those who had just snapped – nervous looking men who had suddenly struck out at something or someone for reasons that were as mysterious to them now as they had been in the moments of their impulses.
Powell fell into line with them and shuffled to the steam table to receive a plastic spoon and a segmented plastic tray that contained grey meatloaf, soupy whipped potatoes, and syrupy fruit cocktail. He took it to a half-filled table, sat, nodded a quiet blessing over the meal, and raised his head to the sound of a voice in the seat across from him.

"So you're the new guy, huh? The priest who killed that teacher." *No secrets in jail.* The speaker was a well-muscled white man with slicked back black hair whose thick forearms were tattooed with bullets. "Let me tell you something, padre – in here, you're mine."

So this is the set up. Best to confront it here where lots of people were around. "I have no doubt that you believe that," Powell said. "But you're mistaken."

"Really?" Black Hair tipped his play by setting his spoon

down. "Well believe *this!*"

The man rose quickly, the punch already on its way. Powell deflected it with his left forearm while rising towards his assailant, driving a right hand hard to his throat, squeezing a thumb down hard on his windpipe – old training that was as wired into his neurons as much as the reflex to cover his nose when sneezing. The effect was almost instantaneous. Black Hair managed to get his hands on Powell's arm but with air cut off, he was already passing out before they could help. He dropped heavily back into his chair and when Powell let go, fell face first, gasping into his tray.

"Guard! This guy's choking!" The scuffle and Powell's shout brought three uniforms. Before they arrived to lay Black Hair out on the floor, the man next to him, a skinhead with a flying skull tattoo on his hand, reached down and removed something glinting from Black Hair's jumpsuit cuff. *The shiv.* Not just an opening, Powell thought. *An endgame.* But what was the game?

By now two of the guards had Black Hair back on his feet, still wheezing as they led him towards the infirmary. The third was asking the men at the table what happened and – no surprise – was being told by each of them that he hadn't seen a thing. Powell kept an eye on Skinhead who was warily eyeing him back, a face-off that ended a few minutes later when the guards lined them up to return the trays and shuffle off to the rec area, a boxy gym with low risers on one side, a basketball hoop at one end and weight benches at the other. Powell was making his way carefully across the floor to the risers, wondering where the next strike would come from, when a uniform caught him from behind him,

"Your lawyer wants to see you, Powell."

Powell couldn't think of what Dave Shepherd would want but was glad to follow the grey clad guard out of the rec hall.

What harm could it do? Well, now he knew. If the jail was to be a trap, it would be a hard one to get out of. Shepherd would have to get to someone who could overrule the judge on whatever grounds he could come up with. Maybe then he could find out who he was a scapegoat for. He'd have to be the angel that did come back, and it was that return he was pondering when the guard led him into a small interview room with a table and three chairs.

Two of them were occupied.

Shepherd was there, of course, but Powell was surprised to see Kate Romeo in the seat next to him, looking troubled, her blue eyes sparkling and her jaw set. *But lovely even so.* He sat in the third chair and waited until the guard had shut the door before he spoke.

"So what's going on? Can they hold me?"

Shepherd first. "The short answer to that is yes. But probably not for long. I've called our correspondent firm in Concord to get their criminal law guy up here. The early word from him is that he shouldn't have much trouble getting you out."

"And I talked to Sweeney at Public Safety," Romeo interjected. Powell didn't know who Sweeney was but guessed it was a good thing. "He's going to get the AG to get Sanborn off this case. Might take a few hours but probably not longer than that."

"If it's that easy to get me out, what am I doing in?"

Shepherd and Romeo exchanged a long look before Shepherd answered. "Walter Sanborn has been the police chief in Bethlehem for twenty-seven years. They say he has something on everybody in town, and that may not be far from the truth."

"So how did that get me here?"

Now Romeo's turn. "The judge's wife has a DWI case pending. The stop was made in Bethlehem. And most folks there say that the county attorney's black sheep brother-in-law deals pot. Not in amounts big enough to be interesting to the Anti-Drug Task Force, mind you, but still sufficient for some jail time and a helping of political embarrassment. Don't know what good it does Sanborn to have you in here, though."

"My guess is that there's a lot in it for him." *What harm?* That answer was becoming clearer at any rate.

Shepherd's puzzlement was evident in his furrowed brow and curled eyebrows. "Why? What makes you say that?"

"Guy with a shiv came at me at lunch." Powell surprised himself by how matter of fact the words sounded as he spoke them. "That doesn't come cheap."

"Mick!" Romeo's alarm was palpable, like hands gripping him, trying to pull him back from some edge. "The guards break it up?"

"Not really. They didn't see a thing. Nobody did. Lucky for me the guy started to choke."

"What?" Shepherd was wide-eyed now, wading in water he'd never been in before, but Powell saw cold understanding in Romeo's narrowing stare.

"I'll call Tate," she said, pulling her phone from her jacket pocket. Tate Powell knew, was Sheriff Jack Tate. "Get you put in lockdown until we can get you out of here."

"What's going on?" Shepherd still befuddled.

"It's a set up, Dave." Powell felt himself settling farther into a calm center, a place where focus could only be on what windows each moment proffered and how each of them might be put to use. "Get rid of me here and blunt the momentum of Kate's investigation before it finds something that someone doesn't want found."

The lawyer stared at him in gaping disbelief, not speaking

until Kate Romeo gave a short nod that confirmed Powell's theory. "Why? What could – "

"We don't know that yet." Powell surprised himself with his curtness. "But my guess is that when we do know, we'll find a lot of money at stake on some-thing."

Shepherd turned to Romeo like a child who hoped mom had a different answer than dad. But no luck.

"He could be right. One murder – that might just be a crime of passion. Two might be some psycho serial killer. But a setup here – that'd have to be part of something bigger. And Walter Sanborn is not in it for free."

Shepherd looks so confused and, in a way, hurt that for a moment Powell thought he might begin to cry. Instead, he shook his head, collected himself, and asked, "Okay – what do I do?"

"Get your criminal guy up here ASAP." Powell's brain was in a mechanical modality now, clicking out cold ideas without an intimation of emotion, reminding him of now distant days in tropical climes. *Not good. The past not past.* But no time for rumination now. "Maybe get something in the local paper. If people are looking, it'll be harder to hide this."

"Al Johnson will help you – tell him I sent you." A half hitch in Kate Romeo's voice as faint as the buzz of an insect caught Powell's ear.

"So the press up here is cozied up to law enforcement?"

"He's a friend."

A hint of an edge in her tone and a hint of a blush on her ear lobes produced in the priest a stab of something he knew was envy, pushed him to consciously shake it off. *Of course there's a guy. Why shouldn't there be?* Time to change the subject.

"Maybe a reminder to the sheriff would be good, too," Powell said to Shepherd, "that he's accountable if anything should happen to me. Hard to say how far Sanborn's reach might go but if I remember right, the sheriff's from the south part of the coun-ty, not up here."

"Hanover." Shepherd made a note and tucked his pen back in his pocket. "I'll deliver the message."

Apparently, the message was delivered. For two hours, Powell sat in his cell doing nothing and a sheriff's deputy sat outside, thumbing a copy of Sports Illustrated. Another kind of doing nothing, Powell mused. But both of us being.
And so, not a bad thing, when you considered the alternatives. But if the plan was to affect his *Not Being*, what was its underlying purpose? That it was intended to cover up something about Jan-et's murder seemed likely – *but what*? What secret was worth kill-ing for? And who had the means to pay for it? Eric Ames might, but what he wanted was no secret and killing Janet would likely not help his cause. *Patience.* Patience was all he'd really need. You didn't need to know much about small boarding school finance to know that any available income stream, however small, ultimately was likely to be used no matter how green the trustees wanted to appear. The simple fact was that there was never enough money for all the things that needed doing. Janet may have delayed the water project, but at some point it would go forward. If any-thing, her death would only add to the delay since no one would be eager to proceed while eulogies still hung in the air. But if not Ames, who? And why? And another lingering question – *who was Vladimir?*

No answers, but somewhere in the depths of Powell's mind, just beyond the reach of conscious thought, the name Vladimir was tickling at an association that he could not quite bring to the surface. *Vladimir.* He closed his eyes and considered it again, felt pieces of the puzzle slide into place, saw bits of a picture forming, something that looked like a castle tower in one corner of the background, a dark eye front and center, the rest still indistinct but coming.

"Let's go Father." The deputy's voice pulled him from the reverie followed by a clang of metal as his cell door slid open. As his guard stepped in, holding handcuffs, Powell noted another deputy behind him, cap and winter jacket on, gloves in his left hand.

"Go? Go where?"

"Seems you're wanted in court," the second deputy said. "And, yes, we do have to put the cuffs on you. Nothing personal. Hands behind your back please."

Powell decided that the feeling of cuffed hands at the small of your back was not one that you could ever get used to. *All about power. Who's got it and who doesn't.* And even if faith told you that all power is ultimately God's, the tug at your shoulders and the cold steel on your wrists made it hard to remember.

The guard tossed a jail issued jacket over his shoulders and led him through corridors and past multiple locked doors where a black Crown Victoria that almost shouted COP waited with its engine running. Strange, he mused, that it wasn't a sheriff's cruiser but, sliding out of the cold onto the Vic's wide back seat, he let the thought pass. Until he saw Walter Sanborn step out of the jailhouse door and offer his hand to the deputy who had just slammed the car door.

CHAPTER 15

Wednesday 3:56 p.m.

Powell was gone and Kate Romeo needed a sign.

Snow on his floor provided a first hint but not a message. The two-inch circle of snow was feeding a small puddle in the shadow of a pair of cordovan loafers just inside the door at Powell's house on the school campus – the shoes he'd been wearing at the café and, she supposed, at the jail. So he *had* been here.

Romeo surprised herself by not pointing out the ice melt to Trooper Landry, who was with her for this look around the escapee's pad to see what, if anything, it could tell them about his whereabouts. Sam Robeson himself had let them in, looking well brushed as usual in a camel hair coat that was as out of place on a country road as the wing-tipped shoes that made his progress down the path more of a skate than a walk. His demeanor seemed uncertain, too, as if his emotional center was standing more on ice than solid ground. Or was that just her imagination? Certainly with two corpses edad a half-frozen police chief found in his domain he had some reason for the shakes; more reason say, than said police chief had to be there in the first place. At any rate , he had excused himself quickly and disappeared.

As for the police chief, he was conscious and on his way the hospital. He had been well-concussed, though, and either couldn't or wouldn't say how he had ended up handcuffed to a tree twenty miles from a jail from which he had no authorization to remove a prisoner, his weapon apparently missing, and his cruiser on fire in the parking lot of a vacant tire store two miles from the school next to a note that described where to find him that someone – presumably Powell – had tacked to a pillar.

It was that note that led Romeo to believe that she might find some communication here though she realized that this, too, could just be her imagination. But what was Powell doing? *Not an escape.* If it was, why leave the car so close? Not to mention the car fire – a literal beacon – and the note. *Obviously meant to find it.* But if it wasn't a getaway, what was he trying to do? If he was innocent, trying to clear himself; if he was guilty, trying to cover something up better – but this last seemed unlikely. *Why leave a note?* But either way Powell knew she'd be looking for him, and he had to know that this looking would bring her to this house. *If he needs help, he'll have to tell me where he is.* The shoes and the snow puddle said he had been here, and not too long before. If there was a message for her, this is where it would be.

Todd Landry saw nothing at all, not the puddle or the shoes. "Doesn't look like he's been here. If he had, wouldn't the jail jump suit be here? And his car's still parked out there, too."

"Hmmm." *Best not to tell him.* Once she did it would become a part of a process over which she had little control. "Maybe we shouldn't think about what's here or should be here. Maybe what's not here is what we need to know."

Landry's blank look told her that he wasn't following. "Look, he wouldn't take his own car since that's what we'd be looking for. Maybe he'd try hitching or grabbing a car in town. But both of those are panic moves and this guy seems pretty cool. Wouldn't take too long to come back here – why don't you go ask

Robeson whose cars should be around and see if any of them are gone? I'll poke around here a little longer, and then we'll go see if Sanborn's talking yet."

Romeo watched the trooper work his way up the slippery walk from the house to the road. After he had crossed it and disappeared into the pines around the path that led to the school's administration building, she resumed her scrutiny of Powell's digs. On the surface, nothing seemed out of place. The large closet just inside the door contained both alpine and Nordic skis and boots for both, a daypack suspended from a peg, an assortment of hangers, and a tailored wool dress coat. Gloves and hats were laid neatly on a shelf above. In the kitchen, counters were cleared; nothing on the table except yesterday's mail. The bathroom was tidy, the towels were dry, and a travel kit was under the sink. Razor, shaving cream, and toothbrush were all present and accounted for.

The priest's bedroom was spare and plain with the lingering scent of beeswax. A double bed, neatly made, a dresser full of crisply folded laundry nothing hidden underneath. Feeling her way through it brought Romeo a strange sense of shame, as though she were violating a long-held trust. Odd, she thought, for someone who had searched as many rooms as she had. *And I hardly know the guy anyway.* But the sensation persisted as she worked her way through the hanging cotton shirts and khakis of the closet and the carefully stacked sweaters shelved above. *Damn you, Powell.* But she knew that it was not really him that she was damning. Kate Romeo sat first on the end of the bed and then on a round cushion – for meditation, she guessed – that was situated on the floor beneath a window next to a blue vigil light and a small box of wooden matches. Closing her eyes, she tried to clear her mind of all thoughts but when they refused to stop tumbling and spinning, she channeled them Powell's way instead wondering where he sat now and if he felt as alone as she did.

"Tell me something, damn you," she said, half whispering. "Tell me where you are." But there was no reply. Romeo sighed, rose from the cushion, and moved to the living room to continue her search. *Not making it easy for me.* But in the living room he did.

The wall of books dominated the room, and Romeo gravitated to it the way she had the night before. The volumes – hundreds of them, she guessed – were organized by topic: philosophy and theology, fiction and poetry, economics, history, geography and travel, nature and the outdoors, each section neatly ordered alphabetically by author's last name. Powell definitely had some type A tendencies, she thought. And that was the arrow that pointed to the message. In the history section among the C's a gap appeared – something missing. Glancing around the room she spotted a book on the coffee table in front of the sofa. Author: Couch, Ernie; title: *Presidential Trivia.* Romeo was absolutely certain that it had not been there the evening before. On the cover, a blue sticky note bore this notation – 22, 24. Kate Romeo sat on the sofa and picked up the book.

But if the numbers denoted pages, the entries on them revealed nothing. Jimmy Carter had seen a UFO. Woodrow Wilson's Ph.D was from Johns Hopkins. Truman started wearing glasses at age six. John Quincy Adams had been behind the Coffin Handbill, which criticized Andrew Jackson's wartime execution of mutineers. Robert E. Lee thought Grant a superb general. Van Buren had been born in Kinderhook, New York. Warren Harding had played the coronet as a child. Jackson bore a sabre scar as a result of refusing to clean a British officer's boots. Only Jackson appeared on both pages and the entries did not suggest a place or means of contact.

Gradually it dawned on her that locally 'presidential' referred to the mountain range that started with Mt. Eisenhower on the south, including Mt. Washington in the middle, and ending with Madison and Adams on the north. Romeo had hiked all of it over her decades of summers in New Hampshire but in winter it rightly claimed to have the world's worst weather and was more likely to be deadly than enjoyable – it was a rare year that a body was not carried off one of the peaks. There was a Mount Jackson just east of the main range, not named after the president though most folks assumed it was. Not a place to hide, though, Romeo thought. She recalled its summit as bare and windswept with approaches that would be almost impossibly steep in icy weather. If Powell was an outdoorsman, it would be a place he'd know to avoid after November.

Restlessly Romeo moved back to the bookshelves. Based on the guidebooks and maps there, Mickey Powell did indeed know the local terrain.

Various hikes in the Appalachian Mountain Club's guide to the Presidentials – a bible for local hikers – were marked with penciled notations that included dates and comments. He'd climbed Mount Jackson three summers before but there were winter outings noted, including a three-day snowshoe excursion into the Pemigewasset Wilderness only the winter before.

Which fired a synapse in the lieutenant's mind. *No snowshoes.* There were no snowshoes in the closet where she'd seen the skis. No backpack or ski clothes either. His Pemi excursion could not have happened without them – and that would be what he had come back for now. So he was headed to the woods.

But Mount Jackson? Not likely, she decided. The few trailheads that could provide jumpoffs were a good twenty-five miles away. Even if he managed to get there, the trails, working their ways up steep cliffs provided little room for hiding – it would be fairly easy to track him. *A diversion?* There were a half dozen that would make more sense. Romeo returned to the couch and idly thumbed the trivia book, hoping for a revelation.

And received one.

The inside back cover listed the presidents in numerical order starting number one, George Washington (no middle name), and ending with number forty-two, William Jefferson Clinton, who must still have been in office when Powell had purchased the book. Stephen Grover Cleveland was number twenty-two and number twenty-four. *Mount Cleveland.*

Hardly a mountain at twenty-nine hundred feet, Mount Cleveland was less than five miles from where Romeo sat now and could be approached from a variety of angles through woods thick enough to hide tracks from an air search. There were cabins there, too – hippie shacks, the locals called them – rustic Waldenesque two roomers that went back to the heyday of Franconia College when the Gale River valley was overrun with scruffy kids seeking "alternative" wisdom, now mostly used for high school pot parties in the summer months. If Powell was a hiker, he would know where they were.

So Romeo knew where to look for him – but first there was the matter of Sanborn at the hospital. She radioed Landry to meet her there when he was finished, left the house the way she'd found it except for the sticky note, and pointed her car down the hill toward the highway that would take her around the town to the new hospital on the hill above the reservoir.

It was past dusk by the time she got there but even the winter darkness it was easy enough to recognize her car's twin pulling into the hospital lot ahead of her – a black Crown Vic with a whip antenna and a state government plate whose low number she recognized. DOS 3, indicating the third ranking Department of Safety official – her boss, Major Fredrick "Freddie" Boynton, the Commander of the Investigative Services Bureau. Not a good thing for somebody that he was here.

The major – all six two, two twenty of him – stood waiting for her when she stepped out of her cruiser; grey haired, straight as a fence post, and clearly unhappy.

"Jack Tate called me, Lieutenant," he barked. "What the hell is this about?"

"I don't exactly know, sir." Freddie was usually fairly casual but when he addressed you by rank, you knew you'd better answer by the book. "Apparently Chief Sanborn removed a suspect from the jail who later overpowered him and escaped."

"And you didn't authorize it?"

"No, sir. I don't know who did. I haven't had any conversation with the chief at all."

Romeo noted that the major's stony features softened a bit as he considered this, but he wasn't quite done yet. "But you were present at an off-the-record meeting with the suspect and his attorney."

"Yes, sir." She knew Boynton well enough to know that it was never a good idea to think you could sweep anything under the rug. "His attorney invited me so there was no expectation of privacy. Anything I heard could always be asked again in a formal interview."

"Uh-huh." The major chewed on that a moment before he spoke again. "And is it true that this guy is as dangerous as they say? Assault charges or some such?"

"Charges in New York were dismissed, sir. When I talked to the department down there they said he was instrumental in apprehending a serial killer and that he had saved an officer's life."

Not quite what Hernandez had actually said. 'Powell, that man, he saved my ass. Twice.' Something in her voice had told Romeo that there was more to it than that but she told herself that it wasn't the time to speculate. But couldn't help it, couldn't stop herself from wondering-- just what was Maria Hernandez's ass like? She felt a blush rising to her face and hoped that Boynton didn't notice it in the cold. But if he did, he didn't let it show. Good luck for once.

"Hmmm," was the major's only comment, then a blunt, "So did he kill the girl or not?"

"It's not impossible but I don't think so, sir. He may have had the opportunity but there's no trace of a motive. And we don't know exactly where or how she was killed."

"She was good looking?"

"Yes, sir." Romeo knew that the major was thinking that was all the motive they needed but she didn't think so. *Different somehow.* Or was she just being naïve? She knew how Boynton would answer that one but for now he spared her by dropping the subject and heading for the hospital door, speaking over his shoulder as he moved.

"Well, let's go see what Sanborn says."

A sheriff's deputy whom Romeo recognized from around the courthouse and Steve Cox from the Bethlehem P.D. were sitting stiffly in the hospital's small waiting area like two middle schoolers caught fighting on the playground who were not sure what to do outside the principal's office. Boynton swept past them with only a curt nod, and Romeo stayed in his wake. He stopped at a nurse's station, showed his badge and asked for a room number.

"It's 104 but Mr. Sanborn is resting," the young woman at the desk told him. "The doctor said no visitors."

"We aren't visitors." With that Boynton was off down the hall again, leaving the nurse half standing and totally flustered.

"Guess you better call the police," Romeo said to the nurse before she followed the major, "Or not."

Sanborn was sitting on the bed in a hospital gown, holding a phone and cursing at it. "Pick the goddammed thing up, stupid."

Seeing Boynton brought him up short but only for a moment. He slammed the phone down and fired a question before one could be fired at him. "D'you get that guy?"

Freddie Boynton let the question pass like a wild pitch heading for the back stop, staring at Sanborn for a silent moment long enough to be disquieting. "And what guy would that be, Walter?"

"Powell – you damned well know that!"

"Powell." Another long silence. "That would be the Powell that you removed from the Grafton County Jail with no authorization and without telling the sheriff after the Attorney General told you to stay out of this case? That Powell?"

"You coming at me?" Sanborn's fat face reddened with anger. And fear, Romeo thought. "Guy tries to kill me and you're coming at me!"

"If he was trying to kill you, you'd be dead, Walter – you were down and he had your weapon. Not to mention which, he left us a note to tell us where to find you. So drop that and tell me what the hell you were doing."

"I got nothing to say to you." The chief's piggy eyes were narrow and bloodshot. Cornered. And dangerous, too, Romeo thought.

"Suit yourself. But next time it won't be me who's asking." Major Boynton left the chief glowering, and Romeo followed him back into the corridor, hustling to keep up with him.

"Major?"

"What?" His tone said *this better be good*. Better to tell him than not to, though – he'd be pissed if he heard it later. Romeo took a deep breath and spoke.

"Powell told his lawyer that someone came at him with a shiv at the jail."

Boynton stopped, cocked his head. "Anyone see it?"

"Someone must have – it was in the dining hall. None of the guards, though. The attorney was going to bring it up with Tate."

"Which Tate neglected to mention to me. So what happened?"

"Well, Powell said the guy choked."

The major actually smiled at this. "And this guy is a priest? Glad he wasn't at my high school."

"Sir?" Romeo wasn't sure what to make of the smile.

"Walter Sanborn is a corpulent creep and a bully." Boynton was all business now. "Wouldn't figure him as part of a death plot, though. Tell you what – I'll chat with Tate while you see if you can find out who Walter's been talking to. And be in touch – I hate surprises."

With that Major Freddie Boynton turned and left her standing in the dim light of the hospital hallway. She followed his route but slowly so that her own thoughts could catch up with her. It had obviously occurred to her boss that someone might want Powell dead. *Who? And why?* Was something from his past catching up with him here? And if it was, what did it have to do with Janet Debian?

Before any answers caught up with her, Trooper Ted Landry did. He was coming in the door, hat and gloves still on, slightly out of breath.

"Did you see Boynton? He was-"

"Yes, I did see him, Ted, "she interrupted. " The major and I had the pleasure of arriving at the same time. What have you got?"

"Robeson gave me a list of all the cars on campus and they're all there, including Powell's. Also, the needle Powell found? Joanne got the trace on it. It's from Canada –same with the one in the Brooks O.D. Most of them went to something called Hema-Quebec, the rest went all over in small shipments. I called the Mounties and they'll get us a list. And the M.E. called to say he's faxing a preliminary report."

Kate Romeo heard what he was saying, processed it, and mentally filed it but all the while another voice was telling her it was time to take a walk on Mount Cleveland. Landry's last comment, though, caught her full attention.

"One thing, though. The M.E. said they were able to get a little blood out of her liver. Found flunitrazepam – and on top of that, she was H.I.V. positive."

CHAPTER 16

Wednesday, 9:09 p.m.

Something about the winter sky on a clear night pointed beyond itself. The black and grey of snow laden trees against the deep violet of a firmament broken by the shimmering of a thousand stars – all of it evoked something more, Powell thought, something ancient and measureless, purposeful and majestic. One could, Powell guessed, conceive of it as simply a collection of facts, a body of data to be analyzed and quantified. But it was far easier to say *God* and to listen for the message it was surely trying to deliver. Which was something about the vastness and interconnectedness of being, he thought. Take out any one part and everything was changed. *But you can't take them out. Not really.*

That was a point on which the mystics and the physicists were agreed. Matter and energy were always conserved. One could become the other, but the totality remained the same. Janet Debian, the Naked Man, Jesus Christ, Moses. What is, is. Atoms and their particles could reconfigure themselves, but they did not cease to be. But what was it about a winter sky that roused such thoughts? Powell laughed – it occurred to him that it was probably a defense mechanism to take your mind off the cold.

And it *was* cold. Teens or lower, Powell guessed. Where he sat was out of the wind, his back against a boulder on a slope above a cabin visible through the thick scattering of birch and pine trunks that continued the climb to the summit above the line not far below where the oak and sugar maples quit. His carefully layered clothing kept the chill out – polypro next to the skin, then a fleece layer, then Gore-Tex to keep out the wet and wind, mittens over gloves to retain hand warmth – but the small oval of his face that his balaclava left bare had long since gone from stinging to numb while the sweet smell of woodsmoke told him that the fire he'd laid in the cabin's iron stove had not yet gone out.

But it wouldn't be much longer now, he was fairly certain of that. Once they found the car and the note they would be looking for him and Powell was confident that Lieutenant Romeo would want to take a peek around his place. He was less sure that she would decipher his Cleveland clue but she didn't miss much so it seemed reasonable to believe that she'd come looking – and an experienced hiker wouldn't have much trouble picking up his trail. But would she come alone? His uncertainty about the answer to that question was what had him nestled out of the wind and not in the cabin below where a candle he'd lit raised a flickering light in a window on this cold clear January night. There was little doubt the police would assume correctly that he had Sanborn's gun, and even less that Sanborn would have some tale about assault and escape, making him officially 'armed and dangerous.' Would Romeo play it by the book with back up and S.W.A.T. teams?

Something told him no. Or was that just wishful thinking? *Loneliness, like desire, could bend your thought.* But her helpfulness at the jail, her ease with him that morning in the café, her intent listening the night before – could all of that have been an act? Powell wanted to believe that there was some caring there, some care. Glue, he thought. *Caritas.* The stuff that holds us together.

Ubi caritas Deus ibi est. An echo from a chant or a seminary lecture. Where care is, God is. But God or not, it was hazardous to believe something only because you wanted to believe it. Better to sit in the snow and wait to see what came.

What came was a voice. "Good evening, Father. Aren't you a little cold?"

Romeo's voice, emanating from a silhouette on snowshoes about fifteen feet away slightly behind him and to his left, a shadow that began with a gun, a nine-millimeter from what he could see, held in two hands extended at arm's length.

"Good evening, Lieutenant." Powell wondered if his voice showed the alarm he felt at the suddenness. "Are you planning to shoot me?"

"If that was the plan, you wouldn't be asking." Her voice was tense, he thought, but more nervous than angry. "But I would feel a lot better if I knew for sure where Chief Sanborn's weapon was."

"Fair enough." *Armed and dangerous.* "It's tucked in the back of my pants. If you've got a light there, I'll show you."

The hard stab of light that hit Powell's eyes blinded him for a moment but he thought the voice behind it had warmed a degree or two. "That would beat shooting you all to hell. But let's do it like on TV – put your hands on your head and lay face down on the ground."

Powell hesitated, decided there wasn't much to lose. "You didn't say 'Simon says.'"

"That is funny, Mickey, but I have to insist."

The name told him that it would be all right. Placing his hands on top of his jacket hood, he rolled into the snow. "This isn't just some dominatrix thing you do with the guys, is it? 'Cause if it is –"

"Shut up, Powell," she said, but there was a chuckle beneath the words. He felt her hand under his jacket, felt the weight of the gun being removed from his waistband, heard her move two steps back in the snow.

"Okay to sit up now?"

"Yeah. Tell me what happened."

The light was off now but Powell could make out her dark form six feet away as he rolled back to a sitting position against the boulder. "What happened was I let a state police detective sneak up on me like a fox on a chicken. Pretty damn embarrassing."

"Isn't it just? But I like being called foxy. Now tell me what happened with Sanborn."

"Not much to tell. He took me out of the jail, said we were going to look at the crime scene, and when we were in the woods, pulled out his gun. I disabled him and got out of there."

"After he drew his weapon you disabled him? How?"

Powell noted that her hand was down now, the automatic pointing at the ground. "Listen, Kate," he said, "I don't mind answering your questions, but couldn't we do it inside?"

"Fair enough."

Was she smiling? He hoped so but couldn't see her face clearly enough to know. *No matter,* he told himself. But even as the thought formed he felt the untruth of it chafing like a minuscule pebble in a shoe. Somehow her smile would make all the difference, a fact which – even now that he was admitting it – made the pebble chafe all the more. Standing, he brushed the snow off his clothes and began a half-hopping walk through the still deep snow down the steep slope to the cabin. Once there he shouldered the sticky door open and stepped into the warmth. The candle he'd left lit on a plate had nearly guttered out, leaving a hardening pool on the tabletop. While he reached up to a high shelf for a replacement he listened to Romeo muttering as she loosened her snowshoe bindings.

"Little trouble there, Lieutenant?"

"Nothing I can't handle, Father." She was standing up as he turned, her face glowing even in the candlelight. "You had a pair of these coming up here. What did'ya do with them?"

Powell pointed to pegs on the pack wall where his snowshoes hung. "They make too big a track. I went out the window there and up past the outhouse. Covered up as best I could but I guess you spotted it anyway."

"No." She shook her head, removed her hat, tossed her hair. "I just didn't figure you to be in here."

"Why not?" Even as the question formed, Powell found himself wondering how old she was, braked the thought, tried to turn himself back to the moment. "I practically sent you an engraved invitation."

"Yeah, right." Full smile, there it was, fleeting but lovely. "That was clever. But I guessed you probably didn't know me well enough to know for sure what I'd do. Seemed like a safe bet since I wasn't too sure myself."

"And do I know you well enough now?" Old emotions stirring, warm and fluid in channels well below consciousness. *Slow. Slow.*

"I don't know." The smile again— *how* to read it? "Do you?"

At the edge, he thought. To jump or not? In the end, he did not. His eyes let loose of her open, steady gaze, and returned to it with a question instead of an answer. "Well," he said, grinning. "You're here alone. Why?"

Something in her expression - an eyebrow, the corner of her mouth - seemed to signify hesitation or indecision, a split second where a step towards some deeper self-disclosure was possible. *Or is that just what a fool hopes?* But that moment passed and her voice, though friendly, was only matter of fact. "That people consider you worth killing made me think it might be useful to keep you around. So how'd you take Sanborn down?"

My own fault. Could have stepped closer. What fear was it that had held him back? Even as that question formed, the answer to another was tripping off his lips. "You might say that Sanborn took himself down."

"Really? He handed you his automatic, handcuffed himself to a tree, and hit his own head against it?"

Romeo was still smiling but Powell knew he was exasperating her so he put his words together more quickly. "First, he didn't draw his weapon until we were in the treeline which let me know what we were doing there. I mean if I'm a threat, why not take the piece out at the car? Mistake on his part - nothing gets me focused like the thought that someone wants to kill me."

"But that doesn't turn you loose. What else happened?"

"He made another mistake and assumed that I couldn't get to him. But if he knew what happened at the jail, he should've considered that maybe I could. Anyone who ever saw a *Karate Kid* rerun knows not to stand within range of a kick."

"So you know karate?" Romeo's voice was now more cop and less woman, and Powell wondered if he had a good read on her.

"At one time I did - now I just practice tai chi as a centering exercise. But I noticed up there - " inclining his head toward the door " - you weren't standing close enough to find out what I knew."

"Well, I'm standing there now, Mickey." She said, stepping toward him. Her upturned face was perhaps eighteen inches from his, both weapons were on the dusty table, her hands were at her sides. "And I think you're skipping the part about being afraid."

Her words were a supple branch, stinging as it lashed across some exposed part of his psyche. *Because they're true.* "With Sanborn or you?" he asked.

"Both."

The startling luminosity in the blue depths of her eyes in candlelight was both a challenge and an invitation. *Accept,* Powell told himself. Aloud he simply said, "Yes."

"Yes, what?" Her tone even and encouraging.

"Yes, I was afraid – with both of you." A hand inside him was clutching at his throat but he pushed syllables past it. "But it was different – I thought he might kill me. I was afraid you didn't believe me."

A narrowing of her eyes and a slight movement of her lips produced a look of puzzlement that seemed genuine to Powell. "What do you mean, believe you?"

Good question. When she'd found him, he hadn't said anything to be believed or not but that really wasn't what he was getting at – it was something deeper than that. "I meant," he said, his eyes dropping as the thought formed, "that I was afraid you didn't believe *in* me. A raised handgun doesn't say much for trust. Or maybe you were afraid of something, too."

When Powell brought his glance back up, he saw that her eyes were now averted and that when they came back to meet his there was a kind of pleading there, even as she said, "Police procedure – that's all it was."

No conviction in her voice though. She couldn't even hold his gaze, glancing instead back over her right shoulder toward the iron stove. "No point hiking out now. Probably we should get the fire going."

Powell smiled, wondered if she intended the double meaning, concluded that she didn't – but went there anyway. "That's not an offer I get from many women, Kate."

The lieutenant snorted. "No? And you so smooth and all!"

If intimacy was a moment in which you might share your fears it was a moment now gone. Good-natured teasing was comfortable and shallow, like a cool stream you might wade into in the middle of a hot hike, and Powell noted that he had used a wisecrack to back away from deeper water. Maybe his fear wasn't just that she wouldn't trust him, the priest thought, but that she would. *And what would be wrong with that?* To avoid grappling with this unvoiced question he busied himself with sticks and yellowed newspaper to rebuild a foundation for a log on the embers in the dusty stove while Romeo claimed the shack's one rickety chair.

"Got the tox report back on Debian." Her tone had slipped into professional timbre. "I probably shouldn't tell you this but she was positive for flunitrazepam and – "

"Fluni . . . what?" His match had just touched the paper.

"The street name is a roofie. It's a date rape drug."

As the flame curled around and up the paper to a pitchy strip of birch bark that popped and sparked as it ignited, a synapse in his brain fired, too, bringing an unfocused memory with it. "She was raped?"

"Could be. There was no bruising, though. She might have been drugged after sex. And the other thing – she was HIV positive."

The image of the castle wall resolving itself now, and something on it, something black, moving stealthily down. The fire was spreading now, catching sticks and pinecones, reaching up around the log that Powell had set on the kindling.

"Kate?" He hoped the revulsion he was feeling wasn't evident in his voice. "I know who Vlad is now."

VISITATION

She wasn't jonesing when the snow angel came – the dose from the methadone clinic hadn't worn off yet – and she was glad of it. When you were thinking of a fix you couldn't see or hear or smell or taste or feel anything else. And she wouldn't have wanted to have missed any of this. Not the way he just showed up, appearing at the door as if from nowhere. Not his look of grave concern. Nor his opening. "I heard about Todd. I came as soon as I could."

She had never seen him before but something told her who he was. "Are you Onjoe?"

The man had smiled, like you would to a friend. "Andjeo. Todd used to call me that. In my country it means angel. But actually my name is Josef. May I come in?"

So polite and all. In the dingy trailer living room he told her that he had come to make sure that she was alright, and had listened – actually listened to her – when she told him about the cop and the clinic and the rest of it.

"It's not right that someone as young and lovely as you should have to face this alone." That's what he said, and in that smooth sort of foreign way of talking. And then he said he could give her something that would make her feel good, and she took the pill and it did, and then he was stroking her arms and face gently, and then they kissed and he asked if he could make love to her, which Todd had quit wanting to do months ago. And after he had said he would draw her a bath, just like that: "I'll draw you a bath."

And the hot water made her feel so clean for the first time in a long time. And then Josef gave her another pill to help her relax, and now she felt like she could just completely fall asleep right here in the tub, and she let him take her arms, first one and then anothcr, and heards him say that something would maybe hurt just a little but didn't feel a thing letting her arms fall back into the water and seeing something red before her eyes closed.

CHAPTER 17

Thursday 7:54 a.m.

Dracula.

That's who Powell thought Vlad was. Vlad the Impaler, The Romanian prince, son of Dracul, the historical inspiration for the fictional vampire. "Think about it," he'd said. "All of her nicknames are from popular culture. Obiwan, Underdog, even L.C. for Lon Chaney – her nickname for the Naked Man. You know, like the Wolfman actor? I should've thought of it before."

Even now, twisting along the highway that followed the Connecticut up to its headwaters, the idea seemed bizarre to Romeo. But in the dark cabin, lit by the flame of a single candle and flickers from through the woodstove's door, it had been almost freaky. She knew her voice had sounded startled when she'd replied. "What in the world made you think of that?"

"I'm not sure." Powell had turned, set another log on the fire, and poked it for a moment with a long stick he'd dug out of the firewood in the corner of the cabin. "I think because you mentioned H.I.V. and that got me thinking about blood and the fact that Janet's was gone."

Vlad the Impaler. A picture formed of Jason Francis naked on a cold night, his blood splattered and pooled in white snow. *Impaled on a rusty nailhead.* "Mickey," she had said, "You gave me the impression that this Janet was a nice girl. Why is she hanging with a guy like this?"

"Could be we're seeing connections that aren't really there. All we know is that she was seeing someone who she nicknamed Vlad. Maybe he worked nights. Maybe he had funny teeth. Maybe he's got nothing to do with her murder."

"But you thought of it because of her blood."

"Yeah."

A silence had settled on them then like a cloud on a mountaintop, chilling the space between them in spite of the fire, bending them into themselves like hikers in the rain, each plodding through their own thoughts without regard to the other. Romeo's musings were all questions: What had Janet Debian stumbled into that had gotten her killed? Why was someone now after Powell? What was it about Debian that concerned him? Why did she care?

Now in her cruiser on the bright winter morning , she was able to grin at this last memory – even while shaking her head – and admit that she had kind of a thing for Powell. But in the dark cabin all she had were the questions. Finally, when the stillness there was weighing on her like a smothering blanket, she had risen from the cabin's chair to shake it off and stepped over to the space in front of the stove where he sat staring intently into the fire. Sitting cross-legged next to him and without trying to catch his eye, she had spoken into the blaze.

"Janet Debian was more than just a colleague, wasn't she?"

Powell had nodded, without looking away from the blue and yellow tongues dancing over the orange embers of the burning logs. His voice had been almost a whisper. "Perhaps not what you think, though."

"You don't know what I think."

The priest had glanced sidelong at her and had then turned his pensive attention back to the flames, as if considering how far into the fire he wanted to go. Only its crackling between them for a moment and then his near whisper again. "She reminded me of my daughter. Or of the young woman I hoped my daughter would be."

"*Your daughter?*"

Powell's laugh had sounded genuine but his voice had more than a dollop of irony in it. "Good to know I can still surprise people. It's quite a tale – more of a novel than a short story. But the Reader's Digest version goes like this: when I was overseas I knew a woman, a French doctor. We lost touch but years later I found out that she had died and that she had had a daughter who was a student here at Seven Springs. That's how I heard about the school in the first place."

"And she was your child?" Romeo had caught his eyes then and had peered into them, discovering for the first time a pool of sorrow welling there.

"Very likely. But I never really learned. The girl knew nothing about her father and avoided the topic. It didn't seem fair to just spring something on her after seventeen years. I got to watch her for a year – I was a full-time sub then – before she went back to Martinique where her guardians were. As a former teacher, I get a post card now and then."

Powell's voice had cracked on the last phrase, a soft, ragged echo of something torn deep inside him. Without thinking Romeo had clasped his hand and leaned towards him. He'd closed his eyes then but the flickering light was bright enough to sparkle on the tears that were rolling down across his cheeks and his fingers had tightened around hers. After a long moment, he had released them, wiped the tears away with a sleeve, and spoken again, his voice tighter then, as if he were working hard to control it.

"Janet Debian was a smart, idealistic young woman. I miss her."

Romeo had let the words hang in the air for a moment before she'd given voice to the only tribute possible for her. "I wish I'd known her."

"You would have liked her."

"I'm sorry about your friend. The doctor, I mean."

"Thank you." Powell had nodded acknowledgment almost solemnly. "And what about you, Kate? Has there been anyone special?"

"No," she'd answered quickly, reflexively, but then without thinking added, "well, once, sort of. I'll tell you sometime."

He'd given her a look that was at once interested and respectful but had given voice to only one word. "Okay."

Not much to say after that. They had stoked up the fire and let the quiet rise around them with the heat. When Romeo's head began to nod, Powell offered her the sleeping bag from his backpack.

"You probably have to work tomorrow," he said. "Don't know what I'll be doing."

Romeo had taken the bag and spread it on the cabin's dusty floor. "Seriously, Mick, what *are* you going to do?"

"Maybe it would be better if you didn't know." His voice as ordinary as buttered toast.

"Listen, Powell, you need stay out of our way in this. Just come in – "

"No, you listen," he'd interrupted. "People are trying to kill me and some of them are cops. Until you've sorted that out you can't protect me. So I'm not going anywhere with you."

Not what she'd wanted but he did have a point. "Okay –
then just stay put. Could you do that?"

"Well I am staying put for the night," he'd grin. "Maybe in
the morning we can talk about what's next?"

"Okay." She'd nodded and there had been no more talk.
She had slipped into the sleeping bag and he had curled by the
woodstove before blowing the candle out. The reassuring crackle
of the fire had lulled her to a sleep from which she'd wakened with
a blurry memory of a dream about a long trek in a green forest
following someone whose backpack looked just like Powell's battered old Kelty. The fire had been stoked up again. The grey light
of dawn was just beginning to lighten the cabin's grimy windows.
And both Powell and his beat up backpack were gone. She'd
bolted out of his sleeping bag then and had found her flashlight to
inspect the rest of the rustic space. His snowshoes gone, too – and
Sanborn's automatic.

Powell, you bastard. But even as she'd thought it, Romeo felt
worry more than anger. Someone wanted him dead, and she knew
clearly now that she wanted him to remain alive.

The trail had been easy enough to follow – a winding track
through the woods to an old logging road that descended in easy
switchbacks past two more shacks to the road, a sanded gravel
two lane east of Bethlehem. Beyond that, though, no trace of him.
At that point he might have hitched a ride or simply followed the
pavement toward either town. No way of knowing how much of
a start he had, so no point in trying to guess which way he might
have gone. Romeo fished her radio out of her pocket and called
for a car to come pick her up.

"What the hell are you doing out here, Lieutenant?" Trooper Landry had asked through his open window when he rolled to a
stop on the shoulder a quarter hour later.

"Got a tip that Powell might be holed up in one of the huts up there." *That was true enough.*

"Find anything?"

"Well, someone had been up there. Not there now, though." *Also true.*

That had been enough to satisfy Landry's curiosity. He drove her to the side road where she had dropped her car, and she now pointed it east toward the Troop F barracks.

Where she learned from Joanne that Major Boynton had called, that Amy Ashton was waiting to see her, and that Janet Debian's phone records had come in, this last with a hushed tone that might as well have been a wink.

"Anything interesting there?"

"Well, I thought so, Loo." She reached across the desk to hand Romeo a manila file, half smiling as she did so.

"Okay, Detective Fillion, what have we got?" The title wasn't far off, the lieutenant thought.   "Well, Debian's recent calls weren't anything special – incoming there was one from a Red Cross number, one from her parents' phone, two from other teachers here – except one the afternoon before she died which she returned just a bit later. It was from a cell phone with a Montreal number. When we went to run it down, we found out that it belonged to a young woman up there who reported it lost the next day. But you want to know what's really interesting?"

Fillion's dramatic pause was annoying but Romeo knew that this was her moment and that playing along would pay a dividend. Forcing a grin, she said, "Actually, I do want to know. Were you planning to tell me?"

"Okay." Joanne's serious face now. "I got thinking about the way those syringes matched up and that they were from Canada – you know, the one up in Colebrook and the one at the school

– so I decided to run Todd Brook's phone, too. And guess what? He got a call from that same Montreal number the same day. Didn't return it as far as I can tell."

"Hmmm. That *is* interesting." Lieutenant Kate Romeo could almost feel the mechanics of her mind shifting into gear. A junkie and a schoolteacher, she thought. Where and why did their paths intersect? "Maybe a visit to Miss Julie Tuite would be in order."

"Maybe so." Joanne's smile brimmed with self-satisfaction. "But don't forget Ashton and the Major."

Ashton. Romeo shook her head at the thought-penetrating pitch of the reporter's voice but also knew that cooperating with the press was the best course since the stories would run with speculation if they couldn't run with facts.

"I'll call the Major. Send Ms. Ashton in when I'm off the phone."

Brusque and to the point, that was always Freddie Boynton's style. They had the jailbird who'd come at Powell, he said, and the guard who turned him over to Sanborn. The bird, a lowlife who was being held for trial on an arson and murder rap, wasn't singing. The guard was lawyered up and stonewalling, but Boynton was sure they'd break him since they had the moron on tape leading Powell out to the fat prick's car. When he turned, they'd pick Sanborn up. *Any clue where Powell was?* he asked. *None,* she told him, which was true enough. *We'll find him,* and then a dial tone.

A knock, and her office door swung open to reveal the Daily Record's reporter, a bit breathless as usual, strands of her streaked hair breaking free from her side combs like dotty dowagers wandering away from a tour group, speaking before she'd crossed the threshold.
"Lieutenant Romeo, could you answer a few questions for me?"

"Good morning, Ms. Ashton. Have a seat." Recalling the

scene as she drove, Romeo wondered what it was about the woman that so annoyed her. *Maybe the total focus on her own agenda? Or the klutziness?* In the car, she smiled at the thought and remembered the rest of the scene – Ashton sitting, dropping her pencil, picking it up, breaking the lead, fumbling in a purse as big as a suitcase for another. "To tell you the truth," she'd said when the woman finally looked up, "I doubt that I can tell you much but ask away."

"Okay then." The reporter now a bit breathless but somewhat focused. "Can you confirm that there have been two murders at the Seven Springs Academy?"

"Amy," she had replied. "I know that you know that *murder* is a word with a technical meaning under the law. I can confirm that there have been two deaths on the academy's grounds. It'll be up to the district attorney's office to decide if they were murdered."

"The victims' names?" Ashton scribbled even though she was hearing nothing new. Must be reflex, Romeo thought.

"We have already released a statement that Janet Debian, a teacher at the academy, was killed. We haven't yet reached the second victim's next of kin."

More scribbling, then, "I've heard that the second vic was a patient at the New Beginnings Center, Jason Francis."

"Is that right? Well, you didn't hear it from me." Which had to be what Ashton knew she'd say.

"Okay." Then the real question. "Can you confirm that the prime suspect, Michael Powell, escaped police custody yesterday?"

"There is no prime suspect in this case at this point." Even in her memory the phrase sounded clipped. "So, no, I can't confirm that."

"Really? Because Chief Sanborn said – "

"This isn't Chief Sanborn's case. But for the record, Mr. Powell is a person of interest. The sheriff's office and my superiors in

Concord are investigating why he was taken into custody and how he came to be out of custody."

"But you don't know where Powell is?"

"No," she said. "I don't."

But I wish I did. Slowing for the cluster of buildings at Route 105 that was North Stratford on the New Hampshire side of the border and Bloomfield on the Vermont side, Romeo observed that her emotional thermometer was a bit warm on this one, partly because she'd slept through his departure and partly because she was worried about what he'd do next. And under both parts a growing sense that she liked him. *Stupid. A priest, for God's sake. Stupid, stupid, stupid.* And yet she noted that she was smiling.

After 105, the highway straightened a bit and continued up the broad valley of the Connecticut River. Occasional houses crowded the edge of the road, their chimneys sporting plumes of grey-blue wood smoke, and the winter fields were marked only with snow machine tracks. A remote but beautiful part of the state, perhaps all the more beautiful for its isolation. She had often daydreamed about quitting her job and moving here to the northern forest, to hike its low uncrowded mountains, to fish its still clear streams, to watch its days dawn from starry darkness and its nights fall into crimson dusk from the porch of a house set at the base of a forested hill. But in the dream, there was always someone on the trail behind her or casting up the stream a bit or in the doorway of the house. She could never see who it was, could not see him now, and this failure always turned the reverie towards melancholy.

And then too, she thought, the hard reality was that the north woods were not nearly so idyllic as all that. The whole area was saturated in alcoholism and domestic violence, and it wasn't so long ago that a town crank had shot up Colebrook, murdering two of her colleagues and two civilians, while even more recently in

Pittsburg the high school principal had hung himself in the school's tiny gym when his trove of juvenile pornography had been revealed. And now she was on her way to find a junkie who might give her a clue about who and where Dracula was.

Romeo wheeled her cruiser southeast off the highway on Lime Pond Road, which followed Simms Stream up towards its headwaters on Baldhead Mountain. She knew it well, having often left her car along its shoulder to wade the stream in dry fly pursuit of the brookies that made their home there. According to Landry, Julie Tuite occupied a trailer about three miles off of Route 2 at the intersection of Lime Pond and an abandoned gravel logging road.

She found it easily enough, a twenty-five-foot green and white mobile home sagging on an uneven foundation at the back of a weedy, overgrown lot, a clone of hundreds of others scattered across New Hampshire's North Country and the Northeast Kingdom of Vermont. Tuite's rust-flecked Chevy Malibu sat rutted in the snow of the unplowed driveway from which a narrow path of footprints led to wooden steps in front of a dingy white door.

Which swung open at Kate Romeo's knock. She leaned into the room and called out, "Julie? You here?"

Only the clicking of electric baseboard heaters in response. "Julie?"

Romeo stepped into the cluttered confusion of Julie Tuite's living room, passed through the grimy kitchen, and through a cracked door from a narrow hall that led to the bedrooms and spied Julie's pale sleeping face resting on the edge of her bathtub. The drug nod, Romeo thought, but when she pushed the door open she saw that she was mistaken.

Julie Tuite was not sleeping. And the water in the bathtub was blood red.

CHAPTER 18

Thursday, 8:47 a.m.

"**W**e take the fight to the enemy."

The voice belonged to a burly lieutenant colonel whose voice was as clipped as his hair. The time was just past midday, a sweltering August afternoon in 1968; the place a clearing in the woods somewhere within the two hundred thirty-two square miles of Fort Bragg, North Carolina. The listeners were a team of hard-bodied young men in full battle dress, helmets on, faces painted, M-16's slung back but ready. Powell knew that he was one of the listeners but as clear as the memory was, he did not recognize his younger self in the semi-circle of warriors. *Still a believer then.* That younger self, like each of the other soldiers in that circle, still believed in the righteousness of the cause.

"We do not wait for him," the colonel was saying, "We find the enemy and we capture or destroy him."

Waiting in the cold darkness of the musty barn, Powell heard the colonel's voice as clearly as he had heard it in that sweltering summer day thirty-five years gone, just as he had before dawn when it had him tiptoeing around the cabin in near total darkness, when it had had sent him into the arctic cold well before daybreak could etch pine branches against the sky, had brought him through the woods to the Swazey Lane – a shorter

walk than the six miles he'd logged the day before – just as a swell
of grey appeared in the east above the black line of the mountains.
The enemy – who is that? The question had dogged him as he snow-
shoed down the mountain and had dogged him still as he hiked
the empty, icy lane towards the main road, the snowshoes now
strapped to his pack.

On the macro scale, of course, there was only one enemy,
the Evil One – not a person as Powell conceived it but a kind of
negative energy that pulled one thing apart from another and
sucked all of them into an emptiness beyond comprehension. He
had had tastes of it himself from time to time – during his early
days in Egypt after leaving the horror of El Salvador, in New York
when his best friend had been killed in a firebombing, here in the
mountains when his putative daughter had shown no interest in
her parentage – but always some aspect of the particularity of life,
some small, beautiful thing had caught him and pulled him back.
A beggar child's shy smile in the marketplace, the wry, limpid sadness in the eyes of a friend at a funeral, the startling red of a fallen
maple leaf at his feet as his daughter had walked by him – in each
of these and in an infinity of other infinitesimal joys – Powell had
found salvation even in the midst of the world's pain.

And on the micro scale there was no doubt that Sanborn
was an enemy. Now that Powell had escaped him, Sanborn was
in deep – the major, according to Romeo, was not one to let anything go. But the question was between macro and micro – Sanborn was not crazy nor was there any obvious pathology there, no
addiction or deep-seated hate that anyone talked about. So what
motive did he have?

Rationally, the only answer that Powell could come up with
was that Sanborn or somebody with whom he was in league was
afraid that a continued investigation into Janet Debian's murder

would bring to light something that he – or they – would prefer remained in darkness. If there was a fall guy – especially a dead fall guy – perhaps those turning rocks over would stop their turning. But what was it that was hidden?

Sex, money, and power – those were the perennial obvious candidates. Powell grinned to himself as he trudged up the icy, rutted lane recalling that a seminary colleague of his had published an extended, nearly incomprehensible essay on Christian ethics entitled just that: Sex, Money, and Power , and that his own quip at the time was that at least the title would sell books even if the style was lacking. Though maybe finally it was just about power, money being simply the symbol of and means to it, and sex – for many men, anyway – the ultimate experience of control.

But was it always that way?

Considering sexual intimacy, Powell first conceded to himself that his own experience was nearly ancient history now, more than twenty years in the past. *Still vivid, though.* The memory of thick tropical air, of warm fingers on warm skin, of sweat beading and pleasure rising toward an ecstasy where no self existed but bliss itself. Not a gathering of the reins of control but a letting loose, a letting go, a physical taste of that spiritual transcendence that had later visited him in Egypt and that had led him away from the flesh and towards the joys of the soul. The sublimity of that surpassed all else but the infrequency of its visitation often left him in doubt, which was, he knew, an experience as old as the spiritual life itself. And so, the memory of other joys remained, sometimes as a rejoinder, sometimes a comfort.

Was it enough? Mostly it was, he thought; enough and more than enough. But there were days when some simple sight would grab and confront him – a woman's bare shoulder on a hot summer day or an old couple picnicking at a concert in the park –

with the naked fact that there were joys he had not known.

And now , slipping on the road, he admitted to himself that the sight of Kate Romeo's sleeping face was one such reminder of all that he had missed.

"For Christ's sake," he said aloud, the reproving words escaping into the cold air in a cloud of vapor but an echo in his mind replied, *yes – for Christ's sake*, and Powell laughed in wonder at how the synapses of his brain had moved him from a question of why someone was trying to kill him to the memory of a woman asleep to the basic fact of his faith. And of course, he told himself, the basic fact was that in God all questions, all memories, and all facts were one. *So return to the question already.* What would his death cover up?

Money would have to be part of it – Sanborn already had all the petty power he was likely to get, and Powell could not recall that anyone had ever turned up the faintest hint of sexual scandal around him, the one thing that could sink any ambitious man in the gossipy puritan milieu of small-town New England. No, someone had to be willing to pay him, and the price would not be low. Ames apparently had money, and had some reason not to appreciate Janet Debian but it was hard to imagine that his bottling plant wouldn't ultimately be built in any case. Could there be enough money in water to need to kill someone? And then the developer with the wetlands issue – what had happened with him? Certainly there were dollars involved there but now that the issue was raised, it wouldn't go away whether Janet was dead or alive. And what could he do about any of it anyway?

Find Sanborn. That had to be the first step unless Romeo's major got to him first. But, Powell conceded, it wouldn't be easy to do. No matter what was up with Sanborn, the police would be looking for him, too. He had knocked out and handcuffed a police chief after all, had set a police car on fire, had escaped, was thought to be armed. He couldn't just knock on doors in Bethlehem and ask where the chief was. Best to regroup and make a plan – and the best place for that would be the one place where no one would expect him to be now. At home.

Getting there proved to be surprisingly easy. He'd stood on the roadside where Swazey Lane hit Route 302 for only a minute or two when a semi slowing as it came into town stopped to pick him up.

"Winter camping?" the driver, a burly man in his forties, had asked gesturing at Powell's backpack and snowshoes.

"Yeah. Just out a couple of nights."

"Don't you freeze out there in a tent?"

"No, no tent – snow shelter. Like a little igloo. You make it right it's as snug as this cab." Small talk was the social currency of the world, Powell reflected, its way finding common ground and comfort zones. "Whatcha haulin'?"

Electronic components for industrial scales, Powell learned over the next few miles, picked up at the docks in Portland off a freighter from Malaysia and bound for the Fairbanks factory in St. Johnsbury where they'd be put into finished products to be shipped out of Montreal for the European market. He let the driver's voice slide just below his consciousness like a winter stream beneath the ice while they rolled through the village of Bethlehem and he considered the best approach to his house on the campus. Though it was not yet seven and school was still closed, some of his colleagues would likely still be in the school groove, up and moving early so there'd be more than a fair chance that one of them would see him along the road. The woods would be a safer bet, and he was well equipped for snow.

"If you're going to St. Jay, could you drop me at the interstate?" he asked the driver. "I left my car a couple exits south."

The teamster complied and Powell bid him good day, waiting until the semi had rounded the curve that took the road toward Littleton before he skipped off the entrance ramp across the pavement over the plow mounds and into a cluster of maples that climbed the gradient above the highway. After post-holing fifty yards give or take to get out of sight, he stopped and sat on a snow-capped stonewall, a remnant of the area's estate days, to strap his snowshoes on and plot his course. The forest, he knew, swathed a slope that ran above the site of Ames' factory development and below West Farm Road where the academy was. A mile or less from where he was now he could pick up the school's trail system, used for cross country skiing and mountain biking. The trails would speed transit to his home, which was at the far side of the school property, but there was a chance that he'd run into some young teacher, out to ski or give a dog a morning run, a risk he'd have to take.

As it happened, he encountered only winter birds and a single deer, a lovely doe, hooving quietly at the base of an oak for some edible moss beneath the snow. Her head had come up at the sound of his approach, an eye had turned toward him, and she was gone, disappeared among the brown-grey trunks, her tracks the only sign that she had ever been there.

And so too with Janet Debian, he reflected, as he worked his way across the winter landscape. There were tracks and traces to be sure, but her image was already becoming indistinct. How did her hair fall across her face when she removed her hat? When she smiled which of her teeth was slightly out of line? What exactly was the timbre of her laugh? Gone now, and not to be recovered.

But the why and how of that could be found, Powell thought, and in that there would be a grim satisfaction. *What is unknown can become known. What is hidden can be found.* He stopped behind a tall pine at the edge of the field behind his house, half knowing that his determination about Janet's death was an echo of and a cover for his failure to find his daughter – or more precisely, his failure to be found by her. Nothing to be done now about that loss, he thought, but we'll see about this one. No one in sight on the road or across it or near the house itself. He crossed the field unhurriedly on the well beaten path that students and teachers used to access the trails, unlocked his door, and ducked inside.

The rooms showed signs of a search but not an intrusive one – some books out of place, closet doors open, the neat pile of his mail scattered a bit on the kitchen counter. Probably no warrant, Powell thought. Just Romeo looking for some clue as to where he might have gone. *Thoughtfully provided.* He smiled at both his own cleverness in leaving the presidential clue and at Romeo's in having figured it out. *Great minds.* Or, he thought, perhaps just strange minds. Whichever it was, now was the time to turn his own strange mind to the computer. First, to choose good ground for an encounter with Sanborn, and then to find out what he could about the economics of bottled water.

The first task turned out to be easy enough. It would be simple to find Sanborn at the Bethlehem town building but that was obviously not the terrain on which to meet him. His wife owned an antiques shop on Main Street, but Powell couldn't count on the chief showing up there – town gossip was that the couple was barely on speaking terms, the wife tolerating the husband only for the money, and the husband tolerating the wife only because she knew which closets the skeletons were in. No listing for them in the phone book and a broad search turned up 434,000 hits – more than a few about the chief – but no address. The online town tax maps, however, were more helpful. They listed a large property with a house and barn held in the names of Walter and Violetta Sanborn across Wing Road from the Amonoosuc River and just off Route 142. Bingo. At some point he'd be able to find the chief there. And he knew the area well enough – the school used a put-in just below the 142 bridge for its paddlers in the fall and spring.

His second search, on bottled water, produced 5,240,000 hits. Way too much information, he thought, but this much was clear – bottling water was big business. Depending on whose numbers you liked, the market had doubled in less than five years with about nine billion gallons of water being sold the in the previous twelve months for something like thirteen billion dollars. And while there were still small bottlers, the big boys were in the game too – Coke and Pepsi and Nestle. With that kind of competition, the margin for a new entrant couldn't be much, Powell thought, and initial capital requirements were fairly high. Even if the water itself was cheap, you'd need a plant, bottling equipment, a truck fleet – and all that came before you'd figured out how to crack a crowded market. Did Ames have that kind of money? If Powell was recalling it correctly, his giving to the school was nothing special – perhaps in the thousand dollar per year range. A nice donation but not close to what some of the other trustees put up. But if he wasn't the enterprise's chief investor, who was? Powell googled Seven Springs Bottled Water but got nothing that made sense – maybe Romeo would be able to find something out; best for him to doze a bit and then to focus on Sanborn.

The alarm pulled him awake at eight-ten, achy and stiff,

and too disoriented to remember what his task was. He had to walk his mind through his jail experience and his escape and his night with Romeo before he could recall that finding the chief was his goal.

How to get there? The maps said it was six or seven miles to the Sanborn place by road but it could be a good bit farther than that if he stayed in the woods and followed the twists of the river – maybe four hours each way on top of what he'd already walked. Probably more than he could do even without the snow, but he couldn't exactly call anyone and ask for a ride. He knew where the school van keys were but he doubted that he could snag one without being seen. Even if he managed it, it wouldn't be long before someone noted that it was missing.

Gazing out at the dawning day across his snow-covered lawn towards the road and the small parking lot on the far side, the answer came to him. *No one looking for my car.* Since his Subaru was parked when he'd disappeared, there would have been no need to put out a bulletin on it. Romeo might think of it when she woke up and walked out but her solo trek suggested that she wouldn't want him caught by anyone but herself. Hoping, that he was guessing right about her, Powell put on his coat, hat, and gloves, found his keys, surveyed the road again, and – seeing no one – briskly crossed to the lot and calmly slid into his vehicle as if it were the most usual thing in the world. If anyone had seen him, there was no sign of it.

Fourteen minutes later he was through Bethlehem, at the put-in, and feeling much less clever. The small parking lot there was two feet deep in snow and the plow banks at the roadsides were easily twice that high. The only place to leave a car was on the road itself, far too conspicuous to be safe. Without knowing exactly what he would do, Powell drove on down the road, past

Sanborn's driveway, past a cleared house lot, then back into new growth woods.

A quarter mile past the lot, the plowing ended in a tight circle where the snowplow driver had turned his rig around. Not an ideal spot to leave a vehicle but at least there were no houses around and no sightlines from the 142 bridge.

Powell locked the Subaru and floundered his was into the woods, wishing that he had brought his snowshoes along.

Twenty minutes to the back of Sanborn's lot. The house, a rambling, weathered wood framed box that needed paint, was directly in front of him, it's chimney billowing with fuel oil smoke. A teetery barn, attached in the New England style, ran off the house to the left, a loose hanging door at its center. Access.

Powell worked his way through the woods to the far end of the barn to let it cover his movement across the lot, then edged along its back wall to the door, which was, as he'd suspected, unlocked. Cracking it just enough to admit him, he slipped in and let it close behind him. The space smelled of ancient hay and crankcase oil. Too dark to make much out except the outline of another doorway to his right. There the colonel's voice spoke in his memory blending with loud voices from behind the door in his ear. He tiptoed through the inky space towards those sounds and pressed himself against the wall there, sliding the chief's automatic out of his waistband as he did so.

"Goddam it!" Sanborn's voice, as belligerent as ever. "He created this mess, I didn't."

"True. But it's only going to get worse if we don't do something." The calm tones sounded familiar but were too soft for Powell to place them. "And we have a lot at stake – especially if the czar decides to get involved."

"Okay, okay. I'll take care of it."

"That's what you said about Powell."

"That bastard suckered me – but he won't get a chance to do it again when I find him. And anyway, I was just supposed to get him to the jail. His guy muffed that. Now where's our man?"

"That is the complication – I don't know. He said something about an errand in Colebrook last night. Today he has one of his events at a church in Vermont – Newport or Derby Line or somewhere, I don't remember. Someone at the bloodsuckers should know where he is."

Bloodsuckers? Thoughts of Vlad and the sounds of a car door slamming Then the sudden rattling of a chain, then barking close by, and a snarl even closer – and bared fangs suddenly lunging at him from the darkness and paws pushing his chest. And a doorbell in the midst of cacophony and Sanborn yelling, "Wolf, shut up in there." And the doorknob rattling, and the gun tight in his hand.

CHAPTER 19

Thursday, 9:31 a.m.

"Did you feed him to his own dog?"

Romeo had watched as Powell's head had snapped around to where she was standing in a birch copse, his eyes first wide with surprise then narrowing to focus on her.

"No, I didn't feed him to the dog." There'd been a slight edge in Mickey Powell's voice and Romeo had had to struggle to keep her face as impassive as the state's native granite. *Serious now. Be serious.* "I didn't even know he had a dog until you slammed a car door and woke it up," Powell had said, his countenance as earnest as an acolyte's. "That damn thing scared the hell out of me."

"Well, it's a good thing you didn't sic it on him. That'd have been a problem." His eyes searching hers, not fearful but worried.

"Why? Sanborn *did* try to kill me."

"*Why?*" Trying to sound incredulous, not sure she could bring it off. "In case you didn't know there are laws in New Hampshire against abusing dogs."

"Oooooh." Head down, shaking back and forth, face coming back up with a grin. "Now that was just mean, Kate."

She had smiled. "Serves you right, ditching me at the cabin. How did you know it was me at the door?"

"I didn't until just now. I was out the back of that barn and into the woods in no time. Where you didn't have any trouble finding me again." His voice sounding a little rueful on this last phrase.

"You might as well have left another note. You had clearly been back at your house. Your computer had been logged onto Mapquest, which will show recent searches even if you clear it – so I knew you were coming here. Your car was gone. It's tire tracks were in the dusting of snow on the road here – which is a dead ender in the winter. Figured you might be watching it from somewhere until I left so I stopped around the bend and had one of the ambulance guys take my car. Then it was just a question of dropping down to the river and doubling back. Figured you'd follow your own tracks to the car."

"Probably good that I was that obvious. Chances are the dog would have waked up on its own anyway. That wouldn't have been pretty." Sounded like he meant it, Romeo had thought. Unusual for a guy to admit the need for help. She'd listened again for the of what he was saying . "Is Sanborn okay?"

Powell's tone serious enough to make her think he might really care. "The mutt chewed him up pretty good – lotta blood," she said. "Which is a little strange considering it was *his* dog."

"That thing was seriously worked up." Powell had paused and looked at her cautiously. "And it *could* be that he tripped on something coming through the door and fell right on the mutt."

Meaning, she knew, that he had tripped him. "Did he see you?"

The priest had considered this. "I don't think so. He probably saw that somebody was there but I don't think he could have seen it was me. Who was the other guy anyway?"

"Other guy?" Romeo had felt a hollow forming in her gut,

like the circle at the center of a whirlpool. "I had to break a window to get through the front door when I heard him screaming. There wasn't anyone else there."

Powell's eyes on her, so intent that she felt herself looking away but they'd still been focused on her face when her glance came up again and his gentle voice started. "He was talking to another man. That's why I didn't go in. Sounded familiar but I couldn't say who it was – someone I've heard before, though. They were talking about getting me and about someone they called 'the czar' and maybe about another guy but that was when the dog woke up and went crazy."

Damn it. She had been so focused on getting the dog off Sanborn and then getting an ambulance out to him that she had not done what she would have reamed any rookie for – she hadn't secured the premises. If there had been anyone there it would have been easy for him to duck upstairs or into a closet before she got in. *Too late now to do anything but backfill.* "Was there more than one car out front when you drove past?"

Powell had tugged at his lip momentarily before answering. "I think not – but I really couldn't say for sure. There were vehicles in that barn, though."

Kate Romeo had nodded. "You said they were talking about this czar and maybe someone else. Why the maybe?"

"They could have been talking about this czar man himself – there was no other name mentioned. But Sanborn referred to someone as 'our man' – which didn't seem to fit. Anyway, whoever he is he's supposed to be in Vermont somewhere today."

Romeo had listened carefully as Powell told her about the mention of the church event, about the bloodsuckers, about the man at the jail – and about 'the errand' in Colebrook, the last reference hitting her like a punch, tipping her against one of the birches for support, pushing words out of her like a desperate prayer. "Oh, God."

"What is it?" Powell's hand gentle on her elbow.

"Oh, God," she had said again, closing her eyes tightly and swallowing hard against the bile rising in her throat. "I know what the errand was."

As she'd opened her eyes, she could feel angry tears welling in them and she'd blinked to stay them, concentrating on holding her voice steady as if the need to calmly tell Father Michael Powell about a dead junkie in a bathtub was all that held her together.

A soft squeeze of her forearm from Powell. "You knew her?"

"Not really." Shaking her head, feeling her voice drop almost to a whisper as if she were telling an awful secret. "But I've probably known a thousand like her over the years. Life starts bad and gets worse and they're caught in it, but still there's something sweet there that persists in believing that it will all get better, that the next guy will be the prince, or that the frog they're with will turn into one. You know the type I mean?"

"I do. Saw them in Indochina, and I saw them in El Salvador, and I saw them in Egypt and in New York, and even here at the school, these well-off kids - I see them here, too. Guys just get mad and ugly but with women it's different.
No matter how much the world treats them like Its, women hang onto the idea that there is a Thou out there for them who will see them as they really are."

Romeo had found herself agreeing with him and found it odd that this celibate priest could describe women so well, with such an intimate knowledge. *But it's true. You want that yourself.* And that was precisely why her fling with Al Johnson had never gone anywhere. Nice guy, fun to be with, not a bad lover. But he saw only his idea of her and not what was really there. She clasped Powell's hand and given it a squeeze, tossing her head as if to shake loose sorrow's grip on her.

"What now?" Powell had asked, as if he knew that she needed to move on.

Thinking, *he reads my mind.* Briskly saying, "Tell me the part about the jail again."

"Not much to tell. Apparently, Sanborn was just supposed to get me in there, which he did. The inmate with the knife – that was this czar's guy. What do you know about him?"

"Hardly anything. Name's Butch White. Set fire to an old warehouse in Lisbon – probably insurance fraud but we can't make that part of the case yet. Didn't know there was a drunk sleeping it off in the backroom. Before that, a bunch of petty dealing and assault offenses. Been in jail ten out of the last twenty years. Not tied to any murder that we know about, though. He's not talking, and no one inside is willing to talk about him either – at least not for the record. His only visitor this week was his lawyer – a suit from Manchester – so he's probably the one who delivered the order, but those conversations are privileged so he's not giving us anything either."

"How does this low life rate out-of-town counsel?" Powell was focused, she'd noticed, chewing his lip and stroking his jaw with a thumb.

"Good question. From what we can tell the firm does mostly real estate and commercial work. Major Boynton has some people looking into it."

"Want a suggestion?"

"Sure – what have I got to lose? I'm already way out of bounds with you." Though she hadn't said it, she appreciated that he was asking and not just telling her what she should do.

"Leave a note in his cell when he's not there. All it needs to say is, 'you missed.'"

Romeo had seen the implication and had smiled wryly. "Should a priest be threatening people like that?"

"Actually, it's not a threat, just an observation of fact." Powell grinning now, too. "But if it makes Butch think his demise is possible, that would be completely in accord with scripture, wouldn't it? 'You know neither the day nor the hour.' Perhaps confession would come to him more easily then. And that would be good for his soul."

Romeo had stifled a laugh. "One problem, O holy one – what do I do with you?"

"Why do anything? I'll go home and say my prayers and wait for a revelation."

Smiling still but shaking her head. "No can do. Robeson knows we're looking for you, and if anyone sees you and reports it, I won't be able to step in. Until we get a judge to give us an all clear you are still an escaped prisoner. I've got an idea, though."

Romeo had fished her phone out of her parka and punched three buttons. When Al Johnson's voice answered she said, "Al, I need to borrow your house for a while."

"For what?"

"Perhaps better that I not tell you. But there could be something in it for you."

"If it's you we're talking about, Lieutenant," Al said, "then I'll throw in my car, too."

Romeo chuckling. "Do you ever give up, Al? But what I was thinking about was a story – you are still in the story business, no? Is the key still in the usual place?"

Al's rejoinder had been typical of him. "You want to know how reporting and sex are alike? Persistence pays off in both.

And, yes, you know where to find the key."

The detective had turned back toward the priest who was watching her curiously. "Okay, I've got a place to park you while I go down to Corrections in Haverhill. With any luck we'll have lifted the bulletin on you by the time I'm done there."

"Okay." Powell's voice strangely flat. "Where to?"

"A friend's house in Littleton. But let's stop at Sanborn's first and then you can drop me at my car."

Sanborn's house had given Romeo nothing. The barn door was open, literally and figuratively, and nothing was inside except the chief's own pick-up. Even the snarling dog had been hauled away by animal control. Kicking herself all the way, she dropped a too quiet Powell at Al's place and had headed for the jail.

Where her fortunes improved. Sheriff Tate reluctantly agreed to run Powell's scam on Butch White, and within an hour he had asked for a meeting.
The thug was as jumpy as a dog on a just tarred road when she came into the interview room.

"Mister White," she said, hoping she sounded brisk, "you asked for a meeting but your lawyer can't get here. I'm here just as a courtesy to let you know that we'll get back to you as soon as he gets here."

"I don't want him. He's not my lawyer." White's words were quick, almost panicky.

"At the moment, Mister White, he's your attorney of record and he stays that way until you sign a statement appointing someone else or declaring that you renounce your right to counsel. Which I advise you not to do."

"I'll do it. Get me the paper. I'll sign it."

"Mister White, I'm telling you to think twice about that.

You are in a lot of trouble. We've got you on the Lisbon fire – the forensics are clear, and that means at least manslaughter if not murder two. And we've got you right here in the jail on assault with intent to commit murder. You're going to need all the legal help you can get.

"What the hell are you talking about intent to commit murder – all I did was take a swing at the guy." White was agitated, almost coming out of his chair.

"Again, I remind you that you shouldn't be speaking with me until your lawyer gets here – but I believe you're forgetting the shiv in your sock, Mr. White." Romeo let that sink in for a second or two before she went on. "Isn't it funny how much more people were willing to say when they found out you wouldn't be here long?"

"He's not my lawyer! And whaddya mean not here long?"

"Seems there's also an open warrant on you north of the border." A complete shot in the dark – but Joanne had said the phone calls were from a Montreal source. "We're going to give you to the Mounties first and save the taxpayers of New Hampshire a little money."

The prisoner's face went as white as his name. "You can't do that! I have something for you."

Close to it now. Looking at her watch, turning to leave, speaking dismissively: "Sorry, Butch. I don't think you have anything that I need."

"Wait! I do!" His voice desperate now.

Romeo turned at the door and said nothing. White was leaning forward, his cuffed hands raised, his whole posture a plea.

"What if I told you I could give you the czar?"

CHAPTER 20

Thursday 10:41 a.m

Except for one thing, Al Johnson's world was all male. The books on the shelves were military history and sports, the pictures were outdoor photos and action shots from baseball diamonds, basketball courts, and football gridirons.
Bats, skis, boots, backpacks crowded one closet and the bottles in the recycling bins were red wine and beer empties. The housekeeping was tidy but not fastidious. There was nothing low fat in the refrigerator. All male except for this: Kate Romeo knew where the key was.

Powell knew that there was no reason that this should bother him. But knew, too, that reason had little to do with feeling unless you peeled back layers of emotion to reveal the hidden truths. Envy was close to the surface, of course. He wanted what Johnson apparently had – that was true but it was not the truth. What he wanted was interesting but why he wanted it was important. *Because I'm fifty-six. Because I'm lonely. Because I'm afraid.* And even deeper was bedrock. *Because connection is what's intended for us. Oneness is fundamental.* How many times had he heard the scripture read – 'Hear, O Israel, the Lord our God, the Lord is One.' The preface to the first great commandment – to love oneness. And in it the echo of the Creation story... and the two shall become one flesh.' Mix those two passages with loneliness and anxiety, shake well, and you created a perfect cocktail of doubt. *Maybe it has all been a mistake.*

He knew the reasoning: celibacy was a gift you lived into, and that when you did, you reached a place of true intimacy that transcended the sexual tension or competition that commonly existed between man and woman or man and man.

And most of the time it was so – men did not consider him a rival nor women a prospect, and so a kind of openness was possible that permitted disclosures that might otherwise be unspoken. And so, men would tell him about their fears of aging and women of the deep, misplaced shame they felt about their bodies and he could sometimes lead them further into a place of peace that the quotidian world did not offer. Mostly it worked.

But sometimes not. Sometimes the aching for simple human touch crashed down on him like a rogue wave, capsizing the fragile craft of his daily existence, tumbling him into the deep waters of longing, leaving him spent on some unfamiliar shore. Now Al Johnson's small house was that strange beach and the flora which rose to greet him beyond the strand was envy – green tendrils of covetousness that wrapped themselves around him like some mutant ivy. *Thou shalt not.* Powell smiled wryly. It had been more than two decades since he had known a woman's intimate touch but clearly the desire for it had not decayed but had merely lain dormant like some desert seed that rests unbroken beneath the surface, waiting for moisture to swell it open. And wouldn't it again be a cop, he thought, who would be the one to water it. Maria Hernandez, the New York cop, the last one. Unavailable as it turned out – but now Kate Romeo. *Why should that be so?* Because she was a woman? Because he admired her no-nonsense self-confidence? Because there was a hint of vulnerability just beneath the surface of her persona, not quite visible but present nonetheless?

Powell sighed. All of the above perhaps – or none of the above. And no matter in either case. He was in the home of her lover, and there was no reason to think she needed or wanted another. As for what he wanted or needed himself, he knew that what he wanted did not matter and that what he needed would be provided. A rueful grin crossed his countenance. *Take my yoke upon you and learn from me, for I am gentle and lowly in heart; my yoke is easy and my burden is light.* Aloud he said, "Not *so* damn easy."

Poking around Johnson's apartment restlessly, Powell knew he needed to find something to do before his latent sexual tension added itself to the confused stew of emotions already in the kettle – about Janet, about Sanborn, about the naked man Francis and the would-be killer at the jail. If the whole mess boiled over, there'd be no predicting what the result would be – but bloody specters of his past reminded him that even a seemingly placid, centered life could explode in spasms of violence.

He found coffee makings and brewed a mugful, examined the books and photos again, sat down on the couch, stood up again, found a road atlas, opened it indifferently and let its maps flip by from the back – Washington (state), Washington (DC), Virginia, Vermont which his thumb reflexively before his mind knew wh y. And then the thought was there – according to his overheard conversation, someone was going to be in Newport or Derby Line today. He vaguely knew where the towns were – north and somewhat west of Littleton – but the map pinpointed them for him – both about sixty miles from where he stood, . Newport, the bigger of the two at forty-four hundred, smack at the bottom of Lake Memphremagog; Derby Line, home to fewer than nine hundred souls, snug on the border where I-91 became C-55 en route to Sherbrooke.

Small towns, Powell thought. Small enough that someone – or everyone – would know about a 'gig at a church.' What could it hurt to go take a look while Romeo was at the jail or questioning Sanborn again? She might have tipped her counterparts in the Green Mountain State but since she knew he was here at her pal Al's, no one would be looking for him there. Maybe he'd see someone or something there that would fire a 'missing piece' synapse and make the whole puzzle of Janet Debian's death come into clearer view – and get his mind off Kate Romeo and Al Johnson to boot!

Which was not what transpired – at least not as far as Romeo went. She was with him, in his mind, on the causeway across frozen Moore Dam Lake, and with him on the steep climb out of the Connecticut valley towards St. Johnsbury, with him above the dairy farms that edged the Moose River, and with him still as the highway left St. Jay behind and sped into the hills of the Northeast Kingdom. Powell tried to slow down the mind tape playing in his head to deconstruct it – the way he taught students to analyze film. What do you see? What do you hear? What is actually happening? What is truly happening? What does it signify?

What he saw was her dark hair, her inquiring eyes, surprisingly blue, her square, solid shoulders. What he heard was her no-nonsense, matter-of-fact voice, neither accusing nor suggesting, only asking. What was actually happening was a complicated sequence of electro-chemical reactions in his brain, the counterpart to the vision that was created by light, sound, and nerves in a darkened movie theater – Kate Romeo was not actually in his head any more than actors were actually on the screen, but the *truth* was not actual. The truth was in the story he told himself about who he was and who she might be, just the way the truth of a movie – or the lack of it – lay in how well those ephemeral images told a story that viewers comprehended. And the truth was not black and white but was as nuanced as the rolling winter landscape through which he now drove, both black *and* white, and a thousand shades of grey under a brittle blue winter sky.

The story was in part physical, the body itself whispering from beneath the level of a consciousness that it tolerated but did not obey, its urgencies tempered, perhaps, with the passing of years but still insistent on its pleasures.

And the story, Powell knew, was part emotional, arising out of that complex interplay between organism and ecosystem that humans simply knew as 'culture' but which they experienced primarily as fear. *Be afraid*, culture said. Be afraid that you're getting old, getting fat, getting grey, getting bald. Be afraid that you're not smart enough, young enough, or hip enough. And while reason told him that these fears were false, Powell knew well that he was not immune to them any more than his predecessors, the desert fathers, assaulted by demons of carnal desire in the sandy wastes of Egypt nineteen centuries earlier – no matter what reason said, the vanities of the world pursued even those who, in faith, sought to leave it.

But that stream of faith was part of the story nonetheless, no matter how much the glittering, empty promises of the world polluted it. Faith called one to another, and each to all like an ocean calling to a river and a river to a stream, to create between and among them an awareness of and participation in the Oneness that was God. So if fear and loneliness were the progenitors of desire, oneness was its fulfillment. And if this was profound, Powell thought, ; it was also funny. Grinning as he took the Newport exit, he imagined himself propositioning Romeo. *So Lieu-*

tenant, how about some oneness?

Absolutely no telling what kind of response that would get – but it was fun to think about and it kept a smile on Powell's face as he eased his car into town, first passing modest saltboxes and weathered capes, then blocks of grand wood-framed Victorians and lacy Queen Anne's, now frumpy and mostly converted to apartments whose yards sported rusty pick-ups and compacts, signs of a town whose prosperity in an earlier era had the faded, unkempt look of a poor dowager's aging, elegant wardrobe. Like most of northern New England, he thought.

Before Powell had quite settled on a specific destination, the graceful lines of the red brick library caught his eye and he instinctively pulled his car into a parking place at the curb. The midday sun, just now appearing through the clouds, was surprisingly warm for winter, signifying the beginning of January thaw, and Powell found he needed to jump a small river of snowmelt to make it to the sidewalk below the pointed three-story turret. He circled to the front of the building and made his way up broad granite steps through massive oak doors and into a spacious entrance hall with a gleaming red marble floor and a beautiful circular polished maple desk to one side behind which sat an equally beautiful woman whose carrot top was a shade more orange than the floor's red, the perfect antithesis, Powell thought, to the mousy stereotype of a librarian.

"Good morning." The greeting offered with a wide smile before he was halfway the echoing space.

"And good morning to you. What a lovely place!"

"Isn't it?" The woman looked around as though she hadn't seen the room before. "We're on the National Register."

Powell liked her – the smile, the affability, the pride. *Real – like Kate Romeo*, he thought, and then winced a little that the lieutenant had returned so quickly. To reroute his train of thought he said, "I wonder if you have a local paper."

"Sure do. In the reference room there, just past the stand of magazines. The Newport Daily Express."

Powell found the paper and took a seat at a polished wooden table. Not much was happening in Newport - the high school basketball teams had both lost, the police report highlight was a pair of simple assault arrests of two women fighting in a tavern parking lot, and the economic headline was that SAQ Ltd., a plastic bottle manufacturer, had decided to locate up the lake at Stanstead, Quebec. The attorney speaking for the developer had thanked the city council but had stated that the transportation options were a little better since it was on the main highway. There didn't seem to be any church news at all.

"Looking for anything in particular?" The librarian, in soft-soled shoes had crossed the marble floor without making a sound.

"Not really - just in town today with some time to spend. Thought I'd see if there's a church supper or music somewhere or something."

"Not so much of that on week days - most weekends someone will be cooking and the Haskell Opera House over in Derby Line might have a concert. But, say, if you're not squeamish, you can get a nice homemade sandwich and a cup of soup at the blood draw today."

Blood. Powell felt his heart rate tick up a notch. Wasn't this whole story covered with blood? "That so? Where is it?"

"At St. Mark's - that's the Episcopal Church."

A gig at a church. "Really? Is it hard to find?"

The librarian smiled. "You practically trip over it going out the door. It's just a block down on Second - a little white church with bright red doors. The draw's in the parish hall in the basement. Simple."

Simple it was. Powell covered the distance in less than five minutes, thinking of Janet's pallid face emerging from a drift, thinking of steam rising from red snow beside the Naked Man's contorted body and of a woman bathing in crimson water, thinking of veins and arteries, and of the words of consecration – 'This is my blood.' *Vlad the Impaler.* Exactly the nickname that Janet would give someone who drew blood for a living. At the corner, a sandwich board with a red cross in one corner and a red blood drop in the other indicated the entrance through which Powell would find him.

And do what? Even if he could guess exactly who the man was, what could he do about it? Call the police? Unless Romeo had brought them completely on board – and with what little she had, why would she? – his story would sound ludicrous. He fumbled in his pocket to find his phone, punched up her number, and waited.

But not long. "Powell! Where the hell are you?"

"I'm standing on a corner in Newport, Vermont. I know where Vlad is."

"Jesus! How?"

Powell explained briefly. Cars passed on the street. A middle-aged couple emerged from the church basement. Romeo was talking but Powell felt himself being drawn to the curb to cross the street, down the steps to confront the devil.

"Are you listening to me?" Romeo's voice buzzed like a hornet in his ear. "Do NOT go into that room! This guy is dangerous! I'll get help there."

"He doesn't even know who I am."

A black sedan pulled to the curb in front of the church.

"You don't know that. He could easily have seen us chasing

Francis."

Crown Vic. New Hampshire plates. Powell's stomach knotting.

"Oh, God."

The car's door swinging open.

"What?" Romeo insistent.

Walter Sanborn, his face and one hand bandaged in white, standing on the sidewalk.

VISITATION

Focus not possible. The world seemed to sway, as if some seismic shift was occurring but there seemed to be no rumbling. A dull throb pounded at the back of his head and a sharper pain had somehow seized his immobilized ankles, stabbing at his knees, too, and his hips. His arms were extended above his head and caught there as if unseen talons had had gripped them. Words would not come when he tried to shout, only a raucous subhuman keening.

The scene at which he looked was upside down; a table stuck to the ceiling, a bare light bulb rising out of the floor. An inverted man came through an inverted doorway and crossed the room to slap him.

"Do you think you know the world?"

Though he tried to form an answer, he could only manage a squeal and the man struck him again.

"You have no idea."

Then a swirl of movement, light glinting off something shiny and something stinging beneath his chin, warm liquid like a balm that flowed across his face and up towards the top of his head.

CHAPTER 21

Thursday, 3:52 p.m.

"**A**re you always so damned pig-headed?"

The January air was still warm even in the falling dusk, and a sweat from the hike up the hill in heavy snow was breaking on Kate Romeo's forehead but she paid it no mind. All her attention was on Mickey Powell who sat easily in the snow ten feet in front of her behind a double birch whose split framed a small farm below a white field that sloped down to it from the woods.

"I hope it's the smell," he said, his look almost bemused, "and not the sight of me that brought you to that particular turn of phrase."

The breeze blowing toward them did indeed carry the pungent, sour smell of the four hogs that moved idly about a pen next to a small barn that stood between a tidy white house and a frozen pond formed where an earthen dam blocked a small stream, but Romeo was in no mood for more than a glance at the swine.

"You're killing me, Powell," she snapped. "Bad enough that you didn't stay put but now you're conducting surveillance on a private citizen in a foreign country." The last phrase was actually Major Boynton's and she could yet hear the incredulity in his voice as his words burned through fiber optic cables to singe her ears.

"That may be true for you, Lieutenant," the priest offered equably, "but at worst I'm only trespassing and since there were no postings, I doubt that even that would stick. The rules can't be that different even if they are in French. And, anyway - you're here. You wouldn't be if you didn't think this was interesting."

He was right - that was what irritated her. His call from the blood drive had pushed all her buttons but it *was* interesting. First the Hema-Quebec connection - while tracing the blue syringe her office had learned that H-Q was the Quebec blood organization, founded in the 1990's after a contamination scandal had induced the Red Cross to leave the province but they had not discovered that Hema-Quebec and its predecessor's American affiliates were cooperating in collection drives in far northern New England and the eastern townships of the French province, sharing equipment and personnel - but not the blood itself - across the border. She remembered Todd Brook's words to Julie - their heroin supply was 'as sure as blood.' Could it have been coming across the line in an equipment van or mobile donation unit? And a blood collector certainly fit with Janet Debian's crazy nicknaming and Powell's Dracula theory. And then Sanborn - it seemed clear that he was looking for this 'czar' or one of his minions, and where did he turn up but at a blood drive in Newport? Romeo sighed. There was no point in arguing with Father Michael Powell - she had to acknowledge that she would have tailed the chief herself.

"Okay, so I'm here. Which I shouldn't be. Tell me again what happened after you and Sanborn got to the church."

Powell spoke without turning away from his downhill view. "He went into the church's parish house where the drive was. Came out again about five minutes later, got into his car and waited. About ten minutes after that another guy came out - white lab coat, glasses, tallish, maybe six feet, dark hair, young – thirty tops – pretty trim, coulda been one-eighty. They drove off together and I ran back up to Main Street where my car was and spotted them heading to the highway. I followed them across the border but lost them after they got off 143. Told a guy at the feed store at the crossroads in Hatley – did you see it? The one opposite the old closed cottages? Told him I was looking for a young man who worked for blood services, that I had picked up the wrong pair of glasses after a donation and that I wondered if he had mine. He told me the guy's name was Josef Morevich and that he lived out here. Came out, found the place, circled up here through the woods, spotted Sanborn's car, tried to call you – no cell service. Went pack to the highway to pick up a signal, called, came back. The car's still there, and about an hour ago, maybe a little less, they came out of the house and went into that small barn or shed – see where the lights are in the windows? Not long after that, smoke started rising in the chimney. That's it. You get your car off the road?"

It was a good surveillance report – detailed and no speculation. "Yeah," she said. "Put it up that last farm lane where yours is and followed your tracks through the woods."

"Hmmm." Powell said nothing more and Romeo let her gaze follow his through the tree trunks and across the darkening field to the lit windows of the small barn. Almost a calendar landscape, she thought – the farm buildings silhouetted against a sky tinged red in the west and going to deep, deep blue, in the east, pinpoint stars visible overhead in a moonless sky. A tranquil scene made more so by the unseasonably balmy air of the southern weather system that had pushed its way as far north as this part of the St. Lawrence watershed. She idly guessed that the temperature was probably still over forty on a day when the mercury must have touched fifty before beginning its slide back down. But beneath the warmth and tranquility, like cold granite beneath the thawing ground, this hard, inescapable fact: Janet Debian, Jason Francis, and Julie Tuite were dead and Todd Brooks was a victim as well – either of an accidental overdose or of a homicide made to look that way. And whatever was going on at the quaint farm in front of her likely had something to do with all of them. The question was how to find out just what that was.

"Look!" Powell's voice, low and urgent, but she didn't need the prompt to notice a door opening on the house side of the small barn – light where there had been none, a silhouette moving through it then quickly gone again as the door closed. She could just make out a form of a person crossing the yard towards the house in the darkness. *Not Sanborn.* The figure's movement was too sprightly to be the corpulent chief. What had Powell said the guy's name was? *Joe something.* She heard the faint sound of footfalls on the wooden porch and the solid *chnnk* of a door shutting a moment later. Lights came on in the first windows and went off in the barn. *Switch in the house?* Or had Sanborn turned off the lights in the barn? Why would he do that? And if he had, where was he?

"We need to go down there," Powell said.

Romeo had been watching so intently that she had almost forgotten he was there. "Yeah – when it settles a little more. But not *we* – you're staying here."

"What good would that do?" An edge to his voice now, quiet but honed. But then a soft chuckle. "And, anyway, I'm not in your chain of command. Which probably told you to stay on your side of the border. And which you ignored just like I'll ignore you."

His read was so good that he could have been standing

between her and the major, Romeo thought. She couldn't decide whether to snarl at him or chuckle with him. *But right is right.* She put a shrug in her voice. "He didn't tell me not to, but he would have if I'd asked. Which was why I didn't. To tell you the truth, I think he was glad."

"He had to know you'd come. Obviously he trusts you."

"He does. But trust is easy to lose and hard to get back. This had better not blow up." And, she thought, there was no reason to believe it would. Let night fall farther down on them, go down for a quick look around, get out. If there was something to see, good; if not, let Boynton convince the Mounties to keep an eye on it.

"So what's the plan, Kate?"

She liked the familiarity his tone was pitched with, as though he was talking to an old friend. Without knowing why, she knew she wanted that. *Not now. Not the time for that.* Annoyed with herself, she hoped it wouldn't sound like annoyance with him. "We wait. When it's time, we work our way around the edge of the woods and come up under the berm that forms the pond. If there's no door there, I'll go around to the house side while you cover. You do still have Sanborn's weapon, right?"

Romeo could just make out his nod in the rising gloom. The sky had gone to black now and the trees around them were barely distinguishable, shadows in shadow. She settled herself in the snow a few feet from Powell and felt the chill of the breeze one her face – still not January cold but the air would cool fast under this clear sky. Her parka and snow pants would serve her well, and the Kevlar she wore over her uniform shirt would add another buffer against the falling temperature – she would just need to keep flexing her hands and feet to keep them from numbing before they made their move. She turned to Powell to remind him to do the same but his soft voice was in her ear before she could speak.

"Hey, lieutenant – did you bring the dominoes?"

She could barely make out his face but she knew that he was smiling now, as she was herself. "Little dark for dominoes, wouldn't you say?"

"Lucky for you. I'm deadly at dominoes."

"Really?" Romeo could almost feel his grin. "What else are you deadly at?"

"Lotta things. You should be careful around me."

Still jokey – but was there something else there now? "That I believe. You might be the guy my mother warned me about."

Then one beat more of silence than she expected and a delivery that had slowed almost imperceptibly. "What was she like? Your mother?"

Romeo felt herself leaning back, physically moving away from the intimacy of the question even as some part of her psyche fled even faster. "Whoa," she said. "Snuck over to the serious kinda quickly there, didn't you?"

"Maybe." His voice an open and warm invitation. "But I really do want to know. And I did give you a mini biography last night. But I understand if you – "

"No. It's okay." Her own quick agreement surprised her; the rational part of her mind was reminding her that she was way outside professional bounds, but something deeper down overrode it. Her words spilled out nervously as if they needed to scoot before some net fell around them. "She was a saint, my mom was. My dad was a good guy, worked in a foundry for twenty-five years, provided everything we needed. I think it just wore him out. But my mom was special. Taught high school, math and science, but always had time for us. Took us to lessons – swimming, piano, dance, whatever – made us special clothes, baked cookies, made a fuss over our friends. They all loved her and the way she laughed all the time. At least until . . . well . . . she was great, that's all."

"You were going to say something else."

Mickey Powell's voice was even and reassuring but Romeo felt the net tightening, one part of her closing off another like a picture she'd seen of a fowler's snare closing around bright colored birds in a jungle somewhere, their wings beating towards a sky they couldn't reach. *Why tell him?* But the darkness helped. She couldn't see his face now, and her words in the chilly air might have been addressed to no one, or to the sky or the stars.

"I was going to say until my sister died. She didn't laugh much after that."

"We never found out, not really. She drowned in a quarry where kids went swimming sometimes. She was a strong swimmer, but she wouldn't have gone there alone. No one knew who she was with, though. And there was bruising on one of her arms that shouldn't have been there."

Silence for a long moment and then another. Finally, "I'm sorry, Kate. How old was she?"

"Sixteen. Two years younger than me." Heat rising then with embarrassment and, somehow, anger. "And no need to feel sorry. It's nothing to do with you."

"Maybe that's true," Powell said, his voice now gentle, his words as soft as the cool breeze on her face. "But the longer I'm alive the more evidence I see that the world is just one thing, one whole, with all the parts twined together in surprising ways. So maybe it is something to me."

"That some kind of church bull?" The words were out before she knew it, harsher than she wanted them to be.

"Actually, the church has been pretty slow to recognize it," the priest replied quietly, "but eventually they'll come around."

Then he was still, letting the silence build between them less as a wall, Romeo thought, than as a path along which they might meet. On it her sister Susan appeared for a moment, alive and smiling, and she felt her anger dissipating into the winter night. She sat with her memory a moment longer before Powell spoke again.

"Is your sister the reason you became a cop?"

Kate Romeo looked towards the spot where Powell was sitting but could not make out his features in the darkness. "I used to deny that," she found herself saying, "even to myself. But, yeah, I think it did have a lot to do with it.
I just couldn't take the fact that my sister's life was taken, and my mom's too."

"So there's the twining – your sister died, you became a cop, and now you're helping me find out what happened to my friend Janet." Then a more urgent tone: "Hey, look!"

The lights had gone out in the house below them. Sanborn's car had not left. Where is he? Had he gone into the house earlier, unseen by Powell? Was he still in the barn? If so, doing what? "Okay," she said. "Time for us to be moving."

Their progress around the perimeter of the field was painfully slow, a tree to tree groping in inky darkness. Stopping at the bottom of the hill, Romeo could hear water singing quietly beneath the snow where the pond outlet flowed from the bottom of the earthen berm that sloped perhaps eight feet up in front of them. She could barely make out the shed's roofline silhouetted in the night but remembered that the forest crowded the bank of the pond to their right while the left side, below the hog pen, was clear. "I'll go up first," she said. "If nothing happens, you follow. Got it?"

"Yeah. Got it."

Powell's voice as calm as if she had asked him to pick up milk on his way home from work. *But what are we doing?* She didn't wait for an answer to her own question but angled her way up the berm to the pond's bank, jogging bent over to the hog pens wooden fence, then along it to the shed's wall. Pressed against it, she could hear the pigs stirring for a moment, then only the deep silence of the winter night. When she picked up the sound of Powell's crunching steps in the snow, she began feeling her way along the rough board wall. The swine stirred again, and one squealed loudly – *Powell coming* – as Romeo found what she was looking for, a handle that turned readily and a door that opened at her push.

The darkness inside was darker than that without. Drawing her weapon with her left hand, Romeo clicked its safety off with her thumb, and eased across the threshold into the shed with her right hand extended like a blind man's cane, her steps an inching shuffle into dead air and a rancid sweet-sick smell that was at once familiar and strange. Perhaps eight feet in, her fingertips touched something vaguely cool and clammy. But before she could discern what it was time blew open.

Sudden blinding light, a sense of something hanging in front of her.

Shattering glass and the thud of something hitting the wall behind her.

The light gone again, and Powell's voice hissing, "Get down!"

Without thinking she dove backwards towards the door where his hand grabbed her parka and pulled her into the night air.

"Go," she said to Powell, "Give me some cover when you

you're in the trees."

"No, you go. I haven't shot in ten years at least."

No time to argue. Running to the left where the woods met the bank. A flash from up the hill and a brutal punch to her back that spun her off her feet, sprawling. Something hard, something breaking, icy fire. No breath. Nothing.

CHAPTER 22

Friday, 10:28 a.m.

The images alternated like slides on a screen – on one a woman's bare, pale arm curving towards a sleeping face edged by dark, tousled hair; on the other a pallid body hanging upside down, its tied hands dangling to nearly touch a tub of dull red liquid below it. Mickey Powell shook his head but could not lose them; it took an act of will to bring himself back to the present moment.

That moment was illuminated by the flat, cool glare of long fluorescent bulbs in fixtures recessed in a suspended ceiling. Beneath it, two women behind a counter – a bottle blonde and a brunette – tapped computer keys and shuffled papers as they processed car registrations for an elderly man in an Arctic Cat cap and a gum-chewing, twenty-something chick draped in a too big Groveton Eagles letter jacket. A rack of forms hung on the wall opposite the bench he sat on; above it a poster warned of the consequences of driving while intoxicated. Next to the form rack a window looked across a parking lot to a sign that identified the building as the North Country home of the New Hampshire Division of Motor Vehicles and of Troop F of the State Police, a continuing source of jokes among those old enough to remember the idiotic western sitcom of the mid-Sixtie s of dufus soldiers at a sad sack fort. D.M.V., where Powell was parked now, occupied the top floor of the structure, accessed from the upper parking lot where his Forrester now sat; the police barracks, off the lower lot behind the building, did not have a public waiting area. Kate Romeo was there now, in what was likely a less than pleasant encounter with Major Freddy Boynton.

His mind wandered back to her, to the bare arm curving over blankets in a room lit only by the flickering of a broken chair burning in a fireplace. The how of their being there was foggy – was the door open or had he forced it? Was the chair already broken or had he smashed it? What had he used for tinder? For matches? Where had he found the blankets? What he did recall was stripping her, his shaking fingers fumbling at buttons, peeling wet cotton from her cold skin, layering dusty cloth on her before struggling to keep enough focus to get a fire started, finally sliding in next to her and wrapping his shivering arms around her still naked body, falling asleep with the thought that it was his fault, that he was too late.

When Romeo's body began to tremble, he'd known that they would make it. By then his own shuddering had stopped and feeling had returned to his fingertips. Her quivering indicated that she was moving out of cold shock and towards a milder level hypothermia. It was only then that he had allowed himself to think of the events that brought them to the musty cabin.

He had come up to the small barn as she was easing its door open. One of the hogs squealed as he had entered, groping into pitch darkness. After an eternity that could not have been more than ten seconds, he heard a soft grunt from her – and then the lights! *No more than a two count before the shot.* Windowpane shattering, the thump of the slug into the wall to his right, the sound of Romeo on the floor, fumbling in the black air to find her, yanking her out. Alive! Some exchange about cover then, and she was gone towards the pond. A flash close by, and the *thnnk* of a bullet in a duet with her cry followed by a muffled splash. Then a lack of clarity, as some instinct below consciousness took hold. There had been a scuffle, a body on the ground, instant clarity of vision. Kate half-submerged in the pond, in the water then and pulling her to the shore, then somehow at his car and driving, realizing how little time he had as his headlights hit the feed store, pulling into back of the cluster of cottages at the dead motor court across the road. Nothing clear until her shuddering had awakened him.

The chair had been reduced to embers by then but their glow had been sufficient to show him a bedside table which he had quickly reduced to pieces and stoked to flame, wringing their soaked clothes and draping them from the mantle before sliding back to join her in the narrow bed. When the shivering ceased he knew that her core temperature was out of the danger zone. Pink was streaking the eastern sky when his mind had turned from the possibility that she might die and had begun considering the softness of her skin – a sure sign, he'd told himself, that it was time to get up.

Now, sitting on a bench under the flat fluorescent glare of the D.M.V. office, he considered the serenity of the dawn, of quietly dressing in the smoky warmth of the dilapidated cabin and sitting on the foot of the fusty bed until Kate Romeo had stirred – eyes opening slowly, then widening in alarm as she propped herself up and moved to throw the blankets off before Powell held her back with a firm hand on her shoulder.

"You probably don't want to do that yet. I'll go out to the car and wait."

She had emerged a few minutes later, dressed, pale, tight-lipped, and a quick, purposeful movement like a bird coming down on some dead thing on the highway.

"Tell me what happened."

Powell had heard her inflection as demanding rather than curious. *What you'd expect.* Best to just state the facts. "The guy in the house shot you. Your Kevlar stopped the slug but the impact must have knocked the wind out of you. When I got to you, you were through the pond ice and out cold in the water. Fortunately not breathing much or I think you would have drowned."

Powell had watched as Romeo absorbed this, the diamond hard glint in her eyes softening by only the smallest fraction. "Where did the guy go?"

"The back of his head had a hard collision with the side of a barn. I tossed his gun and took those from him, too." He pointed to a set of night vision goggles with a head harness that lay on the car seat. Romeo had glanced at them but in a split second her eyes were back on his. "I left him there but when I looked back – after I pulled you out – he was gone."

"And at some point you thought it was okay to take my clothes off?"

Easy. Go easy here. Powell heard himself trying to keep his tone flat. "You were in hypothermic shock. There wasn't much choice."

"You didn't think a hospital might've been a good idea?" Still only flat anger in her voice.

"Lieutenant, I didn't see any hospitals on the way up here. Did you?" *Sometimes pushing back is all you can do.* "Because after immersion in ice water you have maybe a half hour before organs start shutting down. if If I didn't get those clothes off and get you warm and dry... Or would you have preferred that I rolled the dice on that while I drove around for a while?"

For a moment, it had seemed as if they were playing a

child's staring game but finally there was an almost imperceptible movement in her irises, no greater than that of the very tip of a leaf breaking through its bud, before her eyes had dropped, coming back up in a damp confusion as her head shook and the tight line of her lips slackened. All she had said was, "Let's get going."

"Okay. Where to?"

"Back to pick up my car. Then we'll go see this prick in daylight."

Looking back, he suspected that his dismay had shown. "Is that a good idea? Shouldn't you get some back-up?"

"Look," she'd growled, "If Walter Sanborn and this Canadian fool think I'm going to back down easy, they should think again. You don't want to go, fine."

She didn't know. It had not occurred to him before than that she might not have fully processed what the flash of light before the shot had revealed. "Kate," he had offered quietly, "do you remember something hanging in the shed before the light went out?"

"Yeah." Her brow knitted a purl or two. "There was something. I touched it"

"*That* was Sanborn – hung to bleed the way you'd drain a hog."

Now the blonde behind the counter was on the phone, saying something like *okay I'll tell him.* Something below consciousness told Powell that she meant him, that she would be coming through the door to her left to cross the room and deliver the message. As that thought surfaced, another lens projected across his mind the image of Walter Sanborn's pale, fat body, suspended from the rafters in the cold barn while some more elemental part of his wiring reminded him that he was hungry – but that transmission ended as the woman leaned towards her gum-chewing customer for an instant, straightened, and moved towards the door. Within seconds she was standing in front of his bench.

"Are you Mr. Powell?" Her toned arched like a gothic buttress.

"Well, *Father* Powell actually."

"Mmmm." As if to say, *not my father.* "They want you in the barracks. The stairs are through there."

She indicated a door in the wall opposite the counter that bore a sign that read Authorized Personnel Only. Romeo had disappeared through it nearly an hour earlier after depositing him on the bench following the long quiet ride from the border station from which she'd called in a situation report. Getting back into the car there, her jaw had been as tight as mortared stone and her dark eyes smoldered like the wreckage at a fire scene, still smoking over a blackened foundation.

She didn't look much better in her office at the Troop F barracks, sitting stiffly in a guest chair while a uniformed hulk – Major Freddie Boynton, Powell guessed – glowered from behind the desk.

"You're Powell?" The man's voice was surprisingly quiet but his look was as hard and glittery as a diamond tipped drill. Powell nodded and said nothing.

"You don't have to be here, Powell. As far as I can tell you're not guilty of anything more than rank stupidity – though my associates in Canada may have a different view. If you choose to stay, I would like to speak with you – but I will not pull any punches. Is that perfectly clear?"

"It is." Couldn't be more straightforward than that, Powell thought. "And I would like to hear what you have to say."

"Good." Boynton indicated at the chair next to Kate Romeo's, waiting for Powell to sit before he went on. "First, I understand that you pulled Lieutenant Romeo out of a pond last night and got her out of harm's way which I'm grateful for if it's true. Is it?"

"More or less. I'm mindful that I got her into harm's way in the first place."

"I'll get to that." *Not a love fest, not at all.* "One thing her report didn't say, though – how did you manage to carry her back to your car? What was it, a quarter mile or so?"

Powell nodded, remembered the heft of her slung over his shoulder, thinking then that they'd never make it, remembered muttering a prayer as he started. "The answer," he said, "is that I don't know. I'm pretty sure I couldn't do it now. But I do know this – in certain circumstances the human organism can do more than we commonly imagine. You may have seen that in your work."

Boynton considered this carefully, as if hearing a familiar language in a foreign land. "I have," he said, before leaning back in his chair and folding his hands together on the desk. "Now perhaps you want to tell me what the hell you thought you were doing up there. Playing Rambo?"

That was an image that never went away, Powell thought. If people heard you were a Special Forces vet from Vietnam, their minds conjured a picture of a bare-chested, muscle-bound idiot in a headband who couldn't get away from explosives and automatic weapons. *Something to it?* Powell shook his head to reject the thought. "Hardly, Major. I was following a man who may have killed my friend – and who certainly did kill Walter Sanborn."

"So you say. There certainly was no sign of it at that farm when the provincial police got there. No body, no car, no shot out window, no slug in the wall, no bullet hole, no gun. Now the S.Q.

has filed a protest with the governor, as have the R.C.M.P. and the Canadian Foreign Ministry with the Justice Department and the Secretary of State. Let's just say that no one is very happy – including me since I have had to put one of my better investigators on leave pending a review of the whole mess."

"But we saw – "

"No," Boynton snapped, "you saw. Lieutenant Romeo saw a car that could have Sanborn's but she didn't get a clear look at the plates. She didn't see what was hanging in the barn – eyes didn't adjust to the light. And Mr. Morevich doesn't deny that Sanborn was there – says he brought him there to give him his glasses. Says he took them and left."

His glasses. His own reason for being there. The man at the feed store must have called Morevich. *He knew someone was coming.* "He's saying he left work and drove twenty miles to give someone his glasses?"

"No. He's saying they were overstaffed for the number of people who were showing up in Newport and he volunteered to leave early since Sanborn offered to give him a ride home. His supervisor confirmed that."

Boynton's voice was calm as a taped customer service voice telling you that operators were busy assisting other customers. *We're sorry. Please hold.* Powell wondered if that was good or bad. "So where's Sanborn then?"

"That I do not know." Same calm voice. "What I do know is that you acknowledged assaulting him when you were in his custody and that you may have again when you were trespassing at his home."

"So you think I got him?" A sense of here-we-go-again in Powell's thoughts – another turn of the carrousel.

"Given the circumstances, would that be an irrational

thought?"

Mickey Powell leaned back in his chair and considered the major for a moment. He was obviously in a tricky situation – a man on a bureaucratic tightrope juggling chainsaws – but he was not jumping to conclusions one way or the other. The worst time to jump, Powell thought, but few people knew that. "No, major," he said, "that is not irrational. But my question was about what you think."

Boynton tipped his head a bit to the left and squinted slightly like an artist trying to bring his subject into focus. "You're a Jesuit, aren't you, Father?"

"I am." Boynton would be Irish, Powell thought, and therefore most likely Catholic.

"My uncle was a Jesuit, my mother's older brother. Taught sciences at the high school I went to in Detroit. John O'Rourke."

Why tell me this? "I don't believe I know him."

"Dead now – a bone cancer about five years ago. Very smart man, though. A bit of a mystic at times but a very disciplined thinker. Always told us to make all the pieces fit. So what I think is this: there is a bullet in Kate's vest and I don't know how it got there. And that leads me to the question I wanted to ask you."

Powell waited, wondering whether Boynton thought he might have shot her himself, but the major's grave question gave him his answer.

"How many hogs were in the pen?"

CHAPTER 23

Friday, 10:44 a.m.

"Four. Why?"

The voice was Powell's but it could just as easily have been hers, Romeo thought, since Freddy Boynton had asked her the same odd question – about how many hogs had been in the pen – and her answer had been identical. It was a relief in a way, to hear it, a kind of validation that her fragmented memory of the previous night's nightmare wasn't totally imagined.

"You're sure? The S.Q. team said there were only three."

"I'm sure. What's the S.Q.?" Powell's tone perfectly steady and certain, like a New Hampshire post and beam barn resting on a fieldstone foundation. Which is what? Whatever that foundation is, Romeo thought, I could use it.

"Surete Quebec. The provincial police. They found a fourth one hanging in the barn, being bled for butchering."

Romeo watched as the priest took in the information, processed it, asked for more – like a chef adjusting the spicing of a stew. A cool customer, she thought. *Real cool.* What was that from?

" . . . about the other windows," he was saying, "Were any of them broken?"

"S.Q. didn't say but that occurred to me, too. Probably easier to switch out the whole window than it would be to fix one pane."

"So you're saying you think the window was shot out?"

Romeo knew Major Freddy Boynton well enough to know what he would say to that, and he did not disappoint her.

"Officially, Father Powell, I don't have an opinion. But even if I did think that Morevich switched a window – and a wall plank, too, where the bullet hit – I wouldn't be able to conclude that he killed Walter Sanborn." Boynton's face was as frank and open as the winter sky. "First, I don't even know that Sanborn is dead.

His wife says that he was always losing his glasses. And that it wouldn't be the first time he didn't come home. Second, except for the fact that Sanborn gave blood at the last drive in Littleton, he seems not to have had any contact with Morevich. And third, so far we haven't found anyone who ever saw him with Janet Debian either, although she was at that Littleton blood drive, too. Along with ninety-six other people."

"There is the syringe." The faintest hint of irritation in Powell's voice now, Romeo thought, a bit of grit in the flow of it that changed its current ever so slightly. "What about th – "

"There is the syringe." Boynton cut him off abruptly. "Which *you* found."

Romeo watched as Powell's lips parted, closed, tightened. He shook his head before simply offering, "I know what I saw."

"I'm not saying you didn't see it, Father. But I am saying that the supporting evidence is very thin." Major Boynton was on his feet now, reaching for his Smokey Bear hat. "If you two will excuse me, I have a meeting with the public safety commissioner in Concord at one – which will probably be less than pleasant. Lieutenant, best if you get whatever you need out of here and disappear."

And then the major was gone. Romeo looked at the door for a moment as if he might come back through it, then sighed and stood, thinking that she was lucky to be on leave and not suspended, thinking that exhaustion had sunk into her all the way to the marrow, thinking how much she hated both the leave and the fatigue.

And then there was the matter of Mickey Powell.

Who sat looking at her now, not speaking, eyes gone gray and grave.

Who had, she knew but did not remember, pulled her from icy water and carried her through deep snow away from a killer.

Who had, she knew but did not remember, removed her soaking, frigid clothes.

Who had, she knew but did not remember, curled tightly around her naked body to bring her warmth.

Who both pissed her off and attracted her.

And who now asked, simply and helpfully, "Do you need a ride somewhere? Or do you get to keep the cruiser when you're put on leave?"

Romeo shrugged. "I don't know. Never happened before. I'm not even sure they got it back from the S.Q. So probably a ride would be helpful – thanks."

"Not sure you should be thanking me. I mean . . . I – "

"Don't start, Mick." Good to know that he got it, that he was willing to shoulder some of the weight that rested on her like a block of New Hampshire granite. But still, it wasn't simple. "Look – you saved my life. If I shouldn't have been there in the first place, well, it seemed like a good idea at the time. And home seems like a good idea now."

Powell nodded briefly. "Okay."

"Lieutenant?" Joanne Fillion in the doorway now, a sense of urgency causing a slight ripple of disturbance in her tone like a stone just beneath the surface of brook. "There's an Armand Lecompte on the phone who says we're talking to his client without his permission and that – "

"Slow down, Joanne. Tell him that Mr. White says he isn't his attorney and that he's going to have to talk to Major Boynton about it since I'm on leave."

"I know – " Joanne's voice a bit agitated " – but he says he wants me to spell my name for him so he can have me served."

Romeo laughed. "A guy named Lecompte and he doesn't know how to spell Fillion? I don't think so – he's just trying to intimidate you. Tell him what I said and hang up."

"What'd you say his name was?" Now Powell speaking as Joanne left.

"Lecompte." Romeo answered as she headed for the door, glad to have something to talk about, knowing that once she was outside, she wouldn't be a cop anymore, at least not for now. "Armand Lecompte. Why?"

"I just saw his name somewhere. Can't think where, though." Powell's dark eyebrows knitted down to match his frown. "Who is he?"

"You know that guy that came at you at the jail? Butch White? Lecompte claims he's his lawyer but White doesn't want anything to do with him."

"That strike you as odd?"

"Sort of. But it may be smart – Lecompte's not a criminal guy. Mostly does real estate and corporate stuff out of Manchester and Concord."

Her comment flipped a switch; she could see Powell's face brighten like a snowbank when sunshine slid out from the back of a cloud. "Got it now," he said. "He was in the paper in Newport yesterday – something about a plant to make plastic bottles."

"You sure it was the same guy?" In the parking lot now, next to his car, pulling her gloves on. "Lecomptes are thick as ticks in August up here."

"Pretty sure it was Armand Lecompte. Think it said he was a lawyer, too. How many can there be?"

"So what's the connection?"

"I don't know. But if you look at any two things long enough, you'll find they're connected." Powell smiled. "At least that's what I teach."

Pretty big stretch. But sometimes, she knew, a stretch was required. And there was plenty that needed connecting. "Maybe so," she said, and repeated, "maybe so."

"So where're we going, girlfriend?" Powell was grinning, as goofy as a seventh grader at a dance.

"You wish, father." Romeo could feel her own smile forming, even as she knew there was little to smile about. *He just pulls me into it.* "And home is in Warren, back side of Mount Moosilauke. One eighteen from North Woodstock is your best bet."

Powell backed his car up and eased it onto 302 heading west toward Bethlehem and I-93. Through breaks in the trees she could see the Amonoosuc River below the highway to the left, the sun glinting like silver on its rippling water. Farther off the shadowed wall of the White Mountains rose above the valley: the Twins, the Galehead ridge, and the pointy spire of Garfield, fronted by the frosted mounts of Bethlehem and Franconia – Agassiz, Garnet, and then Cleveland, where two nights before she had looked into a fire and then seen tears on Powell's face. *A dif-*

ferent creation up there – things cut closer to the bone. Romeo wondered if there was some of the connection that Powell had mentioned between his tears and that more remote world where the busyness of daily life could not screen him from his own emotions. *True for me anyway.* Nowhere did she feel more alive than in the mountains, and there was no place where her heart was less hidden her head, a state that was sometimes less than comfortable but never without life.

Not like the present moment, she thought. Her suspension left her nowhere, feeling nothing, with a kind of numbness rising around her liking drifting snow and the weight of fatigue pressing down on her like the leaden winter sky.

She was musing that getting away to the back country might be a good idea if she could summon the energy to actually do it when she realized that Powell had said something.

"Sorry," she said. "I didn't catch that."

He looked at her intently for a moment before he spoke again, his eyes thoughtful and calm. "Are you okay?"

"Fine for the circumstances," she said, knowing it was not true. "Just tired."

Powell's look said that he was not convinced but after a short silence he went on, eyes back on the highway. "I just want to talk through something about Janet. Would that be okay?"

"Probably not." She wished she'd never heard of Janet Debian – or Mickey Powell, either, for that matter, but she knew that feeling sorry for herself was a dead end. "But what the hell – can't get in much more trouble, can I? What've you got?"

"I'm thinking that the last time Janet's journal mentioned Vlad was around the middle of December – just about the time she was organizing a group to go to the blood drive in Littleton. I remember because it was during final exams and the academic dean wasn't too happy about it."

"Sounds about right."

"And I think you told me that one of the calls on her machine was from a Red Cross number. Yes?"

"Yeah, but as of Wednesday we still didn't know who it was who called her. They have a lot of phones."

"But probably not Vlad, because I'm guessing he works for Hema-Quebec, right?"

His guessing was good. The S.Q. report had confirmed that Josef Morevich worked for the Quebecois blood agency. Romeo nodded and noted that Powell's voice had dropped a half tone as he spun the web of his hypothesis.

"So I'm thinking – " the priest glanced at her and then back at the winding road " – that you mentioned before that the tox work showed that Janet was HIV positive. But if she knew that, there's no way she would have been giving blood. Just no way. But maybe that's what the Red Cross was calling to tell her – that they screened her blood and found out. And if that's true, what would she do? Knowing her, she'd call her partner."

"And that's Vlad?"

"Yeah." Powell kept his eyes on the highway, but Romeo knew he was trying to drive his thoughts her way – or hers his way. "And maybe he already knows he's positive or maybe he doesn't but either way he doesn't like the thought that someone else knows – namely Janet – and that his employer may find out. Not likely that Hema-Quebec is going to want someone with AIDS drawing blood. And that means no more free pass at the border."

"So he's got to get rid of her."

"And not just that – he's got to get rid of the evidence. Her blood."

Romeo frowned and shook her head. "If that's what he was trying to do, why leave her body right next to a trail? He's gotta know that the M.E. will take tissue samples."

Powell weighed her words for a moment before answering. "Good point. Let's assume that he didn't intend to leave it there, that he had a place to hide it. Say someone saw him. He drops her and takes off and it's snowing like crazy. Even if he can remember where her body is, he can't move it without leaving tracks."

Jason Francis. The footprint in the snow. They were in Bethlehem now, stone churches and inns on the left, the brick school and the town building on the right.

Powell glanced at her, then looked away and spoke quietly. "So maybe he was stalking Francis."

Confusion first, then dawning comprehension, then revulsion. "Fits."

"I thought he had gone back to get the flowmeter but why do that at night? Maybe he knew that Francis used the spring shed for his snow streaking."

"How would he know that? Did you?"

Powell shaking his head, still soft-voiced. "I didn't. But maybe Janet did. She had a soft spot for crazy."

Nothing to say then. The car was through the village now and headed down a long hill and back into the Amonoosuc's valley. *Could be. Could be that all the pieces fit together.* What had Powell said? 'If you look at any two things long enough, you'll find they're connected.' *Could be.*

"Listen," Powell was saying now, "unless you're in a hurry, could we stop at my place first? I'd like to get a shower, maybe change clothes. I . . . I feel sort of, well, dirty, if you know what I mean."

Romeo nodded. Even after a dozen years of investigating

it, she had not gotten used to the viscous sick-slick feeling that homicide brought with it, life's vile side, puked up and unavoidable. "Why not?" she said. "No need for me to hurry now."

No need to hurry. Too true, she thought. No rushing from one crime scene to another, no fast riffle through files, no blasting down a highway with blue lights flashing to find a witness or a victim's mother. Maybe all that hurry was just a way to keep the slime stink from sticking.

Powell made the left on 116 parallel to the interstate and then the right on Edge Road which took them across the four lane towards the school and his place. He was focused on the road or on the stream of his own consciousness, Romeo thought, perhaps looking forward to hot water and the smell of soap and fresh clothes. *Who wouldn't be?* "I know what you mean about dirty," she said.

A hangdog droop flitted across Powell's mouth and eyes as he glanced her way. "Geez, I'm sorry. I mean, I shoulda . . . maybe you'd like to clean up first."

"That's okay. I can wait – nothing to change into anyway."

Now he was smiling, still a bit chagrinned but recovering. "I can assure you, Lieutenant, that men's tee shirts and boxers are very *au courant* in the women's dorm."

Kind of charming, she thought, especially his almost boyish embarrass--ment. And who the hell cared anyway? He'd already seen her naked, at her most vulnerable, in dripping clothes that he had peeled off and then dried. "Well," she said, "a shower would feel good."

And in fact, it did – hot water pulsing against her skin, the sharp, clean smell of Zest, the rough feel of a dry towel – little things that, for the moment at least, removed her worry along with the grime. Dressed again, in khakis and a woman's polo shirt that she found neatly folded on the floor outside the bathroom door, damp hair cool on her neck, she found Powell in his kitchen.

"Better?"

"Much. Helluva bruise on my shoulder where the bullet hit the vest but not bad at all otherwise." She eyed him curiously. "But, Father – you keep clothes around for girls who need a change?"

He grinned and shook his head. "You looked to be same size as our French teacher. While you were in the shower, I ducked across the road and borrowed some."

His eyes gave her a quick and frank appraisal, not quite salacious, she thought, but perhaps appreciative. "Coffee's brewing. The mugs are next to the stove. Something on the computer you should see. Hope you left me some hot water."

Before Romeo could answer he was gone. She found the earthenware mugs, filled two with dark roast coffee from the carafe below the brew basket, and – smiling – took them to the bathroom door.

"Hey, Powell," she called. The door opened a crack to show his lathered face and one bare shoulder. "You're not getting modest, are you, Father? I mean we were in bed together even if I don't remember it."

Powell grinned and the door opened wider to reveal a slim man, lathered for a shave, chest hair graying, well muscled, with a bath towel wrapped around his waist.

Romeo returned the smile. "Not bad for an old man. Here's some coffee."

"Old? Ouch. But thanks for the joe, anyway. Did you check out the computer?"

"Not yet." Still smiling, Romeo left him for the book-lined living room. The screen was in sleep mode but when she hit Return it brought up a page from the Quebec *Registraire des Enterprises.* The listing, for SAQ Plastics Ltd., included a Montreal address. Powell had highlighted three names from its list of directors.

Paul Morevich, Sr.

Armand Lecompte.

And Eric Ames.

CHAPTER 24

Friday, 1:39 p.m.

Kate Romeo had turned her cheek for Al Johnson's smooch and did not sit on his side of the booth. That he noticed – and that he cared – told Mickey Powell that he was far beyond whatever line defined propriety between a priest and a police officer and was well out onto that squishy ground of infatuation that was not much different at fifty-six than it had been at fifteen; characterized, now as then, by a kind of sticky hot embarrassment that clung to him like the film from cotton candy on a summer fair day. Perhaps self-awareness was the only distinction – the adult ability to see his own foolishness even if he could not contain it. He would have liked to think that he could hide it better now too – but that illusion had been shattered like a dropped wine glass with a kiss delivered an hour before they'd met Johnson for lunch in the bustling dining room of the Clamshell restaurant.

At the time they'd still been at his place and his hands full – his own coffee mug in the left and the brewer carafe in the right, which made him, vulnerable and safe at once since he could neither easily fend her off nor pull her closer without making a mess. When he'd come into the study to offer her a refill she had simply stepped in front of him, leaned forward, and planted her lips lightly on his.

"What the . . . um . . . why . . . I mean . . .," was all he had managed to stammer before she had stepped away laughing.

"That's just to say thank you. And yes I would like some more coffee."

"You're . . . uh . . . you're welcome." He reached towards her to pour. "For what?"

She took a long sip before answering. "It occurred to me that Boynton thanked you for pulling me out of that pond but that I hadn't - except in a half-assed way. Very bad form."

"Well . . . okay . . ." Powell felt heat rising over his cheeks, pushing back and up to his ears. "I'm glad . . . uh . . ."

"I'm glad too, Father." Her grin now as wide as a mountain stream in spring. "Did anyone ever tell you that that blush is quite fetching?"

Which only spread it further. "If anyone did," he said, "I'm sure I suppressed it. I feel like a boy at an eighth-grade dance."

"Why?" The lieutenant obviously enjoying herself. "Were the girls after you then, too?"

"Well . . ." He recognized that the word too had his hopes up - but hopes for what? "There was one girl, Karen Mitchell. She was a little fast. She told me she wanted to whisper a secret and then she put her mouth right next to my ear and said she wanted to kiss me and then she licked my earlobe."

Romeo laughed. "You must've been some kind of catch - what were you, the captain of the football team?"

"Basketball actually. Co-captain. But at thirteen it hadn't occurred to me that it might mean anything to a girl."

"Well maybe *she* was fast." Her head shaking now. "But *you* were slow."

"No doubt." Powell reveled in the easy fun of the banter, the simple joy of it – and behind it the forbidden memory of wrapping his arms around her naked shivering body. "I think I probably still am."

"Mmm." A more serious mien now. "That's not what it sounded like the other night when you mentioned the French doctor – even in the Reader's Digest version."

"No." Listening. She had been listening. "No. That was different."

"I don't mean to pry but would you mind if I asked how? I mean you had that thing going, which must have been pretty special – and then later you became a priest. What happened?"

Powell found himself wondering why she wanted to know but did not ask her, hoping, he knew, that it was because she was really interested, interested in *him.* Setting the coffee carafe on the table, he cradled his mug, moved to a chair, and sat down. Her eyes stayed on him as she took a seat on the couch opposite his chair, and he had to swallow hard before he said, "I think it was that I was afraid."

"Of what? Of her?"

Powell laughed. "No. I mean I might have been, but that's not what I was getting at. I'm talking about deep down fear. Where I was in Indochina, people were dying, were being killed or maimed every day. You saw someone one day, you didn't know if you'd ever see them again. You walked out of your quarters in the morning, you didn't know if you'd ever walk back in."

Romeo's blue eyes were focused on his. "That sounds awful."

"In a lot of ways I guess it was. But let me tell you something strange – it was kind of wonderful, too."

"I don't get it." Eyes still rapt, but darker now, wariness moving across them like a cloud.

But who could blame her? It doesn't make sense, Powell thought, even to me. "I guess it's the clarity," he said, trying to find words. "When you're at the edge of life, almost over the edge really, your senses are sharper than you can ever imagine. Everything you see is absolutely clear, every smell, every sound, every touch might be the last one and so it's sharpened, enhanced, completely limpid. And then there's all this death around, so if you can grasp one living thing, you hold on for all you're worth."

Kate Romeo sat back and took this in without taking her eyes off Powell's. After a moment she spoke. "Once I was hiking by myself over in the Presidentials, up a knife edge on the Air Line Trail – do you know it?"

Powell nodded, recalling wind and sunshine and beautiful views into the forested U of a glacial cirque. "That's up on Durand Ridge, right?"

"Right." Romeo's voice clipped as he went on. "Anyway, I'm up there, early fall, calm air, just a lovely day – and I stumble. Don't know if I tripped over a rock or just over my own feet, y'know? But, anyway, I'm sliding and before I can catch a grip on anything I'm over the rim and I drop maybe eight, ten feet where I hit rock and slide again towards the next drop, but this time I get a hand on a stunted pine just as I'm going over, enough to stop me, and my feet are dangling but I pull myself just enough to get the other hand on the tree, and then one foot finds a toehold, and I manage to push myself back up onto this little shelf where the tree was. But for the few seconds that I was hanging there, all I could see was the granite right in front of my face and it struck me how beautiful the lichens were, this lovely grey green color in that bright autumn light, and I remembered wondering why I'd never noticed it before."

Romeo looked for a moment as if she might say more, but before any words formed she shook her head, glanced down and sipped her coffee. Quiet rose between them and Powell let it build a moment before he spoke.

"Did you ever tell anyone about it? The color, I mean. The lichens?"

The lieutenant's eyes met his again. "Not 'til now. Didn't think anyone would really get it."

Still the quiet but now it seemed to Powell not to be between them so much as enveloping them, pulling them towards each other though in fact they had not moved. When he spoke again, his voice was almost a whisper. "'I came that they might have life and have it abundantly.' That's what it said."

A question in her blue eyes. "That's what what said?"

"The voice of truth." Powell was hoping she would stay with him long enough to understand. "In this case it was Jesus – and what I think it's referring to is that feeling of being alive, really alive, really aware. You may have been hanging from a cliff but was life ever more abundant than that?"

An almost imperceptible shake of her head. "No."

"And that's what it was with Nicole – we were both just hanging on. But in every moment we had we were alive." Romeo nodding now but Powell could feel the moment passing as if the mention of his past lover's name had crowded the room. *Fool.* But perhaps it was more foolish to think that the space between them, the cop and the cleric, could narrow at all.

"Can I ask you something?" A curious reticence in her voice, like someone outside a door she might not want to open.

"Sure."

"Was Janet Debian alive like that?"

Powell gently nodding. "She was. I mean, not in that lover's way – but she really saw things, y'know? Really felt them. And if you were with her, you'd start to feel that way, too."

Romeo was leaning forward now, her eyes intent on Powell's face. "In one of her journal entries there was a description of a patch of ferns, maybe a page or more just on ferns, their color, the light on them, the shadows from trees, their movement in the breeze. And I remember thinking it was just perfect, as if I was seeing them myself. Is that what you mean?"

"Yeah. She could make you realize that you'd seen things that you didn't even know you'd seen."

"Is that why you haven't let go of her?"

The priest considered this for a moment and shook his head. "I think it's more that she hasn't let go of me."

He watched as Kate Romeo took this in and thought he saw a glimmer of understanding cross her countenance. Then the analytical detective again, sipping coffee and asking, "You know there's not much you can do, don't you?"

Powell sighed. "I do. But as long as there's anything at all to do I think I'd better do it."

Romeo had frowned a bit. "What do you have in mind?"

"You saw what I left up on the computer?"

"Yeah. I did. It's more than a coincidence to have Ames tied in but there's no real connection between that and Janet."

Powell forced a grin. "Goes to motive as they say on T.V. We know Ames wasn't happy with Janet getting his bottling plant put on hold. And now we find Ames tied to Morevich and to LeCompte who's tied to Butch White who tried to kill me."

"Well," the lieutenant offered reluctantly, "I can pass that through the back door to Boynton but beyond th – "

"Kate," Powell interrupted, "I *know* Ames. *You* met him.

He's a venal money-grubber and I don't like him – but I don't think murder is within his range. I'm going to talk to him. And then there's this plant in Stansted. What's that really about? There must be someone we can talk to."

"Whoa, Father." Romeo leaning back in her chair now. "You just said we. You heard the major. I'm out now."

"I heard the major say that you were on leave from your job. That's not the same as being on leave from humanity."

Powell saw her immediate blush and wished he had the words back. Her jaw tightened as she looked away but she didn't push back. Meeting his eyes evenly, she said, "That stung, Mickey. Maybe I deserved it. But neither of us can go mucking around in Canada – when the S.Q. gets wind of it we'll be sharing a cell up there. I'd be surprised if either one of us could even get across the border."

Thinking of his cell at the county lock up, of Kate in close proximity— *one one could do worse.* Grinning crazily, then remembering her smooth cool skin in the mildewed bed of an abandoned cabin, her body quaking in sudden spasms next to his, then panicking a little, knowing how hard he had just pushed her. "I'm a jerk, Kate. I shouldn't have said what I just did. You've already done more than you should have. But that plant up there has to have something to do with this."

"You're right." An expression smooth as a river cobble.

"You think so?" Relieved, charging back on track like a bushwhacker who has found a trail. "We have to find out – "

Her upraised palm and ear-to-ear grin stopped him. "I meant that you're right that you're a jerk."

Blushing and laughing simultaneously, Powell slumped back in the chair and conceded. "Got me. Got me good."

Kate Romeo was laughing, too, the sound gladdening Powell the way the water of a mountain brook did, singing through the trees. *First time. First time I've really heard her laugh.* There was promise in it, he thought, and a hint of something more.

"And you're right," she was saying, "that I've already done more than I should have. But I may know someone who would go. And in the meantime, maybe we can learn a bit more about our crazy guy Francis – and about the good Doctor Ames, too."

That had brought them to a meeting with Al Johnson at the Safe Harbor Lounge of the Clamshell restaurant. Johnson, a big man about Romeo's age, was sitting at the bar with a half empty Guinness and was clearly disappointed, Powell noted, to see that he was accompanying Romeo.

"Al, this is Mickey Powell. He's the guy I planted at your house on Thursday. I hope he didn't make a mess."

"If he did, Kate, it didn't impact the mess that's already there."

Al Johnson gave him a firm handshake and a wary look before he turned back to Romeo. "So what's it about, Kate ?"

"Right now, I think it's about lunch." Half turning towards Powell. "Father Powell here must be fasting."

Johnson's left eyebrow went up, perhaps involuntarily, and Powell wondered if his own weren't rising, too. Hedging, he thought. She had tossed his title in there to keep Johnson on the line. *Or to keep me off it.* Before he could catch Romeo's eye, the reporter had risen to the lure.

"Father?"

"A Jesuit, Al." Kate was grinning, clearly enjoying their mutual discomfiture. "A good Catholic boy like you would benefit by spending some time with him."

Al Johnson was looking his way as if for confirmation but

Powell smiled and turned from him to Romeo. "Would friends of yours be needing repentance, Kate?"

Her turn to blush a bit, but her fluster was only momentary. "Shouldn't I be in a confessional before I answer that?"

A sparkle in her eyes now that could not be missed, but before Powell could deliver a new bit of wit Al Johnson interrupted. "As interesting as this is, Kate, I'm wondering what it has to do with me?"

"You're right, Al. Let's get lunch."

She felt for him, Powell could see that, as Romeo kept up a steady stream of small talk with the reporter and took the booth seat next to him while they looked at menus, ordered, and waited for drinks to arrive. Settled a bit, Al sipped another Guinness and sat back.

"So what have you got, Kate?"

"What we've got is this – three corpses, a thug in jail, a lawyer, a business or two that may not exist, a police chief gone MIA, and a phlebotomist. And at the moment all that's holding that together . . ." Powell watched as her finger pointed his way. " . . . is sitting right there."

CHAPTER 25

Friday, 2:18 p.m.

For a priest, Mickey Powell was a damned good liar. Kate Romeo had watched with appreciation at the New Beginnings Center, where, wearing the black shirt and clerical collar that he had changed into after Al Johnson had headed north to Stansted he had referred to her as his 'pastoral assistant,' while blandly telling the director that he been contacted by Jason Francis' family about a memorial service and was hoping to learn a bit more about him for his homily, ending smoothly with, "The bereaved find it so much more comforting if it's personal."

The director had demurred. Privacy concerns, she'd said. Confidentiality. Liability.

"We're not asking you to open files," Powell countered, "only to help us understand a little better what made him tick. You can imagine that some of the stories that are circulating about Mr. Francis are quite upsetting to the family, but I suspect that if they understood the context it might be easier for them. And it might help them understand his work with you here better as well."

The implied threat was obvious, Romeo thought. If the

family did not understand his work at the Center they might be inclined to hold it accountable. But this was so well cloaked in pastoral concern that it would be impossible to point at it. Clearly, though, the director – fifty-something psychologist named Deb Something whose gray hair was pulled back in an incongruous ponytail – knew exactly what Powell was getting at. The fingers of her left hand nervously squeezed her lips while those of her right fidgeted uncontrollably on the desktop.

"I take it," Powell went on in the same smooth voice, "that Mr. Francis was making progress here?"

"Oh, yes. Yes, he was." Dr. Deb Something paused to take a deep breath. "Of course, he hadn't completed his work with us, but we were beginning to see changes."

"His mother mentioned his proclivity for nudity," Powell paused for effect, as a faint blush spread across Dr. Deb. "Was that changing?"

"Mr. Francis loved nature." The doctor was trying for a professorial tone, Romeo thought, but hadn't quite found it. "In that respect he was no different than thousands of people, tens of thousands. We were trying to help him recognize what the social boundaries of that behavior need to be, and in that, yes, we were seeing change. In fact, he was beginning to channel some of the creative energy he found there into fabulous art."

"Really?" Powell sounding genuinely surprised now. "I wonder if we could see some of it."

"Most of it has been packed." Dr. Deb's tone truly rueful, as if she now perceived Powell to be an ally. "But I could show you his room – he was painting the walls."

Jason Francis's room was only a little bigger than the cells at County Corrections. It contained a single bed, a dresser, a lamp, and a swivel rocker. The ceiling and two of the walls were white. The other two were an orgy of color, swirling, pulsating color, figures and shapes and symbols that began just inside the door at the baseboard and fanned up towards the ceiling as it crossed the room and surrounded the single window, a cornucopia of impression and hue.

"My lord." Powell had whispered. Then to the doctor, who remained framed it the doorway. "May we spend a moment with it?"

Dr. Deb Something could see no harm in it and had left them there, Powell on his hands and knees, working his way up from the floor, while Romeo began at the other end of the river of color swimming downstream toward him through currents of paint that carried trees and mountains, mythical beasts and rainbow people, fanciful flowers and spinning suns. There, at the furthest shore, sketched but not quite completed, she found what they sought.

"Mick?" Somehow the image shook her in ways that actual corpses did not. "Look at this."

The depiction was of a man in black clothes with a red hat and a bright third eye on his forehead walking with a woman hoisted over one shoulder, her hair painted yellow, her pants blue, her top blue and green, the space around them unpainted white wall. Janet Debian, being carried through snow.

"So he did see something." Powell examining the figures closely now.

The black clad man's face showed dark eyebrows and dark hair beneath its hat.

A prominent nose. A down-turned mouth. "Not a portrait exact-ly, but that is what Morevich looks like."

"He has three eyes?" Romeo knowing she sounded incredu-lous. "C'mon."

"His headlamp, Kate. Or the goggles." Powell's voice was patient, but Romeo felt a bit of embarrassment rising. "This was at night, or so we surmise."

"Of course." Mad at herself without knowing why. "Getting dumb in my old age."

Powell gave her a quizzical look. "You are neither dumb nor old, Kate. I'm ahead of you by a mile in both of those races."

A sense of relief at his comment and a tightening of her throat. But why? *Why care what he thinks?* One voice in the stream of her consciousness told her that she didn't need Powell while another whispered that she did need someone, the two combining in a tight dizzying helix.

"Kate?" Powell's hand on her arm. "Kate? Are you okay?"

No. But she heard her voice say, "Yeah. Yeah, I'm fine."

Mickey Powell's expression said that he didn't believe her but mercifully he didn't push the question, instead offering, "I hope your friend Al can find something on this Morevich guy."

"He will. But in the meantime what do we do?" We? When was it that she had started thinking of 'we?' Romeo shook her head to shake the question and tried to focus on what Powell was saying.

"Ames seems like a key. Let's go see what he has to say."

"Why not?" Knowing that Major Boynton would not approve but not caring, she'd caught his arm as they'd negotiated the Center's slippery flagstone walk.

"Since your French teacher was kind enough to outfit me, I'm not in a hurry to get anywhere else. What did you tell her anyway? That you just happened to have a naked woman at your house?"

"No." Powell grinning at her. "But now that you say it that way, I wish I had. That would've gotten some talk going."

Romeo had smiled back and left her arm in his, pretending for a moment that he was something more than a kind almost-stranger who didn't mind being a steadying presence in a slippery spot. *As if.* As if that could ever be the case, she thought. But she had held on anyway until they got to Powell's car, and then had broken away to ask, "So lying isn't covered in the list of priestly rules? As in 'his family contacted me'?'"

His wide smile again. "We're all in the human family, aren't we, Kate? So even if I had been talking to myself that wouldn't have been a lie."

Laughing hard, shaking her head. "You *are* slick, Mickey, you know that? The kind of guy girls are warned about."

She would see his slickness again later, at Ames' office, but sliding into his car he was all amiable warmth, like a column of air rising in front of a cliff that buoys the wings of swallows. He had called the school office for Ames' Portland address, had asked her if she wanted a cup of coffee for the road, and pointed out the brilliance of the sun on the white peaks, all while guiding his Subaru back through Bethlehem and on towards Maine on 302. The talk had been casual and friendly, as comfortable as well used boots on a familiar trail. Not until they had passed the Troop F barracks in Twin had Romeo had any second thoughts about where they were going, or any thoughts at all except how very easy it was to be with Mickey Powell.

Who noticed her disquiet, speaking softly: "Something wrong?"

"No . . . I . . . " Not sure what she was thinking, what she should say. "I mean . . . I probably shouldn't be doing this."

"Kate, look." The car coming to a stop at the light where routes 3 and 302 crossed, Powell serious now, his voice firm. "You don't have to go – no point in making a bad situation worse. And meeting with Ames isn't likely to be dangerous. I can handle it."

"That's not what I meant." *What do I mean?* Was it best to just spill it? Powell was looking at her, waiting for more. Could she trust him? Could she trust herself? Finally, after a deep breath, letting go. "I think I meant going anywhere with you."

"Oh."

Mickey Powell had been nodding then, but the curved furrows of his forehead told her that he was as confused as she was. In deep. No point backing away now. "Look, Mickey, I like you. Maybe too much. I mean, you're a priest and – "

"Me too, Kate." A skittish glance her way, then eyes back on the road.

"What?" Pulse quickening. "You too what?"

A lovely, lilting laugh. Warmth in the eyes that turned her way. "Me, too. I'm a bit smitten with you, too."

"You are? But . . . I mean . . . you're – "

"A priest?" More serious now, but still a smile. "I'm not sure how good a priest I am anymore. Or that I even know what a good priest would be. I might have known once, in El Salvador or in Egypt or even in New York when I first went there but nothing is clear about it now."

A tide rising from her stomach to her ribcage, moorings shaken, a sense of things swirling, of something about to break loose. "That's bad . . . I mean . . . isn't it?"

Another peal of laughter and his hand now reaching to rest lightly on her knee. "Bad? Could be. Or maybe it's good."

Tears had welled in her eyes then, and she had grasped his hand softly and turned away from him to where the snowy trees rushed by along the road.

"You okay, Kate?"

Nodding but not turning back.

Respectful silence for a long moment, only the rush of the car's tires on the highway. Then, "Tell me your story, Kate."

"Story?" She had turned around, wiping her eyes with the heel of her right hand, leaving the left entangled with his. "What story?"

Powell had looked her way and squeezed her hand gently. "Kate, you're an intelligent, attractive woman – and a lonely one. There's not much chance there's no story there."

She had felt a twinge of hurt as a layer of her shell was cracked away, butaway but had to acknowledge that loneliness was a fact of her life. Was it that obvious? But admitting it to herself was not the same as wanting to lay it out for someone else. "I don't know what to say. I mean I guess that's just the way it worked out. And anyway—"

"Tell me about your mother, Kate."

Wincing, almost unable to breathe for a moment. "W-why did you ask me that?"

Again, the gentle grip of her fingers. "I've been talking with people about their hurts for a long time, Lieutenant." A soft smile, almost sad. "With me and most men the roots of that are with their dads. But it's different for women."

Hanging tight on to his hands, taking a long look into his grey-green eyes before he turned them back to the highway, speaking quickly. "She killed herself. I was eight. I found her body."

Silence between them then, and the snowy trees rushing by as if fleeing a disaster. Powell did not speak but when Romeo snuck a glance his way a tear was glistening high on his cheekbone. Finally in a voice just above a whisper: "Why do you think she did that?"

"I don't know. Nobody talked about it for a long time. When I was almost out of college my aunt told me that she thought my father had been cheating on her. By the time I heard that he had a new wife who didn't like me so I didn't see him much. But by then I had figured out that she was pregnant with me when they married and I started to see that their whole relationship, which looked good to a little girl, was maybe not what either of them expected it to be. I think she had thought he was a catch but in the end he wasn't Prince Charming and she was the one who was caught. What was she going to do with a child to take care of and not much education and her looks going? Maybe she just didn't see any other way out."

Powell had let a deep breath out then as if he had been underwater, swimming for the surface. "I'm so sorry, Kate. No child should have to go through that."

"I suppose not." Watching the forest for a moment, spotting ravens hopping on a carcass. "It leaves you with a kind of hole in your heart."

"How did you fill that?" His voice both curious and sympathetic.

"I don't know." Thinking she should stop but the words coming anyway.
"For quite a while I tried to be perfect. Good grades, no trouble, in church on Sunday. Maybe I thought that'd bring her back or something. Then I had a series of boyfriends who weren't right for me or if they were, were scared away by how needy and clinging I was. I didn't see it that way then – just thought there must be something wrong with me. Then I had a series of flings with married men, which made them happy and made me sad. Then I met this guy Ted. This is maybe ten years ago now. He was . . . I thought . . . maybe he was the one. We did everything together and it felt, you know, *right*. And then one night I told him what I just told you, about my family and my mom and all of it. And

that was it. He was gone. Been a fling or two since then but never too close, you know? So there's work – which isn't so bad. At least it's useful. And when I can I go into the woods and try to lose myself there. Sometimes it works, for a while at least. But that self is wily, she keeps coming back."

She managed a half-hearted chuckle at this – as if to say to Powell or to herself that she was all right now – but he wasn't buying, and in a way she was glad. *No bullshit.* A good thing, she thought. She watched him force a grin but felt that he was listening not to her false laugh but to what lay beneath it.

"Maybe she's trying to tell you something."

"Yeah? What?"

Powell had watched the road for a moment before glancing side long and offering, "Did you know that when St. Paul was probing his own confused psyche he said about it, 'I don't know; God knows'?'"

This time an honest laugh. "That's a great line for dodging a question, Father. Thanks a lot."

He had returned the laugh then. "It may in fact be a dodge but it also happens to be true. Perhaps if both of us keep listening, he'll tell us what she's trying to say."

"Perhaps." *Good time to change the subject.* Adding God to the conversation, she thought, wasn't likely to make it simpler. "But just now I'm more interested in what Eric Ames has to say."

"Fair enough." Powell smiling, perhaps knowing that it was time to back off. "Let's go find Dr. Ames."

Which proved to be remarkably easy once Powell slipped back into his liar's role. Ames' office had not been hard to find once they'd made their way into the city but they had arrived just before five and had been told by a well coiffed receptionist with an almost glowing smile that the doctor had left five minutes earlier and was gone for the day.

"Oh, dear." Powell as mild as Bing Crosby in *Bells of St. Mary's*. "This is his cousin Kate, and I'm afraid we have some news for Eric about his aunt. Do you know if he was going straight home?"

"He didn't say. Let's see . . ." The receptionist clicked keys and watched her monitor. "There's nothing on his calendar for this evening but you might try the Admiral Wingate. I think maybe he was meeting someone there for a drink." She had given them the address and Powell had thanked her with smarmy sincerity, clasping her hand like an unctuous undertaker in a coffin showroom.

Gently holding Kate's arm, he had led her from the reception area and, as soon as the door had closed behind them, had hustled toward the elevator.

"Cousin?" Kate laughed. "What's next? Are you gonna be Michael Anthony with a check for a million dollars?"

"We're all cousins by Adam, Lieutenant. But can you possibly be old enough to remember *The Millionaire?*" Powell grinning, but staring intently at the floor indicator as if that could make it the ride faster.

"The glory of cable, Mickey – everything is on there somewhere. I love that show – always nice to think that some stranger is going to materialize with something that will solve all your problems."

"Happens all the time, Kate," Powell said, still smiling. "They're called angels."

She hurried to keep up with him as the elevator doors opened and he dashed for the building exit. "Hey, what's the rush? If he's there, he'll sit a minute."

"Might be good if we find him before whoever he's meeting

does," Powell replied, charging up the crowded sidewalk toward the Old Port district. "Less chance of a brush off."

And what actually happened, Romeo thought later, was a kind of cosmic brush off – though not by Ames. They had spotted him across a cobbled street walking briskly toward the Wingate past a gold Cadillac with an orange parking ticket on the windshield. Turning to check the traffic before crossing to intercept him Romeo noted a man in a hoodie, standing at the corner with what appeared to be a walkie-talkie.

And then time froze in a bright flash as the Caddie rose into the air while an unseen hand pushed Powell into her and flattened both of them on the wet cobbles of the street.

CHAPTER 26

Sunday, 9:03 a.m.

Visions of angels. Choirs, dominions, thrones. Guardian angels peering down from lacy clouds, Michael and his angelic army, baseball players in the California sunshine, raunchy bikers with winged skull emblems, cherubim chowing on airy cake, a row of seraphs carved in the stone rail of a pulpit housed in a museum somewhere. And with them faces fading in and out: of the dead, his mother and Janet Debian and Nicole. And of the living, Don Teller, and Al Johnson, and Allie from the coffee shop, and Major Boynton, Maria Hernandez and Kate Romeo, somehow near but not quite real, like a hologram you could step through, Kate looming close enough that he could see a tear forming in the sapphire lake of her eye.

Sounds, too, but these less than celestial. A loud curse and a thud, voices shouting, a steady whump whump whump over a whisper that repeated, "hang on, hang on, hang on" as if it were some sacred mantra, shrill sirens rising and falling, urgent tones commanding something just past his understanding. And then silence, resting on him like thick cotton batting, blotting out sound and sight, pressing down like the satin-lined lid of a coffin.

Pushing, trying to push, but not able to, raising his head against the supple dark, and then a sliver of light and sound again, inchoate words, and then a voice he knew, soft and close.

Her voice. Kate again, but this time solid and palpable. Trying to call to her but unable to, then reaching frantically to grip her arm, her shoulder before she slipped away again but hands firm on his shoulders, pushing him back, holding him down, and finally the comfort of her voice again: "Mickey, Mickey. I'm here. I'm here. You're okay. Go easy. I'm here."

And then the sure sense that her hand was grasping his, the light sliver widening, shapes forming, and the dawning realization that he was in a hospital bed with his shoulders pinned by a nurse, and that Kate Romeo was indeed in the chair next to it, holding his left hand.

"Kate?" Hearing his own voice now, whispery and thick with fatigue. "Where are we? What happened?"

"We're at Dartmouth-Hitchcock Medical Center, my friend. You got a helicopter ride. Do you remember that?"

Powell weakly shook his head, and Romeo squeezed his hand gently. "What do you remember?"

It hurt to think, and he struggled to know which of the images crowding his mind were real and which were fantasy. "There was an explosion. We were driving. Snow."

Kate's hand tightening on his. "That's right, Mick. A car bomb in Portland took Ames out. I thought I saw the guy who set it off and we called it in and were trying to follow him but we lost his car outside Norway. The snow was coming down pretty good by then."

"I saw him." A picture forming, a green Jeep Cherokee coming down a hill that they were going up.

"That's right. You spotted him on Route 2 where it climbs

out of Berlin into Jefferson. We didn't know it but Boynton had set a checkpoint there. Now we think he saw it and was doubling back."

Trying to breathe easy, looking for a place to turn around. Romeo trying to find a cell phone signal. Thinking he saw the Jeep pull off the highway onto Dolly Copp Road in the thickening blizzard, following tracks that led back to the Howker Ridge trailhead where the car sat in the deep shadows, its hood still warm. Snowshoe tracks heading into the woods already fading under the white blanket of the storm.

"You had your winter equipment in your car. I wanted you to wait until we could get help there but you didn't want to lose him."

Now Powell remembered pulling on layers of fleece, outer shells, a wool hat and mittens, lacing his Sorrels, strapping on snowshoes and a head lamp, the taut line of Romeo's mouth, the sharp edge in her words. "You called me an idiot."

"I did." Kate's lips now formed a sly smile. "In fact, there might have been a participle in front of that idiot. You didn't listen, though."

"No. I didn't." Feeling surpassingly weary now, he wondered why he hadn't. Something to do with Janet, he knew. Wanting to catch her killer. But something to do with Kate Romeo, too. *Showing off.* He managed a feeble grin. "But I impressed you, no?"

"Oh, yeah. Impressive. About as impressive as cold oatmeal." Some sparkle in her eye and a tone that slid into grudging approval. "You did leave markers at the trail junctions. Without those, and in that much new snow, it could have been pretty hard to find you even knowing where you started. And he had enough gear to be out there for a while."

The trail rose gradually at first but the way became steeper after Morevich had turned up the Kelton Trail and onto the Valley Way, his tracks filling quickly in the near white out, Powell recalled. Knowing they would be erased before Romeo could follow him, Powell had broken branches where his quarry had made turns, and had struggled on up the mountainside, a half step slipped back for each step up even with snowshoes, turning his headlamp on only sporadically, hoping that Morevich wasn't looking back, now guessing that he had finally holed up somewhere to wait out the storm. "So you did find him?"

"No." Romeo's eyes searching his now, their green as soft and inviting as a summer forest. "You did."

"*I* did?" A flat throb pounding at the back of his head; something monstrous just below the surface of consciousness, a maw waiting to engulf him. "I don't get it."

"We found both of you at the Madison Hut." Powell knew the place instantly – a hiker's hostel between the summits of Mount Adams and Mount Madison that he had often visited in the summer months. But it was hundreds of feet above where he remembered being and completely exposed to the worst weather in the world. Blizzards in the Presidentials were legendary and the wind could top two hundred miles an hour. "You were inside, just about gone. Grade three concussion, right hand badly lacerated."

When Powell tried to move the fingers of his right hand and found that he could not, Kate Romeo gently lifted it off the bed and showed him the its bright white bandaging. "Don't worry," she said. "They think they have it all stitched together right."

"What about him?"

"You don't remember anything?"

Powell would not know later if he had managed to shake

his head or if she had just read a no in his eyes. He did recall how controlled her voice had sounded, as if she was trying to squeeze all emotion out of it.

"One of the hut's windows was shattered from the outside. We don't know which of you did it but it was broken before you went down – you were on top of broken glass and your knees were cut up a bit. There was a blood trail from where you were out the door and into the snowfield. Looked like maybe he panicked. There was a long sliver of the window glass stuck in the back of his knee. His popliteal artery was severed."

"He bled out?"

"Probably. The M.E. hasn't made it official yet. You near-ly did, too. Your hand was under your chest, and that put some compression on it."

Whoever sheds the blood of man, by man shall his blood be shed. Powell shook his head at the strangeness of this random thought but somewhere in the fog hunkered down on his mind, a pair of neurons meshed and he located its source. Genesis, he was sure. Maybe with Cain, maybe Noah. A curse nearly as old as humanity. Janet gone and Jason Francis and the junkie in Colebrook – what was her name? – and maybe Sanborn. And now Morevich, too. Tears for all of them began to well up in his eyes.

"Do you think I killed him?"

"You must have. There was obviously a struggle. From what we could see at the scene you were hit hard with a log from the wood rack, probably from behind. He was hardly marked but that glass got into his leg somehow and your hand was cut. The lab should be able to tell if your blood was on it. Then again, your blood was probably on a lot of things – your scalp was split pretty good."

For an instant, a broken sequence of images appeared in

Powell's mind like a marred film clip – the stone wall of the Madison hut appearing in the dim oval his headlamp cast through the swirling snow, a door ajar, stepping across the threshold into the black stillness of the room beyond. And these effects, too: glass crunching beneath his boots, the sound of wind whistling over the roof, a sense of movement behind him, a sharp pain at the back of his head. Then all of them gone, replaced by a fantastic image of kneeling in bright light like a supplicant before the Throne. If there was more, it would not come.

"We thought we might lose you." Romeo's voice again, and in her eyes the limpid green lake forming anew.

Already lost. Wasn't the bleeding man at the mountain hut already gone with that moment just as surely as Morevich or Janet or Romeo herself? What is, is only in the present, Powell though, but the words to say this would not form. Instead of speaking he let himself swim in her gaze, savoring the pressure of her thumb stroking the back of his hand.

"It took forever to get you off that mountain," Romeo was saying, "but by the time we got down the snow had cleared out and the wind had dropped so they were able to set the chopper down on the highway."

"I remember," Powell said, his voice as wobbly as his thinking. "Someone was with me."

"Me." Romeo smiling now. "They brought me along. Found your Red Cross card – lucky you had it. Turns out I have the same blood type as you. O negative. The paramedics wired us up for the flight."

"Direct transfusion?" A little steadier now, rills of thought collecting into a coherent stream. "I thought they never did that anymore."

"They don't." Not looking at him, giving his hand a soft

squeeze. "Took some persuasion."

Mickey Powell imagined a clear tube going red as her blood coursed into it, plasma and platelets, red and white cells, flowing in a pulsed rhythm into his arm. *This is my blood, given for you.* The words of consecration, of 'making holy.' *Making whole.* How many times had he bent over an altar, whispering just those syllables? The two of them become one being. Now pressing her hand gently, he closed his eyes while words read from a lectern echoed in the nave of his mind. *That they may be one even as we are one.* Oneness. What it meant to be holy.

"Thank you," he said. As he opened his eyes again he found hers searching his.

Smiling almost shyly, she answered, "You're welcome. Now get better, so it won't turn out to have been a waste."

A wave of sadness rolled in from nowhere. "Seems like the whole thing was a waste. What was it about, anyway?"

Romeo shrugged. "To be honest, we don't know. The Mounties and the S.Q. are going over Morevich's farm but as of this morning, they only thing they'd found was a stolen cell phone that had been used to call Todd Brooks' and Janet Debian's numbers. And – "

"This morning?" Something out of place in what she said, a detail of the picture wrong. "That's not much time to look, is it?"

"Why? They started yesterday."

Time slipping away faster than he could hold it. "Wait. What day is it?"

Romeo laughing. "It's Sunday, padre. You came off the mountain early on Saturday."

Grinning feebly in response, taking the information in, letting it rest within in him for a moment, finding the question he was looking for. "Did Al come up with anything in Newport?"

Kate Romeo shook her head. "Not much really. The Morevich there is a different man – older, pushing seventy, a relative of our guy maybe but no one really knows. Runs a venture capital firm in Montreal. The Canadians like him for laundering the Russian mob's money there but there's nothing solid to hang on him."

Again, fatigue rising around him, as heavy as wet cement. If they could not find a link, they were no closer to mapping the geography of death that began in a snowstorm at Seven Springs and ended in a blizzard on Mount Madison. Not that the topography would be hard to understand, Powell thought. It was the same terrain that humanity had traversed since it had crossed the river that arose in Eden and had stepped into its own consciousness. Janet Debian was dead because she was inconvenient and in the way. Now she was only a point on a trail that was older than the mountains themselves. And so, too, were Julie Tuite and Jason Francis. *Greed and fear and violence. More for me; less for you.*

" . . . did find one thing, though," Romeo was saying. "Kind of interesting but I don't know what it means."

Powell fought through the thickening weariness to let her voice come to him. "What's that?"

"Well, in his digging around in Newport he came across a retired engineer who'd been on the committee put together to try and bring the factory there, Flaherty or Fitzgerald or some Irish name like that, and the guy gave him an earful about how the Stansted site was just the wrong place, that the ventilation wasn't even close to adequate for the kind of plastic extrusion equipment they said were going to be using. Said he'd mentioned this at meetings but everyone just brushed it off."

"So maybe they were planning to add it later – doesn't seem like too big a deal."

"Maybe – but it was enough to get Al to drive up to Stansted to take a look at the place. And here's the thing – all he found were pallets and pallets of water cooler bottles and covers. But no equipment. That seem odd to you?"

"A little," Powell admitted. "Do they have another location?"

"Not that anyone can find a record of."

"Mmmm." Mickey Powell closed his eyes to give his logy brain free rein, hoping its meandering would lead it to a puzzle piece that matched the pattern he had put together so far. Nothing illegal about storing cooler bottles, not even anything particularly wrong about it. How could it fit with needles and bodies and blood? And why make a pitch about manufacturing if that wasn't the plan?

No answers, though, and no ideas, only fuzzy images of snow. Janet's hand emerging from a drift, shoes crunching on the snowy trail as Sanborn walked behind him with a drawn gun, waiting above the cabin on Mount Cleveland in a forest blanketed white, climbing Madison in a blizzard.

"Excuse me, is this Father Powell?" The voice pulled his eyes open. It belonged to a stocky, silver-haired stranger in the doorway with impossibly dark eyes and an air of command, well dressed in a camel's hair topcoat and brown leather gloves.

Regarding the man coolly and noting that Romeo's hand was inside her jacket, Powell answered with a query, "What makes you think so?"

"It wasn't actually a question, Father, only a courtesy. I know who you are." The speaker's eyes glittered and he took a half step into the room.

"Then you have an advantage on me. Who are you?"

"My name is Morevich. I believe you killed my nephew."

CHAPTER 27

Sunday, 9:03 a.m.

Snowing again. Fat flakes in profusion, dancing in the nearly
still air, swirling veils that caught the eye but did not hold it like
the current in a passing stream. Mickey Powell sitting again in
the woods on the knoll above the pond where his students sat in
solitude and again contemplated the connections between the
Out There and the In Here. Most of them had returned the previous evening and the rest would be coming back today, summoned
from their homes with the assurance that the Seven Springs Academy was, despite its recent tragedy, a place of safety.

Whatever that means. An old prayer drifted through Powell's consciousness: ' Give peace, O Lord, in all the world; for only
in you can we live in safety." And maybe that was right. Perhaps
the whole - or holy - was safe for another day. But safety for the
whole did not mean, couldn't mean, safety for each of its parts.
The holy was dynamic end dynamism implied change and change
change always meant risk. And there was no denying that the
whole included risky parts like the czar, Paul Morevich.

Whose greeting had focused Powell - even through his
druggy hospital haze - like a match struck in a dark room. Atten-

tive and wary, he had answered tersely, "What makes you think I killed anyone?"

"Come now, Father." The man's voice as smooth and cool as a field of new snow, with a faint accent that Powell could not place. "Surely you don't expect me to believe that Josef somehow fell on that sliver of glass?"

"Who said anything about glass?" Kate speaking, her tone hard and cold, like New Hampshire granite.

Paul Morevich had half turned towards her, had regarded her carefully before answering. "And you would be Detective Lieutenant Romeo, I think. If it surprises you that I know this" – the word pronounced more like *these* than *this* – "I can only say that in business information is currency and to have much of it is an advantage. Also, let me assure you that I am unarmed. I would consider it a courtesy if you took your hand off your weapon."

Kate Romeo had returned his look without moving. "Maybe I'd be inclined to do that if you tell me what you're doing here."

Morevich nodding curtly, simply saying, "I have come to express my regrets to Father Powell."

Now, in the forest, with snowflakes spiraling around him, Powell felt a faint reverberation of the astonishment that had slapped him in the hospital room, recalling the question that it had spawned. "Your regrets?"

"Let me explain." Romeo also surprised, hand out of her jacket now, eyes narrowed in curiosity as Morevich went on. "My family, we are Serbs; I was in the Milosevic government. I know what people here think of that but you are now learning for yourselves the dangers of radical Islam. My own brother, Josef's father, was killed by Muslims, as was his wife. Josef found their bodies – not a pretty sight. He was a medical student then but after his parents died, he quit and went into the army instead."

Morevich had dropped his eyes to the floor for a moment and had brought his hands together as if in prayer. "Many, many bad things happened in the war. On both sides. He didn't speak of them but when it was over, he wasn't the same. I brought him to Canada to help him heal. The farm seemed to help but his nightmares never left him."

"I appreciate how hard that must have been." Powell alert then, muscles tensing, leaning towards the man in the doorway. "Is that what turned him toward heroin?"

His visitor's eyes glittering like black onyx. "It is possible that he was an addict. He seemed desperate sometimes. I understand that he may have killed a friend of yours, and for that I am very sorry."

More snow now, the air itself gone white and grey, trees becoming spectral shadows, all sense of depth flattening as if the landscape were being pushed into a picture frame. Now raising his face to feel the pinpoint sting of snowflakes on it, now raising the memory of Janet's body emerging from the snow, now recalling Romeo's brusque question in the hospital room.

"He also killed your partner, Dr. Ames. Will your water venture go forward without him?"

Morevich had regarded her coolly. "Dr. Ames was a backer, yes. As to whether Josef killed him, that is only speculation. I hope that it is not true – but whether it is or not, all of my projects are assessed only on their ability to produce acceptable returns over time. Did you wish to make an investment?"

The bald irony of Morevich's query had not sat well with Romeo, but there had been no basis to push her inquiry farther. After a pause long enough to convey her irritation, Kate had pursed her lips and dryly offered, "I believe I'll pass."

A curt nod to her, and then the dark eyes on his own again.

"I came to tell you, Father, that I am making a donation to the school in Ms. Debian's memory.
Nothing can replace a life but it may help me find some closure. Perhaps you will find some as well."

"Perhaps." The echo of his voice, now heard again with the moan of the wind in the woods. Perhaps. But not likely – no one ever really dies, and Janet would be no exception. Her place in the world had touched his and that could not be altered, any more than the collision of his life with Josef Morevich's could be reversed. No doubt his uncle knew this, too – his brazen shrewdness should not be underestimated. His visit and the gesture of his gift were less an offering and an expiation than an inquiry and a warning.

Romeo had seen it, too. After Morevich's exit, which was as abrupt as his entrance had been, she had turned back to Powell and asked, "There's something he doesn't want us to see. What?"

He had managed a feeble shrug. "Maybe Butch White can tell us."

Romeo's face expressionless – pale and beautiful.

"You know. The guy at the jail."

"He's gone, Mick."

"They got him out?"

"No."

No need to ask more. White had been one more loose end, and it had been tied up just as Morevich had hoped to tie them up. One way or the other. Perhaps to move herself past a similar realization, Romeo had repeated her question: "What is it that he doesn't want us to see?"

Now in the white forest Powell believes he might have managed a weak shrug then, though he is not certain. He is sure, however, that her words had echoed somewhere deep down within him like cobbles dropped in a well, their reverberations wet with meaning that the original syllables did not contain. From that deep place below conscious thought another question had arisen to which he had given no voice: *What it is that I don't want her to see?*

Though he had not spoken, the space between them had changed as if his mind had generated some subtle charge there. Romeo stayed only a few minutes more before mumbling something about work and backing through the door, leaving him rueful at his foolishness and wishing he could unthink what he'd thought and say something that would somehow keep her there. But the hard truth was this: what was done could not be undone and staying where he was would bring him no closer.

Powell winced as he sat up – but nothing to be done about anything in a hospital. Wobbly and uncertain, he eased himself out of the bed and explored the room as far as the tether of his IV line would let him. Two drawers and a closet contained most of his clothes – mercifully they had not been cut off him in the E.R. – and his cell phone, wallet and watch were there, too, in a plastic bag under his shirt. Pulling the needle out of his arm, he dressed as quickly as he could, pulling on his hat and gloves to cover the bandages on his head and hand, hoping that he would not look too odd in the medical center's corridors.

As it happened, the people bustling by in their morning routines were too preoccupied to notice. At the information desk, he got the name of a cab company; from the cabbie, the location of a car rental company; from the rental agent a Nissan Sentra. Before hitting the northbound highway, he punched up Romeo's number with his left thumb and left her a message saying that he was hoping to see her. Driving without a right hand was harder than he'd expected, and his eyes did not want to stay in focus, but he made it home in less than two hours.

The campus was jumping. Some kids were back, hauling suitcases into dorms from double-parked minivans; more were coming on buses from airports in Manchester and Boston; faculty bustling in classrooms, making ready for a fresh start tomorrow. Sam Robeson, the tweedy Head of School, greeted him in the entrance hall.

"Michael – didn't expect to see you back today. Heard you had some kind of accident."

Accident? Hard to think of it that way even if you didn't believe in divine agency. But, Powell knew, absolutely pointless to discuss it with Mr. Bean. Anything not old, English, and moneyed was outside the realm of civilized thought to him unless it bore directly on his own material well-being, a province governed by a more reptilian lobe of his mind.

"Bit of a dust up, that's all," he replied in a mocking British cadence, well aware that Robeson would miss the mockery altogether. "A little shaky but otherwise ready for duty."

"Good, good, good. Won't need to find a substitute for you then, will we?"
Robeson's eyes were already moving past Powell and around the crowded lobby, signifying that his dismissal was at hand, when suddenly they came back, pulled, it seemed, by an uncomfortable thought brought a slight grimace to Robeson's staid face. "Probably should have some sort of memorial for Miss Debian, shouldn't we? I gather she was popular. Will you see to that?"

And if she hadn't been popular? But that question would be pointless to Robeson, too, so he had simply said, "I'll see to it."

"Good. Don't want to keep you from class then."

Robeson had offered a patrician's brisk nod, and had moved away, no doubt looking for another way to restore order to his small universe after the extreme untidiness of a homicide. The Head's brisk ignorance notwithstanding, Powell welcomed the return to routine, which served as a kind of temporal lubricant, easing time's movement in spite of the clawing grasp of Loss that reached into every moment. Greeting students, outlining assignments, leading them again into the forest - none of these made the burden of death easier to bear but collectively they reaffirmed that life goes on. Now in the woods, he now watched the snow accumulate on the back of his mittened hand and reflected on loss and memory. The crystals on his mittens would be, he knew, gone within minutes when he went back inside. And who would note their passing? Janet Debian, Todd Brooks, Jason Francis, Julie Tuite, Ames – even young Morevich himself – how long would their losses be mourned? The vacancy of the It-world would pass quickly of course. The roles they played and the functions they served would be taken by others and the world would go on much as before. But the Thou world was different. In Thou-ness, in the ways their lives had touched and intertwined with those of others; in these they would persist. Todd, Julie, Jason – each of them someone's child, someone's brother or sister, someone's friend. For better or for worse knots had been tied that could not now be loosened. He could not free himself from connection to Janet Debian any more than the icy Paul Morevich could free himself from his nephew.

     The thought brought Powell back to the analytical part of his conscious-ness and to Romeo's final question. *What is it he doesn't want us to see?* She wasShe was right, he thought, that his visit was a diversion. If they were looking at him, it meant that they weren't looking at something else. Which had to be the Ames connection. Or perhaps not. If someone inside had told Morevich what happened on the mountain, he would also know what happened in Portland. And would therefore know that they already knew about Ames – which Romeo's comment had only confirmed. It would have to be something he still hoped to hide.

Nothing came to mind, though, and Powell let his thoughts drift like the snowflakes that swirled around him, dancing and spinning on the light January breeze. Ephemeral, he thought. *Like us.* Laying static in drifts for a time, thawing, flowing, perhaps refreezing and thawing again, eventually making its way to the pond below him. Somehow the thought carried him to Kate Romeo and to wondering whether the flow of her life would intersect with his again. *Not likely.* That sad, stubborn answer embedded itself in the stream of his consciousness and turned it to other currents, to Janet, who had liked to sit on the pond's edge where she could see both water and forest. *What flow now carried her?* Looking idly through the winter wood he could see across the white expanse of the frozen pond to the big oak against which she had braced her back not so many months before. Below it the pond spilled into a woodland stream that had often been the subject of her journaling. And not so far below that, perhaps a half mile away, was the defunct gravel pit where Ames's bottling plant was to rise.

The bottles. The bottles weren't in the files yet. Unless Romeo had written a report, only the two of them and Al Johnson knew about the bottles, and Morevich could not yet be aware of that. Why were there bottles when there was no bottling plant? And why buy them if you were planning to make them?

Before answers could begin to shape themselves, the blur of something moving to his right and up the hill edged across the corner of Powell's eye. A figure in a green parka striding carefully but briskly across the field and into the woods. Romeo. He stood to wave but she made the turn towards his sitting place without looking up, as if she knew exactly where to find him. As she approached he could see that the falling snow made a wet sheen on her warm face. But there was nothing warm about her greeting.

"What's wrong with you, Powell?" Already snapping at him from ten feet away. "You practically fracture your skull and then sneak out of the hospital – what did you think you were doing?"

Powell spread his arms wide like a man expecting an embrace. "And good morning to you, too, Kate."

Romeo seemed to bite back whatever words she was preparing to spit at him, and dropped her head briefly, before bringing it back up with a face that couldn't decide whether to glare or to smile.

"As to your first question," he went on, "I think there must be a lot wrong with me. Let me know when you're ready to hear my confession."

A sheepish smile won; the defeated glare disappeared. And beneath the smile, no detective, no agent of a state, but simply a woman in a snowstorm, hands at her sides, and a startling brittleness in her eyes, that made them look like delicate blue ovals of finely blown glass. Panicked then by her open fragility, knowing that he was attracted to her, and that he was stupid and afraid, knowing his words would be wrong but hurrying to speak them.

"It's the bottles. He doesn't want us to see the bottles."

VISITATION

A strange kind of fear, that's what it was – but it took Mickey Powell a moment or two to realize it. A tightness just below his ribcage, his breathing shallow and coming quickly, senses heightened; the smell of brewing coffee and fresh croissant, the sound of murmuring voices in conversation at the other tables punctuated by the occasional chirp of a cell phone or the *whoosh* of milk being steamed for a latte, the bright gold, green, and blue of Allie's patchwork silk vest as she moved about the room, the painfully slow sweep of the second hand of the clock behind the counter, each pulse reminding him that Kate Romeo was not with him. And perhaps would not be. As benign as it seemed, that was his fear. But several phone calls had produced no answer from her, and finally he had simply left the message that he'd be at the Mug at 8:30.

Your own fault, fool. That was the truth. The voices of the mind were not always right, he knew, but this one was. She had come to the woods to say, in her way, that she cared – and he had responded by telling her about bottles. *Bottles!* Now he was afraid that she wouldn't show but then he'd been afraid when she had. And now the clock's minute hand moved to claim the forty-third mark.

Kate Romeo could see Powell through the café's side window: a slimmish but ordinary man in his fifties, his salt and pepper hair freshly shorn, fidgeting with his coffee mug and watching the front door closely as if he expected an image of Jesus to appear on its frosty glass at any moment. *An ordinary man?* You could think that to look at him but Romeo found her head shaking slightly at the thought. *And this fact: I'm here.* And enjoying the sight, too, just as she had enjoyed the slight tinge of consternation in his voicemail messages. But she hadn't come for that, she knew, but because she missed him. *Simple as that.*

And complicated as that, too. It couldn't work and she knew it, but she wondered if that wasn't part of the attraction she felt. Not a lot of risk if you fell for a guy who couldn't fall for you. But he did make her think and he did make her smile and she couldn't help wondering what it had been like to be wrapped in blanket with him in the cabin near Morevich's farm. Thinking 'bad girl' but smiling, Romeo snuck another look through the café window and worked her away around the back of the building where she waved at Allie through a locked door.

"I want to sneak up on the good reverend out there," she said when it opened. "Could you let me slip through here?"

"No problem at all." The waitress grinning, a co-conspirator now.

Standing behind Powell while Allie watched, bending close enough to startle him when she spoke. "Did you want a refill of the usual, Father? Or maybe something special this time?"

Two women laughing at his startled turn, a splash of embarrassment tinged with annoyance, then a rising tide of delight in seeing Allie and Kate giggling like little girls behind him.

"Something special? You two are something special all right." Grinning, shaking his head, relieved at Kate Romeo's obvious glee. "Allie, get the officer whatever she wants. On me."

"Hard to say exactly what she wants, Mickey." Allie gave them both a wink and Powell felt a blush spreading across his face, noted that Romeo was reddening, too. "But if it's coffee maybe I can help."

Romeo examined her shoes for a moment before looking up to answer.

"Coffee would be a good start, Allie – after that who knows? But since the padre's buying, how about some of that Blue Mountain?"

She sat opposite him, her hands moving restlessly like birds fluttering in a park, first to the tabletop where she set her gloves, then to her collar, then to her lap, then back to lightly grip the table, her eyes roaming the room anxiously as if she was not quite certain of where to let them rest. Finally, Powell caught both of her hands in his and asked, "How's it going, Kate?"

What was it that he was really asking? Romeo wanted it to be about her, her life, her days and nights, where she was going, what she was thinking. Foolish to think that, though. Mickey Powell had a full enough life with his classes and his students, his colleagues and his protégés. Why think he had time for more? Best to just stick with the facts.

"You may be right about the bottles," she said. "From what Al remembered they had a kind of hollow at the bottom, you know, like some wine bottles have? Just guessing but maybe you could put a half pound of powder there. That'd be about thirteen thousand dollars' worth per bottle – and if you sealed it in with the covers Al saw, it would be virtually impossible for dogs to smell. Even a few would be worth a lot – five hundred bottles, say, out of a truckload– that'd be six and a half million. And here's the thing – we passed this thinking on to the S.Q. and they paid a visit to the Stanstead factory. Which was empty. Morevich knew that we knew – because

I couldn't keep my mouth shut at the hospital."

"Being a bit hard on yourself, aren't you? He had to know that Ames's death would turn attention his way." So comfortable to deal with her on the level of their professions, her cool detachment and his warm empathy easily intersecting at a distance far enough from their hearts to risk nothing, a stream of conversation that meandered slowly like a river in a flat landscape. Powell wanted a faster current, a different stream, but drifted on as though paralyzed. "I wonder why they killed Ames anyway."

So this is it? Romeo wondered why she came. To sit and chat about motives and theories? Just as well to say good-bye and get back to work. But noting that he was holding her hands, Romeo neither made a farewell nor an effort to leave. Instead she took in the wrinkles of his wind-reddened face, the warm green of his eyes, and cast another line into the water. "I don't think it was 'they' at all. I'm guessing Ames knew that Junior was poaching product and retailing it. Just like Sanborn. You heard them talking about something. My guess is that after Debian or Jason, one of them, probably Sanborn, threatened to tell the uncle. Maybe not a wise thing to say to a guy with post-traumatic stress disorder."

"Makes sense. Did they ever find the Chief?"

"No. But there was a human tongue in Morevich's freezer."

Powell let her fingers go and reached for his coffee mug, and Romeo immediately wanted her words back, wished she could cram them into a box on a shelf and present with something else, something about the sadness in his voice or her own loneliness or the beauty of the snow on the mountains. But nothing came and Romeo turned away as he spoke again. "Don't guess we'll ever know the whole story now ."

Romeo watched him sip his coffee, touch a blue napkin to

his lips, glance out the café's windows to the busy street beyond. Wishing he was somewhere else. But no speaking that, she thought. Too polite. When his eyes wandered back to hers she simply said, "Probably not."

His look then might have cracked her heart in two had not Allie returned with a steaming mug and a smile. "Jamaican Blue for you, Dick Tracy. And does His Holiness need a refill?"

When Powell accepted Allie's offer he saw her barely suppress a laugh. Good to see her happy, he thought. *But at what?* Handing her his mug, he asked, "Something about us amuse you, Allie?"

"Amuse?" Still snickering, shaking her head. "You guys are way past amusing. Look at you! Anyone can see you're attracted to each other but you're sitting here like a couple of tongue-tied kids. You're hilarious!"

"What . . . I mean who . . . um . . ." Words wouldn't come together as Mickey Powell felt heat rising from the base of his throat all the way to his scalp, and noted that Kate Romeo was blushing as well, the red of her wind burnt cheeks shading slightly towards mauve. Allie walked away chuckling and Powell felt a sheepish grin begin to form. "One thing about Allie is she's given to speaking the truth."

"What?" Romeo's eyes widening, almost alarmed. Are you saying – "

"I'm saying she's right." *Nothing to lose at this point.* "I do find you attractive. And I don't know how to say that now any better than I did in middle school."

A rising and falling then, like the wake wave of a passing boat under a canoe, bringing with it a loss of balance and the sense that she could tumble into cold, deep water. *Like at the farmhouse,* she thought, remembering the impact of the bullet hitting her chest. No breath, legs gone, the icy shock of the water. *He pulled me out.* And out of equilibrium again, his words nudging her to the edge of some steep drop, her mind caught in a tight eddy, flailing for something solid to hold onto.

"But . . . I mean . . . even if . . ." Finally blurting, "But you're a priest."

Powell looking sweetly chagrinned. "I suppose that's true," he said, looking carefully at his coffee mug, as if he expected words to appear there, then shyly raising his eyes. But not always a very good one."

"What?" Was there something there? She thought of hiking above the tree line in the clouds, forms of a mountain revealing themselves then disappearing behind a veil of vapor. "I mean . . . not a good one? I don't know what you're saying."

What am I saying? Powell wasn't sure himself. Was it just that he wanted to be close to her? Or more that he wanted to wrap her in his arms as he had in the ramshackle Canadian cottage or to watch her breath rise and fall in sleep the way it did in the cabin on Mount Cleveland? All of that on one side. And on the other side was the desert – not the searing, dusty plain in Egypt where God had founded him in his pain and perplexity so many years ago but in that interior solitude where Love itself met him, love beyond relationship and beyond all others, and filled him with peace that as St. Paul put it, passed all understanding. Were the two sides mutually exclusive? No answer. But perhaps only one way to find out.

"Kate." Powell let silence sit between them for a moment after her eyes found his, not a wall but a gate that admitted each of them to the other's presence. He touched her fingers lightly on the tabletop and was gratified that she did not move them away. "Being a priest is a part of whom I am. Maybe being a cop is that way for you. But what I'm saying is that if being a priest means I can't be with you, I'm not so sure how important it is."

"Okay." Without thinking Kate gently tightened her fingers around his and wondered what it was that she was okaying – that Mickey Powell was who he was or that she wanted to be with him. Or both. There was something deeply solid about him, she thought, like bedrock. Firm footing there, not the sliding climb through talus and broken shale that so often marked her days. And nights. She thought of sitting shoulder to shoulder with him in front of a woodstove in a hidden cabin and wondered what a life like that would be like. And said again, "Okay."

"What is?" Powell smiling now, bemused, it seemed, and curious. "What's okay?"

"You, Mickey." She did not let go of his hand. "You're okay."

"That's better." Allie again, grinning broadly at the sight of their entwined fingers. And receiving broad beams in return. She rested an arm on Powell's shoulder and spoke to him in a stage whisper. "You've given me a lot of advice over the years, Father. Would you like some in return?"

Chuckling now, nodding, glancing quickly at the young woman in the bright patchwork vest, but bringing his eyes almost instantly back to Romeo as if afraid she might disappear if he were not looking.

"Okay then." Allie patting his shoulder lightly. "This is the part where you ask her over for dinner. Ready? Go."

Trying not to laugh, barely succeeding, watching Kate's eyes watching his, crinkling with mirth at the corners. "Kate, would you like to come over for dinner sometime?"

"Sometime?" Allie pounded his back as if he had something stuck in his throat. "You've gotta do better than that, Padre."

"Um . . . I mean . . . how about tonight?"

Snickering, though she didn't mean to be, happy the way she imagined wildflowers to be happy, Kate nodded and said, "Sure, Mickey. That'd be nice. What time?"

"How's six?"

Powell's wide deer-in-the-headlights eyes were gone now, replaced by the green sparkle she had found there before, telling her that he was back in his comfort zone. *Where I want to be.* She let her fingertips lightly stroke the back of his hand, noting that his skin was surprisingly smooth, and spoke. "Six would be fine. What can I bring?"

Mickey answering now but she doesn't hear his words. Thinking nothing to lose instead, then thinking how good it would be to lose that nothing, to have something instead, letting the pad of her index fingertip tell her that that there was no distance between her skin and his. Saying, "Can I say something?"

Powell heard something new in her voice, something calm but moving, like the current beneath the surface of a still stretch of river. "Sure, Kate. What?"

"Do you remember once you asked me if I'd seen any angels?" Kate glanced at him and at Allie and then to the window. Snow was falling again.

"Now I have."

Acknowledgments

Many people contribute to the making of a book. The author would like to especially acknowledge Kate Anderson at Other Words Press for her support and hard work in trying times, Melissa Volker for her assistance with design, my colleagues over many years at the White Mountain School, where this tale was born, for their good humor and friendship, and most of all my wife, Barbara, for her unfailing encouragement in this and all other endeavors.

www.ingramcontent.com/pod-product-compliance
Lightning Source LLC
Chambersburg PA
CBHW061144210726
48294CB00006B/1570